AF579792

A Feast for Spiders

Kenneth L. Evans

Thomas Y. Crowell, Publishers
Established 1834 New York

 For information address Thomas Y. Crowell, Publishers, 521 Fifth Avenue, New York, N.Y. 10017. Published simultaneously in Canada by Fitzhenry & Whiteside Limited, Toronto.

FIRST EDITION

Designer: *Janice Stern*

Library of Congress Cataloging in Publication Data

Evans, Kenneth L
A feast for spiders.
I. Title.
PZ4.E91594Fe 1979 [PS3555.V218] 813'.5'4 78–22458
ISBN 0–690–01805–3

79 80 81 82 83 10 9 8 7 6 5 4 3 2 1

For Dr. Louise Goldhaber

Tres Santos is hot and dry during the day. The evenings are harder to describe, because they have a special quality unlike any other place in the world: cool, faintly moist, heavily scented with spices, flowers, and the smells of the ocean.

I was there for no other reason than my wanting to be there. That's the big advantage of doing what I do; you're your own man, exclusive, of course, of publication deadlines. A writer writes, and it doesn't matter if he's doing it at home, in a plane, wherever. It's what he is, and it's what he does.

I had finished my interview with the retired movie star–singer who lived in a remote village in Baja, and all I had left to do was put it together. It was the kind of assignment I liked best: travel expenses, living allowance, and enough time in which to do the sort of article that enhances my reputation as a knowledgeable, reliable journalist. I had made a good beginning and I wanted time in which to pull it into shape in my mind. No better place for that than Tres Santos.

I maintained my exclusivity the first day there. I'm sociable enough, but you'd be wrong to call me gregarious. Three marriages and about a thousand misplaced friendships don't make for garrulity, not to mention an open way with strangers, and I was glad to spend the time alone. I sunned myself; I drank as many Margaritas as I could; I plunged into the surf and got out quickly; and I ate my meals in the nearby town, where all the restaurants are suspect but fun to be in if you speak Spanish, and I do. It was a great day, and I slept late into the next morning.

I felt easier in myself that next day, more at peace with all the information the movie star–singer had given me. I decided to have lunch in the hotel dining room; I always liked the place anyway. It's large and airy, open wide to the ocean breezes, and it strives to be Aztecan rather than colonial Mexican, and that pleases me.

The dining room was crowded, as it usually is, with yachtsmen, their women, and all the fishermen who fly down to catch marlin and end up trying to kill hangovers. Not a bad crowd, as such crowds go. I had rarely seen a younger or more attractive collection.

Suddenly I heard a strangely accented voice that carried over the chatter and clatter. It announced in tones loud enough to be heard above everything and everyone, "Let's hear it for Archie!" In answer I heard a small chorus of voices repeat, "Let's hear it for Archie!" Laughter followed, of such passionate amusement that I turned to see who Archie was and what was so special about him.

I saw them in the corner of the dining room, possibly the most remarkable group of people I had ever seen in one place before. In the center of them, unmistakably in the center, was a blond man who can only be described as outstanding. He was classically handsome, burned the color of wet sand, and he generated a vitality that made his presence obvious in that enormous room. With him were nine, perhaps ten, young men and women who were not less handsome but who lacked those ingredients of spirit and energy that made the blond man so special. I knew without having a reason for knowing that he was the one who had sung out for Archie. And I sensed instantly that Archie, whoever he was, was not at that table.

I continued to watch them, not speculating, merely enjoying what I saw. The girls, not one of them over twenty-five, were of assorted types—blondes, brunettes, a single redhead—and they were all fresh and casual and sure of themselves. The men, with one exception, were inferior copies of the blond: slightly less blond, considerably less muscled, certainly less dynamic. The exception was a tiny man with painfully black hair framing an elegant white face; he was truly beautiful—there was no other word for it—and I couldn't help but wonder what sort of mess his face would collapse into when he reached middle age. I carried the thought further, because I wondered about his obvious adoration of the blond and what it would come to when, as it seemed certain, the blond would tire of the adoration and tell him to be on his way.

As I paid my check and rose to leave, I looked a last time at those unusual people, and intercepted a look from the blond. He grinned, waved a friendly hand at me, then turned back to his companions. I left, thinking the blond man's energy was limitless and would possibly not exhaust itself in a lifetime. It was nice to know there was someone like that in the world.

I headed for my room.

I slept through that afternoon and awakened at dusk with the conviction that every idea in my head had shaken into place. I lay quietly for an hour, considering how to use the coming hours and days, and finally decided that I had put everything in proper order and sequence. I could now get out of bed, shower and shave, and look forward with relaxed pleasure to the evening ahead of me.

I left my room and went to the hotel's cantina by way of the footpath that winds along the shoreline, passing through a miniature desert filled with flowers and cactus and uneven flagstones that invite broken legs and ankles. Night had lowered on that piece of land jutting into the ocean, closing over it as warm and moist as a loving mouth. The sensuality of the evening was beyond anything I had experienced, and I intended to enjoy it.

The cantina was almost empty, and I was able to select a table outside the circle of lights and to the farthest point of the free-form veranda. I ordered a drink, settled back, and stared out over the ocean, listening to it moan and give up its ghosts on the sands below me. I had been content earlier in the day; I was now enjoying the pleasure of well-being. All I had to think about was the date and time of my departure for Los Angeles.

Then I heard the accented voice again, hard by my ear, and with it came the brush of a cologne that smelled like oranges: sweet enough, spicy, so elusive that it lingered an instant and was gone.

"Mind if I join you?"

I looked up, and it was the blond man, standing beside me, towering over me.

"Sit down," I said. "What will you drink?"

"I ordered it, thank you."

He didn't sit; he fell into the chair with a gracelessness that made him seem boyish, certainly much younger than his years. I could see now, even in the dim light, that he was not the youth he appeared to be at a distance. He was heading toward thirty-five, had perhaps reached it already. He was at the age when people would begin to say he was amazingly well preserved.

"I'm Carl von Kleinschmidt," he said, extending his hand.

I took it and answered, "David McEndree."

"Any nickname?" he asked. "I have a thing about nicknames. I like them."

"Dave will do."

"I'll think of something."

"Don't bother."

He said, "Don't be put off by me."

"You don't put me off. I'll let you know when you put me off."

He laughed, and said, "You come right to the point. Do you mind my asking what you do?"

"Not in the slightest."

"Well, what do you do?"

"I write."

"Should I know your name?"

"Not unless you read a lot."

"I don't. Only when I have nothing else to do, and then not much. I'm something of a dunce."

I examined him more closely, and decided that he looked nothing at all like a dunce. Spoiled, most assuredly; self-indulged; egocentric, positively, and I couldn't blame him for that. But there was intelligence in his face, a fine tracery of lines around his eyes that made him look cunning and resourceful, a set to his mouth that was both stubborn and decisive. Of the blankness that comes with stupidity and not knowing, there was none.

"If you say so," I said.

"I don't really want you to believe that," he said. "I say things like that, that I'm a dunce, but I don't expect anyone to take me seriously. I guess I'm average smart."

"What do you do?" I asked.

"I enjoy. Not much of a profession, is it? I'm possibly the most worthless person you ever met. I don't take pride in that; it just happens to be a matter of fact."

"Are you always this honest?"

"When I feel on safe ground."

"How do you know the ground's safe?"

"Instinct."

He settled into a silence that was comfortable. I ordered another drink, invited him to have one with me, and waited for him to come up with something else. He moved easily in his chair, adjusting himself to a more comfortable position, and he seemed languorous by contrast with my own tendency to formality and rigidity.

"What do you write?" he asked.

"Articles, things like that."

"Are you writing down here?"

"No. I was interviewing down here. I'll start writing when I get back home."

"Where's home?"

I stared at him, wondering how far he would allow himself to go with his questions. Not that I minded them; I'm used to inquisitive people, particularly those who think there's something magical about the practice of putting one word after the other and coming up with something written.

He intercepted the look, interpreted it correctly, and said, "If I'm asking too many questions, just tell me."

"Let's just say you ask a lot of questions."

"Tell me to shut up."

"No," I said expansively. "Go right ahead."

"Where do you live?" He was persistent enough.

"Los Angeles. And you?"

He grinned, and his whole expression was one of genuine amusement. He seemed to feel I was getting back at him, and he liked that.

"Everywhere and nowhere," he answered. "How about that for an answer!"

"Swell," I said, and gave my full attention to my drink.

"Turn about," he said. He had decided to play it a little straighter. He took a few minutes to ponder what he was going to say.

"I don't want you to think I'm a wise ass," he said.

"I haven't reached that point yet."

He studied me earnestly and frankly. The handsome face was in repose, more or less removed from what his mind was trying to do to it, and it seemed stronger, less petulant and vapid. His eyes were a clear, almost transparent blue, and they scrutinized me without guile.

"I'd like to talk a little," he said, "and I'll do that if you care to listen. That's what I know about you. You're a listener."

"And so I am," I said, not a little surprised that he had arrived at that very accurate conclusion.

"There're few enough," he said. "I can spot them in a crowd. Like picking out a black in a gang of Swedes."

"As easy as that."

"Yes. Anyway, I said I'd like to talk a little."

"You seemed to be doing pretty well earlier today."

"That's not talking. That's clowning around, putting a lot of words together to shut out the silence."

That was a fair enough way to put it, and I was impressed. I had already assumed he was intelligent, and I could now add to that fact another one, having to do with a kind of sensitivity.

Before we could continue our conversation, we both reacted to sounds behind us and turned to see a small procession approaching our table. It was led by the young man with the cruel black hair and the feminine face, and trailing him were two of the girls who had been at the table with von Kleinschmidt. The little man, I could see now, was lightly fashioned and as artificial as a life-size doll; his delicacy was so finely drawn it was unreal. The girls were something else again: large without being raw-boned or coarse, beautiful without distinction, vapid, and, I imagined, dumb enough to be both lethal and predatory; they would have so little going on inside them that they would be capable of any depredation. You use women like that, and you guard yourself against being used by them.

"Continued in our next," Carl von Kleinschmidt said. He was not pleased to see them.

"Who is Archie?" I asked, sneaking it in in that perfect moment.

The blue eyes swung back to me. They were so carefully blank that I knew I had touched upon something.

"Anything you want," von Kleinschmidt said. "Anything you want out of life."

I was introduced to the trio. The little man with black hair was Colin Davenport; the girls were Squeegee and Boomer. Have you ever met two females with names similar to those? I never had, and I was amused, to say the least about it. I tried not to stare as they lowered themselves into chairs and languished in elaborate poses that caricatured elegance. They were with us but not of us, their indifference carried like banners of stupidity.

"Dave is a writer," von Kleinschmidt said to Colin Davenport. Then, to me: "Do you mind if we get on a first-name basis?"

"Not at all."

He continued, "Dave is coming with us tonight."

"I am?" I was surprised.

"Unless you have something else to do."

"I don't. How can I have anything else to do here? But that doesn't mean I'm coming with you."

"Lay it on him, Dorian," von Kleinschmidt said.

I now knew Colin Davenport's nickname and thought it suitable. The beautiful white face turned to me, its eyes regarding me softly from a thicket of lashes, the soft mouth smiling gently. When the mouth opened and the voice sounded, I thought instantly of a famous Catholic priest who is best known for his ringing, resonant speech. I had the impression of being in a cathedral, listening to a voice driving at me from a far distance.

"Carl loves parties, you know?" Colin said. "He's party mad, and he's arranged a special one tonight. He won't tell us what it is. You know, it's maddening."

"That doesn't give me much to go on," I said. "I don't like to be unreasonable, but I do like to know what I'm getting in for."

"You'll have fun," Dorian said. "We all will."

I looked at Squeegee and Boomer, fixed in their chairs like wax dummies posed eccentrically in a dressmaker's shop. They didn't look as though they were having fun or expected to at any time in the future.

"If you say so," I said dubiously.

"Say you'll come," Colin said. "I promise you a good time, you know?"

"Dave is cautious," von Kleinschmidt explained to Colin. And to me: "It'll give you something to write about. I guarantee that."

I looked at Carl, at Colin, at Squeegee and Boomer, thinking about their offer. I was never much of a one for "fun," because other people's fun never appealed to me. It always seemed manufactured and desperate, a grasping after pleasure as a way of relieving intense personal anxiety. But what the hell. I was in Tres Santos, I was alone. Something to do was, on occasion, better than nothing.

"Okay," I said, thinking I could always get out of it if the going got rough.

"Vámonos!" von Kleinschmidt said.

He got to his feet, loping off with the same gracelessness with which he apparently did everything. There was an autocratic quality about him that I didn't like; he seemed to expect to be followed regardless of the direction in which he intended to go. Yet there was nothing arrogant about him. I assumed he led because there was no one else to do the job.

"He's pretty wonderful, you know?" Colin said, rising to his feet.

"If you say so," I replied, and took off after von Kleinschmidt with the others.

We left the hotel and walked to the landing strip that was the northern border of the hotel. There were two Cessnas there, revved up, ready to go, and already partially filled with members of von Kleinschmidt's party. Von Kleinschmidt, Squeegee and Boomer disappeared into one; I was ushered into the other along with Colin. We squeezed into the back of it, past two men and a girl who were already seated and belted in. Introductions again: the two men were Caddy and Belt, the girl was Empress. The nicknames were beginning to unnerve me, mostly because I couldn't fathom their significance. I had to admit, however, that Empress lived up to her title.

She was a girl of darkness: deep-hued hair, skin that was literally bronzed, eyes of a blue blackness, a mouth rich with shadowy redness. She was beautiful, beyond anyone I had ever seen before, and she reflected a maturity that I had not found in von Kleinschmidt or any of his playmates.

As the little plane rushed down the airstrip and climbed lamely into the air, she turned to me. Her eyes narrowed with her smile—a friendly, quite wonderful smile—and she winked in a we're-pals-and-we-understand-each-other way.

"They call me Empress," she said, "but my name is Anna. I think you should call me Anna."

"Done," I answered, and started to wonder if the miserable contraption we were flying in would ever reach its destination. To relieve my nagging anxiety, I struck up a conversation with Colin.

"Tell me about von Kleinschmidt," I said, raising my voice to be heard above the dyspeptic noise of the motor.

"He's quite wonderful," Colin said, "you know?"

"You've already said that."

He smiled gently, and said, "You'll hear it again, because I believe it."

"Doesn't flying in this rig bother you?" I asked. I was unable to account for his composure.

"I'm not afraid of natural things. Only unnatural, you know?"

"What's natural about this abortion?"

"It's sick, but it's not evil. And I'm not afraid of it."

So much for that. I could see that Colin was a great deal more complicated than I imagined him to be. Speaking of unnatural, his calmness was that, as steady and implacable as a perfect heartbeat. I wondered if the same could be said for everything going on inside him.

"About von Kleinschmidt?" I tried again.

"Don't call him von Kleinschmidt; he doesn't like it. Too Germanic."

"He is German, isn't he?"

"A long way back."

"He has an accent; at least, it sounds like an accent." I was thinking of the odd, almost foreign speech.

"That's because of all the languages he speaks, you know? In addition to English, French, Spanish, Portuguese, German, Italian, Russian, and I don't know what all. How would you talk if you had all that going on in your mind?"

"You know," I said, "I don't like to think about it."

Colin smiled appreciatively, and said, "I wouldn't know where to start telling you about Carl. You will call him Carl, won't you?" When I promised, he continued, "You know, he isn't like anyone else. He has dual citizenship, American and Mexican—he was born in Mexico somewhere, I forget where, you know—and I don't think you can really say he has a home like other people have homes. There's a lot of money just about everywhere, he never seems to run out, and he does what he wants."

"He doesn't work?" I asked.

"If you can call it working. Have you heard of H. V. Klein—does that mean anything to you?"

I struggled to bring it into my mind, and it came slowly. Yes, I had heard of H. V. Klein, but I couldn't place it in time or place. I probed further, and it came: a San Francisco importer who specialized in European art objects, with special emphasis on exquisite jewelry. It was the sort of place I would never think of going into; its prices and prestige were too intimidating.

"Yes, I know H. V. Klein's."

"H is for Herman," Colin explained, "V is for Von, and Klein is only part of Kleinschmidt. That's Carl's father. He's alive, you know."

"Sneaky," I allowed myself to say, having in mind the contraction of Kleinschmidt into Klein. For some reason, I found that bothersome.

If Colin heard the remark, and it could have been lost in the roar that was going on around us, he chose to ignore it.

"Carl is manager of the Los Angeles shop," Colin said, "but it's only nominal, you know."

"I didn't know."

"That makes him sound useless, like a parasite. He isn't. You know, he travels a lot and he's always buying. He says you never know when the next treasure will turn up, and I guess he's right. I don't know and I don't bother with those things. . . ." He interrupted himself at that point, and announced, "We're here."

The Cessna was circling, and I looked down at here. From what I could see, we were exactly nowhere. There was a great blackness beneath us, and as I peered nervously at it, I saw something that looked like a coastline, then a little cluster of lights, perhaps the suggestion of a primitive road, then the flare of piercing red lights as an airstrip was illuminated. It was a comforting sight.

The plane landed behind the one in which von Kleinschmidt rode. Hatches opened, we all alighted into the marvelous sweet air, and we started toward two Cadillac limousines.

It looked as though it was going to be some party. I was almost glad I had come.

The Cadillacs in that rough country were enough. What followed was almost too much.

We were bumped for ten minutes over the road I had observed from the air, then driven through the gates of a fortressed wall into the most savage estate I have ever seen. It looked as though a part of the Mexican jungle had been uprooted and planted here in Baja. The trees were enormous and mysterious, with hanging moss and creepers; the flowers, as much of them as I could see, were growing with such aggressive wildness that they seemed determined to kill each other; there were pools and streams in which predatory reptiles and fish would have found myriad delights; and there were hidden birds and animals, making their sounds and screaming their protests.

We drove for several miles through that jungle, and then along a curving roadway that moved in a wide and long arc leading to the entrance of a colonial-style hacienda so forbidding, so rejecting in its closed-and-shut appearance, that it seemed to have formed a perfect marriage with the violent jungle that surrounded it. If I hadn't seen all of it myself, I would have believed none of it.

We left the Cadillacs, passed through the hand-carved gates of the place, then walked into the ravishing heart of Mexico herself; I had never seen her so beautiful. In the best tradition of such places, the four sides of the house—if house it can be called—surrounded a patio garden of fountains, flowers, birds, priceless pre-Columbian statuary; everything, in fact, that gave testimony of taste, extravagance, and fabulous wealth. All rooms opened into this garden, and those I saw had hand-carved and -painted ceilings, delicately pasteled walls hung with treasures, floors of Mexican marble, and furnishings of consummate, staggering luxury.

I was only dimly aware that introductions were being made.

There was our group, of course, and it was promptly absorbed by a fairly large collection of people already there. Some of them were of indeterminate foreign birth, a few were Mexican, several spoke no English at all, others spoke with an accented speech that was hard to identify. No point was made of my getting to know these strangers, and I made none myself. I did, however, meet our hosts, Señor and Señora Martinez y Ochoa.

Sr. Martinez was introduced as owner of the biggest fishing and canning company in western Mexico. I accepted that, and I muttered my *"Mucho gusto"*s in response to his and his wife's. But I reserved judgment. There was something unrefined about them, something coarse and crude that put them not many years away from the feudal peonage of Mexico. I sensed they were uncomfortable in their surroundings and didn't belong there.

I was not given time to wonder further about Sr. and Sra. Martinez y Ochoa. Von Kleinschmidt had given his general greetings like the take-charge prince he was, and he came loping over to me, thrusting his arm through mine and pulling me off and away.

"Don't waste your time with them," he said. "They just own the place."

"You act as though *you* owned it," I said.

He laughed agreeably, and answered, "Not bloody likely. I like to enjoy myself here, but I wouldn't want to live here. No, I'm a stockholder in Pedro's company. Does that explain things?"

I was led to a room that was decorated like a cantina, and we entered to a blast of mariachi music and the lugubrious lamenting over lost love that Mexicans sing about when they're having a great time. As we moved into the group gathered there, von Kleinschmidt stopped me and pulled me a little closer. His smile glittered.

"Are you satisfied with what you heard about me?" he asked.

I shrugged. "Just routine inquiry."

"You were being a good reporter."

"Journalist."

"Snob! You have a human streak. I like that."

His laugh jumped out of him so spontaneously that I decided he was pleased both with himself and with me. I had heard of many playboys, had met a few who were called that and struck me as being merely jaded and bored; but von Kleinschmidt appeared to me to be the real thing. He was born for enjoyment, and what's more, had a full capacity to enjoy himself. I almost envied the way he looked, the way he was, the positive energy he projected.

"Enjoy!" von Kleinschmidt ordered, and left to mingle with his other guests.

I watched for a while, sipping at several Margaritas and eventually reaching the point where I was downing them with alarming frequency. But it was all right. I was gradually being caught up in the movement of the place, drifting toward the other guests, listening to some, talking to others. There was a Serbian scientist who spoke Spanish with the most excruciating accent I had ever heard; a Turkish lady who sounded as though she came from Brooklyn and insisted she was the most celebrated belly dancer in all North Africa; a countess from England who was exactly my idea of what a countess should be; a male ballet dancer, defected from Russia, whose body bulged with muscles.

Anna came to me, hooked her arm in mine, and asked me to dance with her. I protested that I didn't dance, hadn't for a long time, but there was no stopping her. She had me gliding and sliding in a matter of seconds, one hand resting firmly in mine, the other making itself felt on my shoulder.

"Let's not talk about when you last danced," she said. "No apologies, please. They don't become you."

I don't know how she did it, but she made me feel more than competent. I lost my sense of time and place, and I didn't give a damn about them. What was real was what was happening. We ate together, we talked together, we formed small groupings with other people, we broke from them and fell in with others. Always there was the continuing impression, growing stronger, that I first had of her: dark, hidden, brooding, and beautiful.

It was two hours before I asked her who she was and what she was.

"I drift," she said, as though that told me everything. When she caught the frankly quizzical look on my face, she said, "That doesn't tell you very much, does it?"

"Not a lot."

We were strolling in the garden of that magnificent hacienda. There were any number of people rambling around there, but it was still possible to separate yourself from them and feel alone. I had never been quite so alone with such a beautiful girl. Even her scent had a separateness about it, something that increased the quality of her being different. I had to know more about her, and it wasn't the journalist in me seeking her out.

"What would you like to know?" she asked.

"Let's go back to your drifting. Do you mean: small-town girl breaks loose from confinement and sees what it's all about outside?"

"God forbid!" She laughed in a way that was a trill, bubbling out of her as from a soprano who knows she's hit the note. Obviously she liked to laugh, and maybe she did it often.

"If you really want to know," she said, "I guess it's a pretty classic story. That's another way of saying my life is a cliché. My parents got divorced when I was five. Batted from one to the other for about ten years. I first learned what groping was all about when I was twelve, from my father. He was a very stupid and clumsy man; still is, I suspect, assuming he's still alive. My mother was very beautiful, and I thank her for that. It was my only inheritance. She tested her beauty a lot, mostly in bed, sometimes married, most of the time not. I think she's living somewhere in the Caribbean now, but it doesn't really matter." She stopped to think about something, then said abruptly, "I'd love another drink."

I snapped my fingers and drinks were ordered and brought to us promptly. We continued walking. She seemed to like that better than sitting down somewhere and facing me. I had the curious feeling I had trapped her, that she was very reluctant to dredge up all this information and spread it out for painful examination. But I wanted to know more.

"You don't have to tell me any more," I said, "not if it upsets you."

She smiled her deep smile, and I wondered for an instant if everything I had heard so far was a lie.

"I don't mind at all," she said. "I don't think anyone's asked me about myself for, well, I don't know when. People don't really want to know about you; they want you to know about them. The one real exception seems to be their wanting to know if you'll go to bed with them. I sometimes do that, too, but I haven't made a habit of it."

We were getting somewhere, but I wasn't sure where.

"How did you meet von Kleinschmidt?" I asked. "Have you known him long?"

"Carl? Carl the irresistible?"

"Irresistible?"

"I shouldn't call him that. It's just, oh, I don't know. I've seen dozens like him around the world, and they all seem kind of dumb to me. They buy people and think they're using them, when it's really the other way around. *We* use *them.* It makes me very sad, but I don't know if I'm sad for them or myself. I met him in Mexico City."

"Then you haven't known him long."

"Three days, which is pretty long for me." She grinned at her joke, and I could see there was a certain sadness to the lift of her mouth.

"I'm a model," she explained, "and I travel a lot. I guess you could say I'm in demand, which I really am. I had finished a show and a layout for a big Dallas manufacturer, and I was kind of footloose. I fell in with Carl, and that's that."

That wasn't that at all, the way I looked at it. I could see no clear reason for this opulent creature attaching herself to anyone like some leech sucking at bare flesh.

"There's really more to it than that," she said, as though she had gone into my mind and fastened on my disapproval. "I hate to fly anywhere alone; won't, in fact. Carl had a chartered jet flying to La Paz, and I hitched a ride. I really am afraid of flying. Maybe I'm afraid of losing my erection."

She didn't mean the remark to be funny, and I wondered why she made it. It was both defiant and defensive and, I thought, reflected a dislike of her strength and willfulness. I had never before known a woman who appeared to be so completely lost to herself. The only certainty she had expressed so far was her fear of flying, which was in itself significant.

"Had enough?" she asked, and she began to make restless movements with her body. I noticed she was drinking her drink too fast, touching her hair where it needed no touching, smoothing her waist and hips with a restless hand. "Let's see what the others are doing."

I went along with her.

The others were doing what they had been doing from the start: drinking, dancing, talking, moving around the garden and in and out of rooms like animals long caged and at last free. There was no real gaiety here, only a forced explosion of energy that was frenetic and joyless. I had been promised an evening of fun and anticipated one, but nothing had stimulated me so far except the time with Anna. That encounter was troubling more than anything else. It was complicated by the intense pull she exerted on me and my natural impulse to be cautious about any entanglements.

We were wandering, not really comfortable with one another, but reluctant to find ourselves loose and exposed in that pack of greedy, metallic predators. Then Anna led me down a corridor I had not seen before.

The corridor emptied us into a room that stretched the entire length of the rear of the hacienda, or so it seemed. To call it a room is misleading; it was more like the massive assembly room of a Spanish castle. The walls were paneled; the furniture was grotesquely heavy, leather upholstered, and arranged in groupings that permitted minimum privacy; the lighting fixtures were all in the shape of lanterns and dimly lit; there was an abundance of artifacts which were intensely religious and equally primitive in design. We might have walked into the residence of a Catholic official, perhaps a cardinal, or some lesser prince of the church. The only thing that gave the lie to that impression was the pall of smoke that floated lazily over the place, dipping and swirling in a stately dance. I had smelled that particular smell many times before.

It was hard to see what was going on in there. The sounds we heard were muted, murmurings that could have meant anything, sighings, occasional small laughter, movements that were soft and exotic. The atmosphere was rich with suggestion, and yet it was like coming upon the end of the world, when the last people were expelling their last breaths, already resigned to giving up their lives.

"I don't like this," I said.

"Don't rush off."

Her grip tightened on my arm, and she pulled me into the room, maneuvering me as though I were a bull balking at being corraled. I was interested in spite of myself, straining to see through the layers of haze, trying to make sense out of that murky puzzle. There was no pattern to what was going on, nothing that gave a name to the goings on.

Anna jockeyed me around, past individuals, past couples, past groups of no more than three. There was, it seemed, nothing to see. Nobody appeared to be doing anything, and if something was being done, it was accomplished so covertly that it was hidden from sight. I felt strangely disappointed, promised pages of startling pornography and finding nothing but blank sheets of paper.

We rounded one corner of that vast place and saw something that could not be mistaken for anything but what it was. Colin Davenport caught my eye first, a tiny, hunched, white-faced gnome sitting collapsed in an outsize armchair that threatened to devour him as a brown lizard would an insect. His face was no longer pretty, but wizened and slack-mouthed. His eyes were focused and staring, and when I followed their direction, I fastened upon the object of his interest: on an adjoining divan, stripped to the skin, a young man was plowing his way methodically and unlovingly into the naked body of a woman. There was no sound, no suggestion of excitement or satisfaction, no hint of passion. It was sex without relation to human desire, and I wondered why Colin, or anyone else for that matter, could find the spectacle so absorbing.

There was a squeeze from the hand on my arm, and I turned to Anna to see what the signal meant. A look at her face told me the squeezing was involuntary. She had merely reacted to what she was seeing, but there was little in her face that told me what the reaction was. Curiosity was there, and perhaps a small measure of tension. I felt the tension myself as the act was completed and the orgasm was accomplished.

At once, the pull on my arm became directional and we were leaving the room, walking back down the corridor, into the garden, over to the cantina. Anna knew my drink by this time, and she took charge in a new way, calling a waiter over, ordering the drinks, lifting hers gratefully to her mouth as soon as it arrived.

She smiled at me gravely, and said, "We've talked enough about me. What about you?"

It was as though there had been no break between her last remark and that one. There might have been no corridor and no princely den of iniquity or whatever, and no hash and no screwing on the divan.

"Writer," I said indifferently.

"That covers a lot."

"I like to think of myself as a journalist. War stuff when there's a war going on, which happens to be most of the time. I concentrate on human interest, the grabbers that sell magazines and newspapers. I'm very good at that."

"I can imagine." She sipped at her drink and looked at me steadily. "Tell me something else about yourself. Married? Children? Things like that?"

"Three marriages, all of them turned sour. Some of it my fault, some of it not. I'm hard to get along with when I'm involved in my work. I labor at writing and that makes me edgy. I explode easily, at things like singing kettles and the TV too loud, or on at all, for that matter. Terrible."

She smiled, and said, "I never lose my temper, which is one of the really awful things about me. My control is a thing of the gods, or so I've been told. Go on."

"No children, never really wanted them. I think I'd be a perfect father. Fortunately for all my unborn children, I've never been put to the test."

"You're not a fatherly type, if you want to know what I think. At least, I don't see you that way. There's nothing familial about you at all. I like that. You'd be surprised at all the fathers and brothers and uncles I've met, all with the same basic idea in mind, if you know what I mean."

"People are great fools. They're seduced by their own deceptions."

"I'll think about that one."

We both looked up as the commotion in the cantina changed quality. Von Kleinschmidt had entered, followed by several of his entourage. I had not seen him all evening, and was surprised to find that he looked fresher than he had when we left the hotel hours before: his face was sleek with well-being, his blond hair was expertly combed and immaculately in place, and oddest of all, he had changed clothing. I couldn't remember what he had worn when we left Tres Santos, but he sure as hell wasn't wearing it now. What kind of man took a change of clothing to a party?

It was time to go, von Kleinschmidt announced, and then, suddenly, raising a glass aloft, he shouted, "Let's hear it for Archie!"

We heard it for Archie, and we left, filing out to the Cadillacs, piling in and barreling off to the airstrip, climbing aboard the planes, flying back to Tres Santos.

There was something curious about that end-of-the-evening, a dropping off into depression that was swifter than most.

When the two Cessnas unloaded at the Tres Santos airstrip, we all knew it was over, what had been was behind us, and reality sat hunched in the path before us, ugly, indomitable, and inevitable. There was nothing left of the evening, not even the least remarkable of memories. We were sour, half sick with fatigue, sorry it had come to an end only because the future promised to be as bleak as it now looked.

Von Kleinschmidt came to me, as we were struggling to the hotel and our individual rooms, and threw an arm over my shoulder. With it came that whiff of bitter orange, that breezy suggestion of scent that I had noticed so much earlier in the evening. I glanced at him briefly and saw he was smiling, that beatific smile that signaled everything was right with his world, as it always seemed to be.

"It was a doozy, wasn't it?" he asked

"What was?"

He ignored that and asked, "Made up your mind when you're going?"

"Yes."

"When?"

"Tomorrow. The shuttle leaves at nine-thirty, and I'll be on it."

"I'll be sorry to see you go. But we'll see each other again."

"You're sure of that."

"I'm sure." His arm tightened briefly on my shoulder, then dropped away.

We reached the *galería* of the hotel, and peeled off like so many cockroaches rushing to hide from a sudden blinding light. That figure of speech is not inexact, because there was something scurrying and furtive about the von Kleinschmidt group at that late hour. With the exception of their leader, they all looked worn to the nub, a little scrofulous, and manifestly low in spirit.

I said some sort of good night to von Kleinschmidt and went to the lobby. There, drawing on my adequate Spanish, I announced my departure, was assured of a place on the shuttle as well as the jet to Los Angeles, and paid my bill. It was like paying the tab after all the medical tests proved negative. I was going home to familiar and more reasonable territory.

I started back down the long *galería,* enjoying the peace and the quiet and the desert-ocean smells, which now seemed to have adequate breathing space of their own. That was Tres Santos as I knew it best.

I pushed my way into my room, and made an immediate right turn into the bathroom. Clothes off, mouth scoured, a quick shower to get rid of those fetid, lingering smells. I was ready for bed, looking forward to the morning. I now felt well; everything was going to be all right.

Then down the steps to the bed-sitting room, and I turned on the lights on my way, preparatory to inspecting the sheets for centipedes.

But there were no centipedes. Only Anna.

She was outside the room, standing on the little porch that led to my own private garden and the public gardens beyond that. Her back was to me, an incredibly beautiful back that was as naked as my own. It was softened by shadows, and I thought how unreal it was in that diffused light. It looked like part of a painting, soft as the strokes of a brush against white paper. There was no design of seduction here, only a special beauty to be looked at and admired.

I stood quiet, knowing she knew I was there. It was a rare instant in time and I wanted to enjoy it.

She sighed from some deep place, and as she turned to me, I reached for a short robe that had been thrown over a nearby chair.

"Don't do that," she said. She stood there in the doorway, and a sight she was. "Strangers don't cover up, only friends."

I would have to think about that one, and I let the robe drop.

"Why don't you come out here," she said. "It's glorious!" As I started to join her, she added, "Don't ask me why after all I've had, but I'd like a drink."

That was nice. After all *I* have had: that's what the lady said. I had always heard it the other way around: "What d'ya want another drink for, you bum, after all you've had." And I had had a lot, but there was some delicacy in her that refused to include me in her request.

"There's about a half pint of tequila," I said, "and some salt I snitched from the dining room, and a couple of limes that've seen better days."

"Let's make it their last day on earth," she said. "It sounds just fine."

I got the ingredients from the bathroom and joined her on the little porch.

It was all very strange. We were having a party, a nice naked one. Being bare-assed with a lady was hardly new to me, but I had never done it quite so casually before. I couldn't remember a time when I had enjoyed a relaxed drink in anything resembling those circumstances.

Anna was reclining on a chaise lounge. She was clearly to be seen, and I first noticed that she was smiling, a gentle smile that told me she liked me and liked being where the was; nothing more than that, nothing insinuating. Then her breasts, which had not flattened against her chest but were roundly upturned, as though they knew only one position to be in. One knee was raised and had fallen slightly toward her opposite thigh, which took care of that area. I could see she was not about to put on a lewd show for me, and I was pleased about it. That smallest bit of posturing gave her a trivial kind of modesty and made her seem delightfully vulnerable.

I considered my own nakedness, but it had ceased to be of the slightest importance. I was a man, and everyone knew what men were like, and I had no reason to be ashamed. I was not ashamed, except for some minor worry about the thickening of my waist.

I poured some of the tequila into two glasses, gave her salt and half a lime, and away we went. Down the hatch.

"I'm leaving tomorrow," I said. "It's time."

"I'd like to travel with you."

"My pleasure."

She sighed again, and moved restlessly on the chaise lounge. Then she got up, went to the tequila bottle, and poured herself another drink. She downed it, licked at the salt and sucked at the lime before she returned to settle herself again.

"I've had enough," she said, "and I'd like to go back to work. I have a fashion layout to do in Los Angeles, and something's brewing in New York, and then a skip over to Europe, and I'm on my merry, merry way."

"You're never bored?"

"Constantly. But I've thought about all that. I'd be even more bored doing nothing or something else. Anyway, God deliver me from the golden ones."

"You're pretty golden, you know."

"You know what I mean. I was born to be a serious, thoughtful one, and I never made it. Somehow, I'm making it all sound messy, am I not?"

"Messy?"

"Chaotic, then, I'm one person, and I talk about being another. My problem is, I never knew who the hell I was. You don't have any answers, do you?"

"You're very beautiful. Let's begin with that."

She frowned as she thought for a moment, and then said, "I'm not ignoring the nice compliment, but you made me think of something. I was thinking, what must it be like to be ugly but feel beautiful inside, and look out of all your outer ugliness and think how marvelous the world looks and all the people in it, and not realize that all those marvelous people don't see you that way, and that's what's wrong with the way you are. You feel *something* is wrong and yet you don't know it's because people see you as ugly. Now, just reverse all that junk and you'll understand how I feel."

"Very deep," I said. Anna was trying to tell me something about herself, but it was unthinkable that her dark beauty could conceal such an ugliness of spirit or soul or whatever you want to call it.

"Is that all you've got to say?" she asked.

"Pretty dumb, right?"

"The last thing you are is dumb. I think you got my point. Well, what about tomorrow?"

"The shuttle leaves at nine-thirty."

"I'll be on it, and you can hold my hand to Los Angeles. Let's reverse that, too. *I'll* be holding *your* hand to Los Angeles. Scared out of my wits."

"I'll protect you. I've flown so much, I consider planes my second home."

"Do you have a home?" she asked, and there was envy in her voice. "I mean a real home that you think of as home?"

"Oh, yes! Not much of a home by most standards, but the exactly right sort of place for a writer." When I saw her interest quicken,

I continued, "It's a real honest-to-God house, two bedrooms, a den-study, a completely equipped kitchen in which I sometimes concoct poisonous meals for tolerant friends, a living room with a great city view, dogs and cats cared for by the neighbors when I'm not there. What else can I tell you?"

"Nothing, please." She was sad, and I thought of the ugly spirit looking out of the beautiful body, glaring furiously at the ugly world outside.

She sighed again, stirred again, and rose to her feet. Now I could see that the casual conversation of two strangers well met was at an end. An intensity had awakened in her, and it shadowed her already dark face, accentuating the deep eyes and the lavish mouth and the mass of black hair. She looked oddly fierce, like a Medea or an Elektra.

I felt an excitement that shot into my groin. I didn't try to hide it, and she gave no indication that she saw I was aroused.

She walked past me, allowing herself no more than the brushing of her hand across my face. It was a refined gesture that told me she liked me very much, and that was about all it said.

I followed her into the bedroom, and waited until she had laid herself down carefully. Again there was no posing that hinted of seduction; she was doing something naturally, without design or deliberation.

I sat on the bed beside her, less self-conscious than I was when I first became aroused. I looked at her, a little awed by the gift she was giving me without my asking or hinting or conniving or using any of the shabby little devices that almost inevitably accompany making out.

"Light out?" I asked.

"Suit yourself."

"Light on, then, if it's all the same to you."

"I said it was."

She lay still, and I waited.

"Just move your hands on me," she said. "Just move them slowly and gently." And then she added, "I'll tell you when."

I started at her neck, that perfect neck that held that proud and beautiful head and connected it to her extravagant body. I

left up to me. You sure you don't mind it that way?"

I did, but I answered, "Don't mind at all. I think women should make more effort than they do."

"I'll buy that."

I could hear the smile in her voice, and I looked at her. She was bent away from me, her face pressed against the oval of glass that gave her a view of Los Angeles rising to meet the plane. She had smiled, all right, which made it even more difficult to account for the tension I saw in her body. I had never before seen her show any rigidity in any way, but it was there, clearly defined in the angularity of her posture. Perhaps she's just losing her erection, I thought, which is enough to make anyone tense.

The plane landed, and confusion took over as it always does after an international flight. I'm an expert at such things, and neither immigration nor customs holds any terror for me. For whatever the reason, I chose to believe Anna had never been exposed to such mysteries, and I led her through the maze, depositing us finally in the customs shed, where we waited for the luggage of three arriving planes.

I am always surprised at how people behave when they come under the scrutiny of the impersonal, all-seeing customs inspector. They seem to fall to pieces at such times, and I always view with impatience their pulling, shoving, screaming, accusing, lying—you name it.

Anna was aloof if not lofty throughout this display. I had taken two of the coats from her, and she stood to one side, silent and inscrutable, loosely holding a third coat and the makeup kit, seeming not to see anything that went on around her. She relied on me to retrieve our bags.

As we angled our way into line, she expressed regret that I had to be burdened with all her equipment, and I protested that it was my pleasure, which it was. On several occasions, as the line moved forward, she made attempts to take on her own burden, but I continued to resist. Then we were there, at the head of the line and facing a Japanese inspector who happened to recognize me because of the frequency with which I passed through the shed. He nodded pleasantly, and it gave me a charge of vague satisfaction that his familiarity with me was picked up by Anna.

"I suppose you want all of these opened," Anna said, suiting actions to words.

"I suppose I do," the Japanese said.

"And I suppose you're tired of hearing that question, aren't you?" she asked, and her smile was one of the nicest moments of her life.

The Japanese allowed as how he was, and Anna again tried to take the coats from me.

"At least put them down," she said, and she pulled them from my arms and tossed one of them over the opened bags. It was no way to treat sable and mink.

"Oh, God, it's a bother traveling this way," Anna said, and she threw the coats back at me as she plunged into the bag she had covered. She pulled a case from it and opened it to expose the most astonishing display of jewels I had ever seen outside a museum.

"Jesus!" I said.

Anna laughed, and said, "It's just about the best junk jewelry you'll ever see. I'm very proud of it." She took a neatly typed list from her handbag and gave it to the Japanese. "It's all been declared before. Here're the dates of purchase and declaration."

"You're an old hand at this," the Japanese said.

"Traveling the way I do," she said, "I'd better be."

The list was examined carefully and checked against the jewels in the case. The furs followed, scrutinized casually, their date of purchase substantiated by still another list; and again they were piled into my arms as we passed on through and out into the lobby beyond.

I tipped the porter who had lugged our bags out of the customs shed, and then told Anna, "I'll get a cab. You wait here."

"Don't bother," she said easily. "I have to make some phone calls."

"I'll wait."

"I wouldn't like that." She smiled, less charmingly than she had for the inspector. "I've put you out enough. Don't add to my guilt, David."

I was annoyed. "You're not putting me out."

"You're angry," she said, "and you're not very cute when you're angry."

"Angry, no. Annoyed, yes."

"All because you're not getting your way."

She had me dead to rights. "You're sure you'll be all right?" I asked.

"Positive. And thanks, David. You're very kind, and you're wonderful in bed, and I really hope I see you again. I'll remember you're in the book."

"And I'll remember you said that, but I won't count on anything."

"Good!"

Then she kissed me—first time—and those lips did a remarkable job in such a brief instant. I left her then, swinging my bag into a cab, following after it, and slamming the door shut. No backward glance.

"Circle the airport once," I told the driver.

He stared at me in the rear-view mirror, shrugged, and off we went. As we started to make the circle, I felt foolish, not to mention small and mean, because I was deliberately spying. But I had to do what I was doing.

I saw nothing until we came near the United terminal, and then I saw Anna slip something into the hand of a porter, say a few words to him, and hurry into the terminal. Strange, to say the least about it, because I had never heard of anyone flying into L.A. on Aeronaves de Mexico and then heading for Beverly Hills or downtown Los Angeles via United Airlines.

It took a stern face and a ten-dollar bill to get the porter to talk.

"The lady's on her way to San Francisco," he said.

San Francisco? What had happened to that appointment in L.A.?

I have a habit of mind with which I live quite comfortably. That is my ability to put something out of my head once and for all, and to resist any temptation to go back to it again, examine it, and then nag it to death. I did that with Anna, helped by the pressures that were put on me during the next two weeks.

I finished the assignment that had sent me to Baja and my casual encounter with von Kleinschmidt and his troupe, and was immediately sent off on the trail of a rising new film director.

I followed him around for a week, collected my material as quickly as possible, and then retired to the quietness of my hillside home. For two full days I did nothing but find other things to do, important things like crossword puzzles, gardening, which I loathe, making another pot of coffee because the last one didn't taste quite right; I hit upon an assortment of things to do which would have been just as well not done.

Deadline day came and I went to the typewriter. The work went well, and I began to enjoy myself. On the day I finished the article, the pressures of the world rolled away and I felt free. I had nothing to go to immediately, no ideas of my own crying out for development and publication. It was time to take a break from myself, because I had not been free of what was going on in my mind for at least the last year and a half. Where would I go for a holiday?

I was considering alternatives when the Mercedes squealed up my driveway and came to a halt before the open front door. People don't pay unexpected calls on me as a rule, and I was mildly curious as to who it was.

Carl von Kleinschmidt and Colin Davenport.

Von Kleinschmidt was as elegant in the smog of Los Angeles as he was in the crystal clarity of Baja. He was dressed informally, as he had been in Baja, but he had made certain concessions, substituting shoes and socks for sandals and bare feet, preferring a conservative sports shirt and gray slacks to the resort gear he had worn at Tres Santos.

Colin was, as before, more difficult to assess. I wondered if anyone ever noticed how he was dressed. All I saw when I looked at him was the beautiful and tragic face and that unlikely frame of black hair. His overall delicacy always gave him the appearance of being both pathetic and vulnerable.

They stood looking at me, smiling in a way that seemed to come out of pleasure.

"Good to see you," von Kleinschmidt said.

"Come in," I said, backing away from the door.

When they were seated in my living room, I said, "I always expect people to look different in one place than they do in another, but they never do."

"You mean," von Kleinschmidt said, "you'd recognize us anywhere."

"That's just about it. How've you been?"

"Just great."

I said, for lack of something better to say, "Are you here for a while or just passing through?"

"A little of both," Colin said. "Carl has to see what's going on at the L.A. store, you know, then to San Fran to see papa, and then who knows. You know?"

"Do you always travel with him?" I asked.

"Only when I have the time," Colin said easily.

The question didn't seem to disturb him. It would have disturbed me because it had, as I intended it should, several implications. I wasn't exactly sure what those implications were, except for one, which was Colin's sycophancy.

"If you haven't had lunch," I said, "I can knock something together here, or we can go out. Suit yourself."

"We don't want to put you out," von Kleinschmidt said.

"It wouldn't be putting me out. Writers tend to be reclusive and jealous of their time. They need to be yanked back to reality, such as there are such things as eating and social obligations."

Von Kleinschmidt said, "I don't feel obliged to anyone, do you, Dorian?"

"No, I don't," Colin answered. "Not even to you."

"You're not here," I said, being careful about it, "just because it would be unthinkable to come to L.A. without seeing me."

"It would be unthinkable to do such a thing," Colin said.

Von Kleinschmidt said, "Yes, we have something in mind."

He reached into the breast pocket of his shirt and drew out a newspaper clipping. He handed it to me, and I read it. Boiling it down to its essentials, the clipping reported the discovery of the charred body of a woman, age indeterminate, in a canyon of the Santa Cruz Mountains; no identification possible because all areas of identification had been carefully removed, presumably before cremation. I was sorry about it, but it meant nothing to me.

I looked at von Kleinschmidt and Colin, and my face, I was sure, reflected my puzzlement.

After a moment, von Kleinschmidt said, "We think it's the Empress."

Anna? Dead?

Von Kleinschmidt and Colin hadn't changed much in the last minute and a half; they looked pretty much as they had when I last saw them in Tres Santos. But there was a difference, and I was trying to figure it out. It had something to do with their telling me Anna was dead, or at least they believed she was dead.

"Why do you think that?" I asked.

"We know, you know," Colin said, and his voice sounded soft and carefully placed in his small body. "We know what a shock it is, you know. It was to us."

"I'm not shocked," I said. "It just can't be Anna, that's all."

"Oh, yes," Colin said. "It is the Empress, you know."

I was suddenly and inexplicably griped by their insistence on calling her the Empress. I was fed up with Colin's constant use of "you know" as a method of punctuation. I was outraged by what seemed to be their complacent assumption that Anna had been monstrously murdered, they knew all about it, they couldn't be wrong.

"We know you got close to the Empress," von Kleinschmidt said, "and we were sure you'd want to be told."

"What proof do you have?" My tone was even, cold, remote. I might have been asking about the neighbor's dog.

"Clothing," von Kleinschmidt said. "Bits of clothing and fur. Everything hadn't burned. The teeth were gone and prints scored with acid, that sort of thing. But the clothing, that's what did it."

"Did what?"

"Convinced us."

I wanted them out of there. I wasn't aware of feeling any particular hostility or real antagonism, but I wanted them the hell out.

I thought slowly and carefully and said, "How do you know so much about Anna when you knew her only three days? Why are you interested anyway?"

I had obviously said something that amazed them, and they were going to consider it a moment before answering me.

"Three days!" von Kleinschmidt finally said. "More like three years. Whatever gave you that idea?"

Now I knew what I was feeling, but I didn't know at what point in time the feeling came to me. It was a hollowness, a sense of, Well, there goes another one you thought might be a little better than the average, which shows just how wrong you can be, buddy, when you mistrust your instincts. I think I was more bothered by the fact that Anna had lied to me about the length of time she had known von Kleinschmidt and Colin than by the possible fact of her death.

"You didn't come here just to tell me Anna is dead, or that you happen to think she's dead, did you?"

"I'm emotional," von Kleinschmidt said, "but hardly sentimental."

"What does that mean?" I asked.

"He means, you know," Colin said, speaking up for von Kleinschmidt, "he doesn't give a shit if the Empress is alive or dead.

She was a thief, you know, and he doesn't like that."

"That's a strong word," I said inanely. "Thief."

"Not so much strong as accurate," von Kleinschmidt said. "As a writer, you must be an observant man. Did you notice what the Empress was wearing the night of the party?"

"A caftan, mostly oranges and reds, with nothing underneath."

Von Kleinschmidt grinned slyly. "You're not only an observer, you're very specific. Anything else? Was she wearing anything else? Jewelry, for instance?"

"Hoop earrings, large ones. She's a tall lady and they kept hitting me on the cheek when we danced."

"Anything else?"

The district attorney's questioning was beginning to get my back up, but I was determined to be nice until I could politely shovel them out of the house.

"Yes, as a matter of fact. She was also wearing a rather elaborate gold snake around her neck. I remember it because I thought it ugly."

Not so much ugly as lethal-looking. It had surrounded her neck lovingly, and then its body had coiled back and the head was slightly raised in a strike attitude that was all too real. It was quite remarkable as a work of art, I suppose, but I had found it menacing.

"Would you believe," von Kleinschmidt asked, "that it's a very ancient Egyptian ornament, perhaps dating back to the time of Cleopatra?"

"If you say so."

"Would you also believe it's worth at least seven hundred thousand, possibly a great deal more, depending on what the traffic will bear?"

"Okay."

"And would you believe that I own it?"

"I'll buy that, too."

"Then you'll most likely believe that I don't like not having it in my possession. I don't like it one goddamn little bit."

The Carl von Kleinschmidt I was now looking at was a sight to behold: angry but controlled, calculating, insinuating, and implacable. Even Colin seemed wary of him at that moment. In the next instant Carl's face softened into its ingratiating smile, eyes crinkled pleasantly, lips tilted upward. He was something, all right, changing his personality as easily as he drew breath. I've seen his kind before, and I'm still surprised to find so many of them in the world.

I said, "Why was she wearing the necklace if it's yours?"

"When you know someone three years, you think you know something about them."

"She wanted to wear it, you know," Colin added, "and Carl let her. No reason not to."

I had no argument with that, and then asked how I could be of help to them.

"If you could just tell us anything," von Kleinschmidt said. "You saw her last, as far as we know."

True enough, I had seen her last, and there was no reason on earth why I shouldn't tell them what I knew. I omitted her night visit to me and the episode in bed, but I told them everything else there was to know. I was even explicit enough to relate my sense of surprise when I learned she had purchased a ticket for San Francisco.

Von Kleinschmidt and Colin left as soon as they had heard me out. They assured me that they considered me a friend and would look me up next time they were in town. I told them I thought that would be swell, if they telephoned me first.

I received a phone call in the late afternoon of that same day asking if I was interested in a new and challenging assignment: to interview the presidents of four major universities—north, south, east, and west—and arrive at regional similarities and differences as they relate to student attitudes toward the educational process. Not exactly the sort of study I'm accustomed to make, actually a shade rich for my tastes, but I was too flattered to turn it down. I bargained for terms, got exactly what I wanted, and decided to celebrate before getting down to my new job.

Los Angeles is my home, but I really don't know much about it because I'm not there enough to consider myself more than a frequent visitor. But my visits are often enough for me to have made a few close friends on whom I rely for a Los Angeles–based social life. Hiram Rather was one of those.

Hiram was an unlikely friend for me to cultivate because of his profession, which was that of minister; yes, minister, as in minister of the flock. But what a minister! A reformed Methodist, as he told it himself, who could no longer tolerate the strictures of that sect, and who, inspired by a spiritual point of view that came upon him richly and suddenly, kicked over the old and binding traces and started a religion of his own. His religion was like no other and flourished under the noble title Church of Religious Emergence.

To put it as simply as possible, Hiram's religion stressed the divinity of individual and personal rights, or: do whatever you want to with your mind, your body, your entire life, just so long as the evil you're capable of is directed solely toward yourself and never at another person or your environment; better yet, try to keep evil under strict control. It's not as simple as it sounds, but it all makes great sense if you have a mind for such things and a need to pursue such a philosophy in a churchlike atmosphere. I have no such mind, no such need. I just happened to like and admire Hiram Rather.

I called him up early in the evening of that same day and said something like: "I'm between assignments. I need to get a few things off my mind. What do you suggest?"

His great voice and laugh jumped out of the telephone receiver and embraced me. "It sounds as though you need to get laid," he boomed, and laughed again.

"Is that what you tell your parishioners?"

"I do," he said. "It's good for what ails most people."

"You mean that, you really do."

"You bet your ass I do. More orgasms and less hostility, that's my motto."

"You really *do* mean it. My God, what kind of a preacher are you?"

"Lousy. I'm a lousy preacher. But as a minister, there's no one like me. I know what my flock needs, and I know what you need. When shall we meet, and where?"

"You mean tonight?"

He meant tonight. My quite remarkable and hedonistic friend was always ready for anything, and that evening was no different from any other. He suggested dinner at Icelandia on the Strip, and after that, we'd see. See what? Well, he wasn't saying, but we'd see something and I was to leave it to him.

I was cheered by the sight of Hiram Rather, who arrived at Icelandia at the precise moment that I did. He emerged from his blazingly white Cadillac (Hiram always emerged; he was too big a man to "get out" of anything, the way other people do), accepted his parking ticket with a grand gesture, and greeted me like the rosy-cheeked North Wind I remembered from childhood books and cartoons.

Hiram is not actually rosy-cheeked, but he is jolly and God knows he's big. Not a giant of a man, but a larger-than-life man: massive and handsome head, smiling eyes and mouth, a fantastic military posture, and a way with clothes that many a man envied. In spite of his staggering, even overwhelming presence, he is basically simple, always direct, totally unpretentious, and so compassionate that he breaks your heart when his eyes cloud with sympathy. Small wonder that he's the pastor of a wealthy and rapidly growing church.

"David!" he bellowed. "You look absolutely great!"

He grabbed my hand, shook it wildly, and bent close to me. He whispered hoarsely, "Christ, you look awful, but I'm not going to let the whole world know that."

He pulled away then, more or less collared me, and hustled me into the restaurant. During our first drink, I had my personal history pried from me, beginning with the day when I last saw Hiram, which was the day I left Los Angeles to go on my assignment in Baja. Hiram heard it all, down to and including the episode with Anna and the day's encounter with von Kleinschmidt and Colin.

"You should have been a priest," I said when I had finished. "I feel that I can tell you anything."

"I can't compete with the boys in the skirts," he said, "and I don't mean that nastily. They have their place and I think I have mine. They think theirs is divine, and I know mine isn't. Unless caring is a divine quality in itself."

"I think it is," I said. "Anyway, it's good to get it all out. What do you think?"

"I think, without really thinking at all, just kind of feeling my way in the true sense of feeling, that you had contact with a bad lot." He thought for a moment, thought some more as he ordered a second drink for us, and then said, "You haven't said anything bad about anyone, except maybe that Anna may or may not be a thief, which is open to speculation, isn't it? Anyway, you really haven't said anything bad, and yet it all adds up to bad with me. Vibes, as the kids say, bad vibes at that. The flesh crawls and the mind slinks away from the thought of what is behind all this."

I hadn't thought of it quite that way, and I stared at Hiram, seeing in his handsome, strong face a faint cloud of dismay.

"I trust what you say," I said.

"No reason you should."

"But I do."

"It was your experience, not mine. I'm reacting because of my own associations."

"They're more active than mine. I think the experience with Anna, then this news about her death, just about numbed me."

He grinned his big, embracing grin, and said, "We'll have you feeling again, you'll see." He ordered another drink.

At that moment, two ladies came into our lives; well, maybe they were already part of Hiram's, but they were completely new to mine. Not just ladies, either; special ladies. One was Dorothy Denton, a spectacular blonde who had only recently made it to one of the Olympian peaks in the field of entertainment, as they call it. The other was a very cool creature, rather a blunt and earthy beauty, whose name, Cynthia Wallenstein, meant nothing to me when I first heard it. I caught on quickly, because she turned out to be *the* Cynthia Wallenstein, the young and very profligate spender of large sums of money for all the cultural arts: movies, theater, artists—you name it.

They breezed in casually and made themselves immediately comfortable. They were part of Hiram's plan to amuse me and take my mind off myself, and I was determined to reciprocate. It would be my pleasure.

Cynthia Wallenstein said, "If you have Hiram's stamp of approval, you have mine. I've read your stuff, and I like it very much. What are you doing next? If you ever find the time, do something for me, and really expose the capricious idiots who're making the movies and producing the plays these days; I mean really *expose* them. I suppose your job is like most, half good, half bad. We'll have to talk about that sometime; I've always felt there was a lot of journalismese in me, even if that isn't a word. What's everybody eating?"

Cynthia drank her drink, fell into a study of her menu, and was silent.

Dorothy Denton patted my hand and, as a kind of afterthought, my cheek. She said, "I go along with that stamp bit. I love Hiram because he taught me I could be Marie Stark, which is who I really am, as much as I want to, and the same goes for Dorothy Denton. And the public be damned. I never think about who's staring at me and who isn't, and I couldn't care how I look because I think I'm all right the way I am just because I want to be that way."

She certainly looked all right to me, and I told her so. She was pleased, not little-girl pleased, or mature woman pretending to be pleased. She was simply pleased, because someone she had decided to like had paid her a genuine compliment.

"We're all going to get along," Hiram said. "I'm a genius at matching people."

Cynthia looked up from her menu and said, "Your real genius is making it possible for someone to feel alive even when part of him is dead or dying. Is there anything more important than that?"

I have no idea how many hours we spent at Icelandia. We

were there for what seemed a short period of time, and then we were in the study of Hiram's parish house, drinking brandy and continuing our uninterrupted conversation.

I should qualify "parish house," because it's really no more than a converted garage behind Hiram's smallish Georgian church. The death of his wife many years before turned him away from any considerable comforts, and he was quite content to jam himself into three fairly good-size rooms crammed with leather furniture, at least a dozen clocks, thousands of books, and floor-to-ceiling paintings.

It was there that the conversation continued, and then split in half at about one in the morning, when Dorothy suggested I take her home.

Home was a ridiculous shack in Malibu. If there is a relatively expensive ghetto area in that beach city—and there is—that is where Dorothy lived.

The house was perched on pilings, and looked like a mass of mismatched lumber hastily assembled with no thought to style and no concern for architectural aesthetics. It would have been considered a dump in any other location, totally without charm and not fit for human habitation.

The inside was something else again. It reflected Dorothy's effervescent outlook and disposition. Its furniture was nondescript but comfortable, its colors bright and energetic. There were plants in every place a plant could be placed without interfering with through traffic. And then there was its chief attraction: a wall of glass that opened onto a sun deck that overlooked the surging ocean and the far-distant horizon.

"Like it?"

"I'm surprised," I said.

"I'll tell you why," Dorothy said. "You don't think it's a fit place for a movie queen. I am a movie queen, you know."

"I thought all movie stars lived in Beverly Hills or Bel Air or the Colony."

"Not this one. I couldn't handle all that luxury. I was born into poverty and I think poor. But I also think comfortable. Don't you think my place is comfortable?"

I did think so and I told her so. But I also said, "It's like you, but I don't know why I believe that, because I don't even know you."

"Sit down," she said, "and be comfortable and get to know me. Or maybe you'd rather leave. It's almost two. Are you going or staying?"

"Staying."

She smiled, her shoulders heaving with a sigh of relief, and said, "If you'd said going, I don't know what I'd've done. Drunk myself into a stupor, most likely. And speaking of drinking, what'll it be?"

"I'll stick with brandy, and maybe I shouldn't even have that."

"Have it. It'll loosen you up. Do you know you're quite an uptight fellow?"

"Not really, I'm a slow starter, but when I get going there's no stopping me."

"Thank God!"

She left the room, and I wandered around it. It contained more surprises than I had imagined at first glance. Even though it was a hodgepodge of this, that, and the other thing, I could see the piece of sculpture here, the picture there, the odd chair or table that showed taste and care in selection. All of it added up to the further reflection of a complex personality: sophisticated, childlike, mature and immature, and over all was the high gloss of someone infinitely wise. The greatest surprise was a small library that ranged from trashy novels to a row of books covering a variety of historical subjects.

"Now what do you know about me?" Dorothy asked from somewhere behind me.

I turned to see her standing in the doorway of her kitchen, holding two brandy snifters in her hands. She was watching me with an intensity I had not seen before, the questioning look on her face one of interest and perhaps a certain degree of apprehension.

"I'm impressed."

"Good! I hope you realize now that I'm more a person than I am a movie star. Christ! Movie star! How can anyone take that guff seriously? Come along. It's a lovely night and I want you to enjoy my sun deck without the sun."

She walked past me, drawing me in her wake.

"Sit," she said, when we passed through the glass door and walked onto the rickety porch. She nudged me onto a chaise lounge, handed me one of the snifters, then pulled up another chair and sat facing me, her hands cradling her drink and swirling it slowly within the glass. "Tell me about yourself. Tell me everything so we can get that behind us."

"Born in Oakland," I said. Then: "You're sure you want everything?"

"Everything, but try and get it said in five minutes. There're other things to think about and do. Don't ask me what. We'll get to that later."

"Unexciting and unimportant childhood. Nice mother and father, one brother killed in Korea, no family now, which may be a blessing. Educated at U.C. Berkeley, married in my junior year, divorced the day after I was graduated, when we were at last able to admit we didn't like each other very much and had little in common. Worked on a small paper in San Luis Obispo, liked it, married again out of propinquity. I always have the damnedest reasons for getting married, or maybe no reasons at all."

"You're not alone. Go easy on yourself."

"Divorced quickly, left town to put that behind me, and went to L.A. Did some free-lance stories for various magazines, caught on and began getting assignments. Met another writer, thought, This is it, common interests—and that proved to be the worst marriage of all. Competition all the way, and I'd be hard put to say which of us was the nastier. We nastied each other for almost ten years; amazing how much the human body and mind can endure—or allows itself to endure, to be a little more accurate about it. Divorced, taking nothing away from each other except ourselves. Two miscarriages during those years, and I *know* that was another blessing. Can you imagine me as a father?"

She said quickly and softly, "Yes, I can," and her hand reached out and patted my knee, then gripped it gently. She let her hand stay there, and I liked the way it felt, warm and reassuring.

"Not much more. Moved into the house I now have in Laurel Canyon, got bigger and better assignments, put away a little money, made a few good friends, traveled a lot. Pretty boring stuff, actually, and I guess that's what I hate being more than anything else—boring."

Her hand tightened on my knee and she said, "You're not boring to me, if that means anything."

"A lot. Now you."

"One other thing, and it's none of my damned business. What about women?"

"Always. Not frequently or on any permanent basis, but always women."

"I would have hated it if you'd said anything else."

"And now you."

She pulled back from me, her hand slipping off my knee in a soft caress. She settled back against her chair, and threw her head up to look at the sky and take a moment to sort through her thoughts and come up with the best and truest words to describe herself. I felt I could see into her, not because of any transparency she had, but because she was indestructibly honest and put everything she was out in front of her, for the world to see. Looking at her now, her face lifted to the moon and softly shadowed, I saw more beauty than I had at any time in the evening. Her physical beauty was undeniable, there was no argument about that; but I wondered how many other people ever saw the gentleness and the generosity of her spirit. She knew where we were headed, and wanted no other direction; and I knew where we were headed, and wondered with a slow-mounting excitement what it would be like to be folded into and around that body, my face against that face.

"Marie Stark is my name," she said, "my true name, and may I tell you I hate Dorothy Denton—it's so *made up!* But the press and publicity people said it was alliterative—a word they didn't think I knew—and would stick in people's mind. They may have been right. I don't often think about it. Anyway . . ." She paused to ask if I wanted a freshener in my glass, and when I said no, she continued: "My parents were immigrant Czechs, settled in Milwaukee, where I was born into poverty, as I told you, but not grinding poverty. We were just honestly poor. My parents are still living, deeply proud of me, but won't take a cent from me. They won't visit me here, so I go there every Christmas if I'm not on a film, and at Easter if I am. My one brother works in a brewery and he's proud as hell of himself and his wife and his seven children. He won't visit me, either, but he's warm and welcoming when I go home for my visits. He's a real darling, and I love his family. Bright, well-behaved kids. I think I'm going to cry."

She lowered her head and looked at me directly. She was indeed on the verge of weeping, but it would be weeping accompanied by her marvelous, glistening smile.

"I'm so damned sentimental. I weep at everything: weddings, funerals, ballets; I even get tears in my eyes when a baby sits on the potty and grins and gurgles at the wonderful thing he's doing for you.

"I had a baby when I was seventeen. I was married at sixteen, much against my parents' wishes. But I knew better, and so did he, and socko! which is putting it more or less correctly. Along came baby, nine months later. The baby never got to sit on his potty. He died shortly after his first birthday, some congenital heart condition. I was devastated, because I truly loved him even though I didn't truly love my husband; I only loved what we did together in bed." She paused. "Is this getting too sickening? Tell me if it is. It gets cheerier as I go along."

"I'm fascinated," I said, and I was.

"Divorce, just like you, but I never tried marriage again. I didn't sleep around much, either, let me tell you. I did my sleeping around selectively, fulfilling a need, so to speak; how about that for delicacy?"

I said it was admirable, and she went on, "The rest isn't even good soap opera; you couldn't cleanse an ounce of pain with it. I was persuaded to enter a Miss Brewery contest, or some such thing—I really do forget what—and I won. I went on to win a Miss Milwaukee contest, then a Miss Wisconsin, and from there, into the Miss U.S.A., which I lost by a mile. How is all this grabbing you?"

The hand returned to my knee, and pressed more firmly this time. I was beginning to get a solid fix on the idea that she liked me pretty well. And it was nice to know, and feel, that the emotions which were flowing between us were fully reciprocal.

"It's grabbing me fine," I said. "Just keep it there."

She laughed, and it was, to use her word, a cheery laugh.

"Anyway," she said, "it so happened that one of the judges at the contest was an obscure Hollywood producer. He came backstage, asked me to come to California for a screen test, which I did. It turned out well because I had an instinctive ability to make love to the camera. If I do say so myself, the untalented Marie Stark instantly knew the camera better than it knew itself. From there we go to a producer's hand down my front or up my skirt, I don't remember which. And I told him if he ever tried anything like that again, I'd cut off his hand and make him eat it joint by joint. He liked my spirit, gave me a bit role in a bitty picture, and I ran away with it. The critics liked me, the audience liked me, and the rest is history, but you'll never find that kind of history in any book."

She drew away again, and again lay back against the chair, her face turned from me. She had been putting on a show, and now she was sad, or perhaps melancholy would be a better word to use.

"I've worked constantly," she said, "except for those trips back home. Lots of social evenings but always with arranged dates because I haven't found what I've wanted to be connected with—yet. I hope I find it soon."

I put the snifter on the floor beside me, and went to her, knelt beside her, and gently tugged at her face until she was looking at me fully.

"I hope you're down there with some purpose in mind," she said.

"Yes."

"Then be purposeful."

She bent to me as I moved to her, and her lips engulfed mine with a strangely sensual hunger. For years afterward I was able to recall the scent of her: her mouth fresh and moist and smelling of some exotic spice, her perfume rising from her body as though she had recently rolled wantonly around in a flower bed.

"We kiss pretty well," I said. "Shall we see what else we do well?"

Her bed was large and so were our appetites. We devoured each other until she fell into a sleep of exhaustion and I dropped off into a shallow slumber that must have lasted no more than half an hour.

I was dazed with satisfaction and happiness when I started home shortly before dawn. I drove slowly through Malibu Canyon, delighting in the chasing shadows on the canyon walls, sensing that nature was everywhere and I could reach out and grab it and hold most of it in my hand. Those are the magical moments of life, and my state of euphoria was so keen that I knew it would last without any serious interruption for some time to come, perhaps for years.

The thought stayed with me until I reached home, garaged my car, and walked into my house.

I know that house, know it well, and something was wrong. I examined each room carefully, found nothing. Then I stood in the center of the living room feeling the place, trying to determine through my intuitive sense what was disturbing me. And again nothing.

I called to my dogs and cats, venerable creatures who were inseparable and old enough to be totally dependent on me. They didn't come.

I found them hanging by their necks from the lemon tree that stood in the center of my patio.

I have never come completely to grips with that moment. The animals were ugly dead, with eyes bulged and legs contorted with the effort to find contact with something solid and stable.

I was calm, coldly calm. I knew what to do, and I did it. My pets were taken down carefully and laid on the brick patio. Then I went halfway up my hillside and I dug a common grave, poking methodically at the hard dirt and decomposed granite until I was satisfied as to depth, width, and length. I buried my pets in the land they knew so well.

I felt a dangerous and smoldering anger, with hatred not very far behind.

That job done, it was time to think about who had done it and why. The Hollywood hills are alive with more than the sound of music, and it is not uncommon to hear that houses have been vandalized for no apparent reason, burglarized for very good reason, burned to the ground for hateful reasons that stagger the mind, and so on. But I had never heard of hanging animals for any reason.

I considered calling the police, and decided against it. A thorough search of the house revealed nothing missing, nothing, in fact, touched. So what would I say to the police? "My cats and dogs were hanged by an unknown criminal, or criminals, and I've already buried them. They can be disinterred if you'd like to have a look." It didn't make any sense.

I thought some more, decided I didn't have an enemy in the world, so vengeance couldn't be the motive; and finally I decided my mind wasn't going anywhere by itself. It needed some guidance and counsel, and Hiram Rather was there to be called.

I called him, and everything seemed better when that heavy voice rushed to me through the phone to advise me.

I started by saying, "Hiram, what do you think of someone who would come into a house in the dead of night and hang two dogs and two cats by the necks until dead?"

It sounded flippant, but I was trembling with fury, fighting with both hands to keep the phone up to my ear.

Hiram said, "That's a good question, and now I'll ask you one: What do you think of two men who break into the house of a lady who doesn't know them and has never seen them and kick the shit out of her? That's no way for a minister to talk, I know, but facts are facts and should be stated as such."

"What lady?" I asked. "Are you talking about someone I know?"

"You know her passably well. Dorothy Denton."

"Jesus Christ!" What else could I say?

I thought of something.

"I don't understand," I said. "I was with her until five-thirty this morning, and she was just fine."

"That was over three hours ago, and—"

"Lots can happen in three hours," I finished for him.

"Lots did happen in three hours," Hiram said, and there was a severity in his tone that troubled me.

"Are you taking me to task for something, Hiram?" I asked. "There's something in your voice."

"You hear a tone of great concern. Are you all right?"

"Fine, other than angry. Why do you ask?"

"Just wondering. What are you going to do?"

"To start with, go out and see Dorothy."

"I hoped you would say that. She likes you and trusts you, David. Not incidentally, she didn't call the police. She said she wasn't hurt badly enough and she decided neither one of you needed this kind of publicity, now or in the future. How about that for common sense?"

I was touched and said, "She's protecting me."

"Not entirely," Hiram said, his voice rounding out smoothly with wisdom. "Don't be so generous. She's also thinking about herself. You're not the only celebrity, you know."

"I'm not one at all."

"We'll talk about that later. But before you hang up, one last thing. Can I talk to you as an old friend?"

Of course he could, and he did, without my urging.

"There's an aura around you now, David," he said. "It didn't used to be there. But it's there now. It smells to me of decay and corruption, like a lot of the badnesses of the world wrapped into one. I don't know where it came from, but it's there, hanging over you, getting into your home and your work and your life. You've got to do something about it."

"How can I do something about something I don't even recognize? *I* don't smell decay and corruption and badnesses. Quite a way of putting it, by the way. So what do you suggest I do?"

"I really can't help you there. Start using your nose and every other sense you have, not to mention your brain. It's a good brain, David, but you've been putting it down on paper too long. It deserves another kind of life, so let it loose."

That's Hiram Rather for you. That's how he talks, and you'd be wise to listen to what he says. I was listening very carefully.

"I'm going out to see Dorothy now," I said.

And we hung up.

I found Dorothy Denton stretched out on a chaise lounge, taking in the midday sun from her porch. Her face was covered by sunglasses, the mirrored kind that cover the cheeks and jut out past the ears; her body was not very well covered by a bikini; and she looked, all told, very fine indeed. That was at first glance.

"I'm very glad to see *you,"* she said, not moving her position. "Pull up a loose board and sit down."

Looking good and making jokes.

"I heard about you," I said. "Why didn't you call me?"

"I didn't want you to think I was one of those bimbos who sleep around a lot and get beaten in between. You could have, you know."

"Not a chance."

"I like to hear you say that, but I don't believe it. We know each other five hours and we're rolling around merrily in sexual congress. Is that what you call a girl in control?"

I laughed loudly and, to use her word, merrily. I liked that lady lying there, I liked her a lot. She had guts and courage, which are not necessarily the same, and she had a sense of humor about herself. Sexual congress indeed!

"Anyway," she said, "figuring I wanted to talk to someone, I called Hiram. I always call Hiram when I'm hitting around for an answer or I need a little massage for my wounds."

"You could have called me," I said, "and I would have come running. Do you care to talk about it now?"

"Would it make a difference? I know you're not asking out of idle curiosity or because you get a charge out of secondhand beatings."

I was tense again, thrown back all those hours to the sight of my hanged animals, and then pitched forward to Hiram's remark about the aura that hung over me. Yes, it would make a difference if she told me.

"Yes, it would make a difference," I said. "And no, I don't live vicariously, ever. What I do and feel I do and feel."

"Well," said Dorothy, and she shifted position. It was then that I knew she was hurt, because the sounds came out of her like palpable agony. Her mouth contorted with the effort, opening wide and then closing as she bit down on her lower lip.

"Christ almighty!" she said. "Now, *that hurts.*"

"If I promise not to get a charge out of it," I said, "will you tell me what happened?"

"Every detail, if you'll fix me a drink. I know it's too early in the morning, but I don't have anything stronger than aspirin in the house, and I would like to feel a little less banged up."

She needn't have made her excuses, because I was up and away at the word "drink." I was prepared to buy the delusion that a drink would make everything seem a great deal better.

"Well," she said, as she raised her head and sipped gratefully at the stiff one I had prepared for her. "Well, now, where were we? We were lying in bed, that's where we were, after you'd gone. I was thinking how nice it had been and considering the possibility of its happening again. . . . Is that too outspoken for you? I can tone it down some, if you want."

I indicated she had my support, and she continued. "Then I fell asleep. I'm very careless about this house. I'm either dumb or trusting, check one. Whatever, I don't lock doors or windows and I've lived here three years and never been raped or burglarized or molested, child that I am. But all that's finished."

She stopped talking, and I could see she was unhappy; not deeply unhappy, but sort of sad for the passing of days that had been safe and warm and rewarding. She would never feel safe again. As if to show what had brought her to this state, she took off those monstrous glasses and I saw. There was a red welt that lay across her cheeks and nose, in a position just below her eyes.

"That's just my face," she said. "My back is covered with those from my neck down to my ankles."

"Why are you lying on your back?"

"Because I'm a back lier, not a stomach lier, as you may have noticed. It hurt like fury when I lay down and God will punish me to the fullest when I start to get up, but it's not so bad if I just don't move. Another one of these"—she lifted the glass—"and I may even be able to outwit God."

She certainly had guts, and I admired them, and I was guilty because she kept reminding me of Anna. I said, "Well, there you were, sound asleep, and then . . ."

The glasses were back on, but I knew she was studying me, taking all of me in. Close scrutiny of any kind unnerves me, but she was too sensitive to put me off in any way. I didn't bask in that look, but I managed to stay comfortable until she had seen what she was looking for.

"I just want you to know something," she said, "and then I'd really appreciate another drink and a melted cheese sandwich. Are you any good at melted cheese sandwiches?"

"Outstanding."

"That's a load off my mind." She finished her drink. "Well, what I want to say to you is you're a very tender lover and you hardly ever find that kind any longer. Also, you're very personable. If you were really handsome, I wouldn't make any comment about your looks. And I particularly like the way your eyebrows keep their distance and refuse to meet over your nose. Do you realize how many men have eyebrows that meet and carry on in shameful ways? Now the drink and sandwich, if you please. I've run out of pretty compliments."

When I started to say something, she interrupted me. "You're now going to return the compliment, and I wish you wouldn't. I hear enough compliments, but none so fine as the one you gave me this morning in bed, without saying a word."

There's no way to top that, so I took her drink and left her to the sun and the salt air. As I turned in the doorway leading to the living room, I caught a flash of her face at the moment when a spasm of pain crossed it, twisting beyond recognition those features known round the world.

I outdid myself in the kitchen. It was a melted cheese sandwich and then some, perfectly toasted, superbly melted, seasoned beyond anyone's expectation. It was so good, in fact, that I made four and was a little more than generous with the second round of drinks.

We ate silently, enjoying the food, the moment of the day, the pleasure of being comfortable with each other. I had known few actresses, and preferred not to think about those I did know; but this one was different. It had to do, I thought, with her attitude, which seemed to be: Acting is what I do best, it's no big deal but it gives me the money I need, and above all it gives me the freedom to live the way I want to live. In other words, Dorothy Denton is one thing, but Marie Stark is alive and well inside Dorothy. It was a nice way for her to be, particularly since her profession demanded that she be at least two people, and possibly more than that.

I didn't want to get too far away from my reason for being there, and I said, "Your phone hasn't rung once. Isn't that a little unusual for someone like you?"

She said, "I'm not on a picture, I'm feuding with my agent and vice versa, and besides, I turned the phone down as soon as I was able to pull myself together and get off the floor. I called once and that was to Hiram."

She had finished one sandwich and was deep into the second.

Her movements were slower now, almost languorous, and I could see she was less than an hour away from falling into a deep sleep. I decided it would be too cruel to question her about the experience, and I began to make going-away sounds.

She was looking at me again, boring into me through those mirrored glasses. She was only two bites short of finishing her meal, but suddenly she shoved the plate away, grabbed her glass in both hands and started to speak again.

"So there I was, sound asleep, and very soon I wasn't asleep at all. What I was was on the floor in my bedroom. I don't know how I got there, but I was flat on my back, the room was lighted, and I was looking up at two young men. They were lovely, by the way."

"Lovely?"

"Teenage-idol lovely. Tall, very well muscled, very blond, smashingly dressed—in fact, too smashingly for my taste, but good stuff, you know. They could have been twins, only they weren't. Both wearing dark glasses, which seemed a little much at dawn with the sun just threatening to get up, and with identical smiles. Not smiles really; they were more by way of being grins. Yes indeed, those were a couple of grinny boys, I'll hand them that."

I felt chilled. I hadn't noticed before that there was a nip in the air.

"I said, 'And what can I do for you?' " Dorothy continued. "I get terribly cute in difficult situations and it's going to be my undoing."

"You were still on the floor."

"Flat on my ass. What's more, I stayed there, because they weren't quite the gentlemen they seemed. While one of them stood there looking down at me, the other one went into the bathroom, found some linen towels I had stashed away years ago, wet them good, wrung them out just as good, and came back to me and his buddy. One of them rolled me over with his foot, and then they started beating me with those towels. Have you ever been beaten with a wet linen towel? I didn't think so. Well, you just try it if you ever go on a masochistic trip."

She was being very cool, but the coolness was being forced

out of her like juice from a dry lemon; a drop now and then, but nothing there to drink. I wanted to leave before I tired her, and I said as much.

"There isn't much more," she said, "and if I get it said now I'll never have to repeat it, will I?"

"I'll get you another drink. You're getting sleepy, and another drink will push you over the edge. That'll be good for you."

"Later, because I'm getting to the good part. That's the part where they finish with the back and turn me over. I think, Oh, boy, we're going to get it everywhere and isn't that going to be swell, particularly on the boobs, and who needs that. But I was wrong; they weren't working that way. One of them said, 'We're going to give you something to remember for a few days, every time you get near a mirror.' And I swear to God, the sonofabitch took aim and hit me a good one right across the face. You've seen that welt, and I'm vain enough to like it the least of all. The bastard could have put my eye out. Well, it so happens he didn't."

"And that's the story."

"Not entirely. What I just told you was the first time either of them spoke. They were being good little all-American types who were just doing something for my own good. They didn't even grunt. When they were done, they threw the towels into the sink in the bathroom and started on their way. But one of them couldn't resist whatever it was he couldn't resist, and he turned to me and said, 'That'll teach you to sleep with the wrong people.' And they left. Now how about that drink?"

I fixed the drink, omitting one for myself, and I gave it to her after I had given her a very light kiss on the lips.

"That was nice," she said, and she pushed her glasses up onto her forehead so I could see the pleasure in her eyes. I saw pain as well, but there was no doubt about the pleasure.

"When will I see you?" she asked. "I'm not pushing, just asking."

"Will you call me when you feel up to going out, or having me down again, or anything else that comes to mind."

"Sure. You bet."

"And whatever it is, we'll do it."

"You're very busy, I know that."

"I will be. I'll be going away on this new assignment, and I don't know how long I'll be gone. Maybe a month. But I always come back. We'll see each other before that happens."

"I won't make you promise. I hate promises because I never keep them. I don't expect other people to, either. So it'll all hang loose."

"If that's okay."

"It's okay."

She smiled and pushed the glasses down again. I gave her a wave and started to leave.

"David," she said. "I have the feeling that grinny blond bastard meant you when he told me about sleeping with the wrong people."

"I have that feeling, too," I said, and I left.

On the ride home my mind drifted down to Tres Santos, going from my first view of von Kleinschmidt and group in the hotel dining room, to the first and only encounter with blond Caddy and Belt in the Cessna, to a montage of faces at the party hosted by the Martinez y Ochoas, and then back and forth again.

One of the people I thought about a lot was Carl von Kleinschmidt, who was a lovely, grinny all-German boy, but that was an accident of birth. Only fate and a few thousand miles kept him from being a lovely, grinny all-American boy, and that didn't make enough of a difference. The fact remained, he seemed to have a penchant for surrounding himself with mirror images of himself, all of them slightly flawed, to be sure, but mirror images nonetheless. If I was right in my assumption, and I was certainly inclined to believe I was, why in Christ's name would two of them have been dispatched to beat Dorothy, whom I scarcely knew?

I knew I was not dealing well with my dilemma. If I could

come upon a reason, give myself a point of departure, there would be no problem. But there was nothing I could think of to hang on to, nothing that made any sense to me.

Anna, and an antique ornament that cost several hundred thousand dollars? What had that to do with me? Besides, she was dead, which seemed to me to take care of that. I was frankly and completely baffled.

I didn't relish going back home, not with the knowledge that the house would be silent and the grave would look down upon me from the hillside. As it turned out, I had other things than the grave to think about.

I entered my house and instantly knew someone had been there. There was no odor that told me that, no physical evidence of intrusion, no sign of burglary—nothing, in short, that gave the show away.

Yet I knew. Whoever it was, he had left something of himself behind, like a shadow that had detached itself from his person and had achieved a life of its own. For some curious reason, I kept reaching out with my hands as I walked through my house, observing and noting, almost as though I expected them to make contact with the unseen unknown.

I began to face the fact that von Kleinschmidt and Colin Davenport had not visited me solely with the intention of telling me about Anna's death. I began to realize that the deaths of my pets were by way of being either a warning or a punishment or both, that Dorothy Denton was beaten as an indication of how far they would go to intimidate me, to find out whatever it was they thought I knew and needed to know themselves.

And—Goddamn it!—all I knew was what I had said and what met their naked eyes. It was to be hoped that searching my house had brought an end to the wicked charade. But whether it had or not, I was not going to stand idly by and wait for the next move, if any. I was not the sort of person von Kleinschmidt and Colin apparently thought I was; I was not the classically withdrawn writer who is only comfortable with his mind and his typewriter. On the contrary, writing was what I did and was only part of who I was.

Right then, another part of me was furious. I had been threatened, insulted, violated, and I was reacting to all of it. If I was being unfair to von Kleinschmidt and Colin, then that was something I would have to find out. There was the slim chance I had misjudged them, and that had to be determined.

I thought fleetingly of calling Hiram Rather, but decided against it. My mind and body had taken on their own momentum, and I let them carry me where they would go. First stop, the H. V. Klein store in the *galería* of the Beverly West Hotel.

My first good look at the place told me I would most likely never do my Christmas shopping there. I have a quick eye for price tags, and the first one I saw, attached to a crystal obelisk two inches tall, told me I could buy the beauty for one hundred dollars. A silver spoon was a bargain for one hundred fifty, and an enameled brooch was a steal at four hundred. That gives you some idea, and I'm only mentioning the prices for souvenirs.

A magnificent woman well into her middle years seemed to be the only person working in the shop, and I waited as patiently as I could until she finished with a customer. Patience was not really a problem, because the woman was a joy to behold. Her hair was white, her skin was flawless, her figure was astonishing for anyone her age, and her general attitude of poise and dignity was a kind of special beauty. I found myself hoping she was married, had been for most of the adult years of her life, and was still very much in love with her husband, as he was with her. And I also thought that Anna would have looked like her at a similar age, if Anna had lived.

The customer left and the lady came to me, her pretty face smiling, her hands making little movements toward me as though she wanted to shake my hand or embrace me or do something to show how pleased she was to see me.

"I'm sorry I kept you waiting," she said, her voice low-pitched and firm. "I'm Mrs. Perreaux. May I help you?"

"David McEndree," I said. "I'm not a buyer. I'm not even looking. I'd like some information."

"Anything."

"I'd like to get in touch with Carl von Kleinschmidt. Can you help me?"

"I don't know a Carl von Kleinschmidt," she answered, and looked frankly puzzled. I could not doubt her; her honesty was clearly to be seen in the narrow path of concentration that fell softly across her eyes.

It seemed a silly thing to ask, but I asked it anyway: "You do know H. V. Klein?"

"Of course; he's my employer."

"Carl von Kleinschmidt is his son."

"Isn't that strange," she said. "Isn't that really weird."

I waited impatiently as her face tightened and she searched for a way to explain herself.

She said finally, "I didn't know the tall, blond man was his son. He never said."

"What did he say?"

"Mr. Klein hired me about six months ago." She stopped and looked at me openly; she was as guileless as Dorothy. "I feel I can trust you not to repeat what I say. Can I?"

"I'm a professional writer." I grinned and added, "Believe me, I've learned the cardinal virture for anyone, writer or not: Keep your mouth shut."

"That's good enough for me. Anyway, Mr. Klein came in the first week I was here, and with him was the tall, blond man and a shorter, black-haired, rather pretty young man. Too pretty, I should say. I don't know why he made me so uneasy. I kept looking at him, and not wanting to, and then looking some more. I should get on with it, shouldn't I?"

"In your good time."

"Mr. Klein was very angry, not that he's very pleasant at the best of times. He was very curt with me. He told me the blond was to have free access to the shop at all times, to take anything out of it, to put anything into it. I was to obey his orders implicitly—or else. I wasn't about to risk 'or else,' I can tell you. I need this job."

"And that's it?"

"Just about. I've seen . . . von Kleinschmidt—is that what you said?" When I nodded, she went on, "I've seen him three times since I started to work here: when he first came in with his father, again about three months ago, and then yesterday. I must say he's almost as rude as his father. He never acknowledges me, and neither does the little black-haired one. They walk around the shop, talk about various items between themselves, and then leave. They've never taken anything out, but occasionally a special messenger will arrive from San Francisco with some very expensive item that sells on the day of arrival. I find it all very strange. It's almost as though they know there's a customer just waiting for a two-hundred-thousand-dollar ring or a vastly overpriced piece of jade. I can't figure it out, and I suppose I've not been the slightest bit of help to you."

"You've been more help than you know, and I've taken up enough of your time. I have only one more question." She encouraged me with a smile, and I said, "When I first came in, I noticed a necklace in the case near the door. It's the gold one that looks like a striking snake. Can you tell me if it's the real McCoy and how much it costs?"

That time her smile was one that could have been meant for a not-bright child. I could see she liked me and was prepared to explain anything.

"Oh," she said, "if you mean is it authentic, of course not. I don't even know if the Egyptians wore such things, although I think snakes played a large part in their mythology, just as cats did. No, that isn't the real thing, even if there was such a thing as the real thing. It's the work of a New York artisan, and it costs twenty-seven hundred and fifty dollars. Does that answer your question?"

Yes, it answered one question, but, unfortunately, it raised others. If I was mystified before, I was now bemused and befogged. I didn't know what I thought any longer, but I knew where I had to go next.

Before I left the shop, I asked Mrs. Perreaux, "Are you married?"

She gave me a what-a-strange-man-you-are look, smiled, and

told me she was married, had been for thirty-seven years.

"I hope your husband appreciates you," I said.

"For all thirty-seven years. And I've always appreciated him. We've had good times and bad times, but the feeling has never changed."

"That's encouraging," I said, and when I saw the quizzical look that clouded her face, I explained, "I've often wondered if something like that might happen to me at some time during my life."

I called Hiram Rather from the airport, and said, "I'm on my way to San Francisco for a few days. Don't wait up for me."

He chuckled appreciatively. "Am I allowed to ask why you're going there? To my knowledge you haven't been there for seven or more years."

I said, "I'm going to seed my aura, and I'm either going to bring on the goddamnedest deluge you ever saw or I'm going to find it's nothing more than a passing cloud of low density."

"I wish *I* were a writer," he said, "and could get by with things like that! Remember to call me when you get back."

I promised I would, and then I called Dorothy Denton.

"Are you all right?"

"Fierce. I had my welts and wounds and added a sunburn. You didn't spike my drinks, did you?"

"Would I do that?"

"Frankly, no. I guess they just hit me. No matter, because the damage is done and now I ache back and front."

"Is there anything I can do?"

"If you carry any weight up there, pray for me."

I laughed, and said, "I think you'll go to your grave with a big smile on your face."

"I'm on my way now, and I ain't smilin', sweetie."

"You're sure there's nothing I can do?"

"Where're you calling from?"

"The airport. I'm on my way to San Francisco."

"How long will you be gone?"

"Maybe only overnight, maybe longer. I don't know. I'll be staying at the Waterford Court. You can reach me there."

"Only if I need to. Call me when you get back. Is that a promise?"

Of course it was, and I said so. Then I hung up the phone and started for my plane, thinking that Dorothy was very special. It was different with Dorothy, vastly different from the way it had been with Anna. Anna might not have existed, but I never doubted for a minute that Dorothy was alive and well, however sunburned and bruised.

She was an unusual lady, lacking all pretension, remarkably modest, so little concerned with self, in fact, that it was a wonder she had ever become an actress, and a very good one at that. The only thing about her that bothered me was our relationship, which was a little too palsy for my tastes. We had started out just liking each other; we had even gone to bed together as though we were sitting down to a good meal. There's nothing wrong with liking someone and enjoying a good meal, but I wouldn't call it romanticism. I wasn't finding fault with the relationship. I was only trying to determine why it was not wholly satisfying.

Dorothy went out of my mind as soon as the plane touched down in San Francisco. I grabbed up my luggage, battled my way into a taxi, and headed into San Francisco and the Waterford Court Hotel. I love coming into that crenelated city. It's a fortress with identical guardhouses marching up and down the hills in orderly military rows. I breathed in that pure sea air, and wondered why it had been seven or more years since my last visit there.

After I reached the hotel and checked in, I sat in my darkening room looking out over the bay and thinking what I would do for the evening. It was too late to make my visit to H. V. Klein, store and man, and too early to go out on a prowl of the city. I thought of several people I could call on a social level, but opted instead for a quick call to Jay Summerhill, chief of police in Santa

Cruz. I tried him at his office, was told he had gone for the day, and finally reached him at home.

He was pleased to hear from me, as I was to hear his tortured rasp of a voice, the result of a cancer operation performed three years before.

"May and I were talking about you yesterday," he said. "Where are you and why don't you come over for dinner."

"What if I said I was in New York or something like that?"

"We'd hold dinner."

I told him where I was but not my reasons for being there, and he was even more insistent on my coming to dinner. He pretended anger when I refused.

"Then what the fuck are you bothering me for?" he said. "It's an asshole thing to do, making a call just to say hello."

"Is that any way to talk in front of your wife and children?"

"You bet your ass!" he tried to roar. "It's the only way I can keep them in line, being loud and dirty. Well, what did you call for?"

After promising to squeeze in dinner on my way back to L.A., I told Jay I was in San Francisco digging up material on a new story, and I said it might have something to do with an unidentified female corpse found in the Santa Cruz Mountains a week or so before. I asked him if he could fill me in on the details of what seemed to be a more-curious-than-average murder.

You've heard the old saw "A silence you could cut with a knife." Well, the silence I got from Jay Summerhill was so impenetrable it couldn't have been dented by blasting. I waited for something out of him, and when I got nothing, I said, "Jay?"

He sighed, in weariness and exasperation, and said, "How did you know about it?"

"I read a clipping. I think it was from a newspaper in your area, but I can't say for sure."

"It was from our area, and the reporter who leaked it has been silenced like you wouldn't believe. If he ever opens his fucking mouth, I'll tear out his tongue."

"Wow!" Which was all I could say, and I added a little whistle to get my point across. I had rarely, if ever, heard Jay express himself so forcefully. He's tough enough, God knows, but he doesn't go around threatening to tear out tongues.

"You can say that again—wow! What is it you want to know, Dave?"

"Can you tell me anything?"

"We managed to kill the story after that and I never heard that it cropped up somewhere else. Since you know what you do know, and I can't change that, maybe a little more won't hurt."

"Do you know who the woman was?"

"Haven't a clue. Keep it to yourself, Dave, but there were two of 'em. That dumb-ass reporter fucked up. A little too goddamn anxious, that's all. There were two, a woman *and* a man. Fingerprints gone, teeth pulled in the case of the woman; the man had dentures and they were gone."

"Anything at all that might identify them?"

"Bits of clothing, and fur in the woman's case. She must have been one expensive cunt. Everything the best quality; one scrap of material was traced back to a designer in Paris."

My heart skipped once, or maybe it stopped altogether, and I asked, "Any luck there?"

"It was exclusive but no big thing. We couldn't use it."

I wanted to ask if there was anything else, and Jay anticipated me: "Just for your information, and I know you can keep your mouth shut, the reason for all the silence is we hope this leads to something very big. Maybe even international, which is my guess. You see, Dave, it wasn't just the case of two people being mutilated, killed, and then burned to death. Everything didn't burn, thank the sweet Lord, and we know both of 'em were loaded with heroin at the time of their deaths. Are you beginning to see the point?"

I was beginning to see the point, all right. I had to get off that phone, and I managed to do it gracefully and in short order. I promised Jay I would try to make it for dinner on my way down the coast.

There are several physical conditions that horrify me, and leading the list is dope addiction. I couldn't conceive of Anna being addicted to anything, certainly not something as deadly as heroin, and yet there was no logical way I could separate what I had learned from von Kleinschmidt and had learned subsequently from Jay Summerhill. There was ample reason to doubt von Kleinschmidt's word, but not the controlled rage he had displayed when he talked about Anna in my house; he was a man afflicted with a deep sense of betrayal and I have seen much prettier sights in my lifetime.

The haze of dusk had been wiped out by nightfall by the time I began to think about the evening that stretched ahead of me. I had a momentary nick of regret that I had refused Jay's invitation, and then I remembered it was a long drive to Santa Cruz and a long drive back; I certainly didn't need that. There were, of course, the people I knew, some of whom I even liked, in San Francisco. But that meant facing three or more hours of "how've you been" and "what've you done since," and I didn't want that, either.

I settled for dinner on the wharf and a stroll through Ghirardelli Square. I was greeted by the desk clerk when I returned to the hotel, and he said without preliminary, "Dorothy Denton has been calling you for the last hour and a half. I told her we'd give you her message, but she keeps calling anyway."

I got a great kick out of the way he told me that. He was so impressed with the enormity of it all that his young eyes sparkled to the point of being tearful. *He* had *talked* to Dorothy Denton personally, that's what he had done.

I said I would go to my room and put in a return call from there. But the phone was ringing when I opened the door, and it was, of course, Dorothy.

"Where the hell have you been?" she greeted me warmly. "I'm down to my first knuckle with all the dialing I've done."

I laughed and said, "You'll just have to learn patience, Dorothy."

"Patience, my ass. Not with what I have to tell you." The excitement in her voice made it extra husky.

"Has it to do with me or you or both?"

"How the hell should I know? I don't analyze those things."

"Since you won't come right out and tell me," I said, "why

don't you give me a clue and see what I can come up with?"

"You bastard!" She laughed, not really amused, not defensively, but definitely with a trace of hysteria; she was, I could tell, both excited and upset. "What I want to tell you," she said, "is that a little bit of flotsam, or maybe it was jetsam, washed up on my beach today, just around six-thirty. I was oiling myself at the time, and feeling a little better about all my agonies, and suddenly I see this *thing* being hustled ashore by a wave. I couldn't make it out at first, and then I could see it was a person, but I couldn't tell what kind—male, female, you name it. Anyway, I was down there in nothing flat, and the wave gave one last push and threw him practically at my feet. And, Dave! Jesus Christ! You know who it was?"

No, I didn't, but I suddenly felt chilled, as though I did know.

"No," I said, because she seemed to want me to say that. "Was it someone you knew?"

"One of the blonds!" she yelled. "One of the blonds who kicked the bejesus out of me. What do you think of that, sweetie?"

I didn't know what to think.

"Christ, Dave," she went on, "they certainly work in mysterious ways, now wouldn't you say? It happened to be the blond who warned me against sleeping with the wrong people. How about *that!*"

Well, how about that?

Another murder had been added to the list of confusions. I was, of course, assuming it had been murder. It was very remotely conceivable that the blond's death had been accidental or a suicide; and if so, he deserved high marks for giving up his hold on life and aiming himself precisely at Dorothy Denton's beach.

I didn't know what to make of it all, and so I slept uneasily that night. I kept waking, my neck and chest clammy with sweat, my ears attuned instantly to the San Francisco sounds that drifted up the hill and into my room. Normally I love those sounds: the strident staccato of the cable cars, the sad barking of ships in the bay, the laboring grind of tortured automobiles; but I heard them too clearly that night, each one separate and insistent.

The arrival of morning did nothing to lighten my mood. San Francisco was fogged in; shrouded is a better word, covered for burial and ready to be put away. I walked out into that mess in rather an ugly mood, and charged to my breakfast as though I were tearing through some resistant gray wall.

An hour later, fed but not gratified, I was in the center of the city, pushing my way through the door that led into H. V. Klein's. It's worth noting that the San Francisco shop was quite obviously the parent store, father to the son that lived in Beverly Hills. It was housed in one of San Francisco's stately old buildings and was four stories high. It looked and smelled of opulence, dripped with it, in fact, as though an excess of richness had been poured into it and the overflow threatened to seep out through the windows and doors.

It was more geared to the tourist trade then its filial store in Beverly Hills, but I was still not encouraged to do my shopping there. A quick glance told me it had many inexpensive items with which to lure the unwary, but spotted in strategic places were the marvelous beauties that seduced the greedy and the smitten, forced them against their will to buy without regard to price or necessity.

No one approached me as I entered the store. I was allowed to look around, to get my bearings. I very soon saw there were three clerks on that floor, all of them men, and all of them duplicates of one another. They looked alike because they had similarly styled gray hair, wore severe dark suits, and assumed the unsmiling appearance of disapproving undertakers.

There were no other customers in the store, by which I mean there was no one else in the store who could pass as a customer. I found it odd that my presence was not recognized, that not one of the three clerks even deigned to look in my direction, much less inquire as to whether I was just looking or interested in seeing something special. I approached the nearest funeral director and asked where I could find Mr. Klein.

I was rewarded with a look that was as gloomy as the man's suit. I have been examined many times in my life, but never so thoroughly.

"May I help you, sir?" the clerk asked.

"Yes, I asked you where I could find Mr. Klein."

"I haven't seen Mr. Klein today. I don't know if he's in the store."

"Do you think you could check and see if Mr. Klein is in?" I asked.

"If Mr. Klein is in, he'll want to know who you are and what you want."

"I'm David McEndree, I'm a writer, and I would like to talk to Mr. Klein for a few minutes."

The eyes looking at me were, as the saying goes, unblinking. "And what would you like to talk to him about?"

"I'd like to talk to him about his son."

"What specifically?"

"Nothing specific. Just a friendly chat."

"I really don't think that's reason enough—"

At that point our conversation was cut short by another clerk, who came to us, ignoring his fellow employee but taking in all of me. I noticed now that he was the only one of the three who wore spectacles, the rimless variety, which found a precarious perch on his nose.

With his eyes still on me, he said to the other clerk, "I think I can handle this, Mr. Henze." Then to me, speaking as though he were taking words from his mouth painfully, "If you'll follow me."

"You're Mr. Klein?" I asked. It seemed incredible to me that that small, gray gnome of a man could have fathered Carl von Kleinschmidt.

"Is that so surprising?" His body stiffened and he moved away from me as though he was leaving something loathsome behind.

He led me to the double doors of the store, pushed his way through, and let the doors swing back at me. I caught them with my hands and shoved them forward with such force that they hit hard against their hinges. Klein's rudeness was so obviously deliberate and his contempt for me so apparent that it was all I could do to keep from hitting him. But I had no intention of letting the man know he had reached into me so quickly.

When we were on the sidewalk, facing each other with varying degrees of hostility and belligerence, I said, "Is this your office? Is this how you usually meet with people?"

"It suits my purpose at the moment," he answered. "The traffic noises will cover what we say. If you don't like the arrangement, Mr. McEndree, I suggest you be on your way."

There was nothing I could do in the circumstances, and I replied, "Whatever you say."

"Exactly. Now, what is this about my son?" He had little trace of a German accent, but I noticed that he pronounced "son" with a caress, and in such a manner that it came out something like "zone." "What is your interest in him?"

"I met your son in Baja California," I said. "I met him several weeks ago."

"I'm not surprised."

"What doesn't surprise you?"

"He drifts. A vagrant drifts."

"I didn't try to categorize him."

"Nor do I."

"I'm a writer, and—"

He interrupted me impatiently. "I know."

"I don't want to repeat myself."

"You won't."

"You mean you'll see that I don't."

His smile was cold, and I saw his teeth were bad. They were like those of a dog who has chewed too many bones and has eaten too much rich food. They made his smile menacing.

I said, answering the smile, "I take no more pleasure from being here than you do from having me here."

"Then why are you here?"

"I want information. If you can't give it to me, I'll leave."

His look was steady, probing, inquisitive. He seemed not to be in the least offended by my obvious dislike for him. On the contrary, I got the impression he liked facing an adversary and testing his own ability to attack and counterattack.

"I'm not looking for trouble, Mr. Klein. I won't give you any, and don't you give me any."

"What do you want to know about my son?" There was that caress again, that thick pronunciation of the word.

"Where I can reach him."

"What makes you think I can tell you that?"

"You're his father."

His smile was tight and faintly nasty, as he said, "Have you ever been a father, deliberately or not?"

"No."

"What makes you think a father necessarily knows anything about his son?"

"I don't think that. I'm asking you only on the off chance you might know where I can reach him."

"I don't. I know very little about my son. We're not on the best of terms."

"I'm not surprised."

The smile came again, thinner and, in a sense, uglier. "You don't approve of either of us. Like son, like father."

"I haven't taken a position, one way or the other."

"I think you always know your position."

"I'll let that pass. I think you meant it as a compliment."

"I never pay compliments. I was making an observation."

We weren't getting anywhere. "Then you don't know how I can reach Carl?"

"What name does he go by these days?"

I preferred not to show my surprise. "Carl von Kleinschmidt."

"My question surprised you." The man was more astute than I gave him credit for being. "I asked because Carl tends to deny his origin and heritage. He admits to it when it suits his purpose."

"His name isn't von Kleinschmidt?"

"It's von Kleinschmidt."

"Then your name isn't Klein."

"I'm a pragmatist."

"It helps you pass as Jewish."

"It's a business matter, and none of yours."

"I see."

I did not entirely see. What startled me was the honesty. But then, criminals and the insane often feel compelled to confess, and I interpreted H. V. Klein's honesty in that light. His contempt for the world and its people put him above ordinary rules and normal endeavor, and he liked to rub faces in his solidarity. He was, it would seem, a first-class sonofabitch.

"Your son was on his way here yesterday."

"So?" A very Oriental "so."

"He left Los Angeles with his crony, Colin Davenport."

"A sycophant!" He said it with more contempt than he had shown me. "Sycophancy is a loathsome disease."

"Did they come here?" I asked. "Did you see them?"

"Now, that, Mr. McEndree"—and his smile was both wicked and wintry—"is none of your damned business."

"We're wasting our time," I said. "And by the way, Mr. Klein, I like your office but I don't like the way it's furnished."

The smile was now fixed and frigid. "Your approval or disapproval mean nothing to me, Mr. McEndree."

"Good day," I said pleasantly, and started away from him.

"Mr. McEndree!" he called after me, and when I faced him again, he said, "I suppose this won't mean much if anything to you, but be glad you're not a father. There's no heavier burden for a man to carry than an unloving son."

Now, *there* was a thought to carry away with me!

I called Hiram when I returned to the hotel later that morning. He already knew about the blond corpse washed up on Dorothy's beach, and I filled him in on my visit to the H. V. Klein store in Beverly Hills, my informative chat with Jay Summerhill, and the visit to H. V. Klein. I found myself, interestingly enough, trying to explain Klein, trying to find some rational explanation for a man who played out an elaborate charade in his store and revealed such striking ambivalence about his own son.

Hiram said, "It would be interesting if Klein was uncovered as one of the infamous wanted Nazis. He *is* German, isn't he?"

My writer's mind whirled through its acceptances and rejections and I said, "Not a chance. There's nothing great about this man, Hiram. And I don't use 'great' as a complimentary term; I mean in the sense of larger than life. I don't believe he's a great villain. He strikes me as mean, petty, vindictive, jealous, and sly. I suppose he's wealthy, but shrewd and greedy have equaled wealthy more often than brilliant and creative. Klein isn't creative. He's what I call a ghetto snob; that's why the nasty way of being."

"You're crazy about him." Hiram laughed.

"You know, Hiram," I said, "I'm not crazy about much of anything right now. I'm backing off. I think I should leave the dead blond to the police, where he belongs. As for the rest of this mess, I don't minimize the hanged animals and Dorothy's beating, but in a way those things are more aggravating than anything else, like minor punishments that were supposed to bring me into line. I don't know what or where that line is supposed to be, so I have no choice other than to stop looking for it."

"You sound down."

"Very. I always hated games and I never get involved with mysteries. I used to read mysteries because I just plain liked them. Then I began to develop an inferiority complex because people I knew used to be able to figure out the plots and pin down the killer about halfway through. That did something to me, and I gave up mysteries. I'm giving up on this one."

"You think they'll let you alone, whoever 'they' are?"

"I have no guesses. I only have hopes. I'm dealing with some weird behavior, Hiram, and God knows I've tried to find out what's behind it. There's a point at which we all have to give up."

Hiram asked me when I was coming home, and I told him in a day or so. I had just about decided to rent a car, drive down to Santa Cruz, and spend some time with the Summerhills. I was attracted to the place by more than the Summerhills, because

Santa Cruz is just north of Big Sur, which has to be one of the glories of the universe. Its vistas are staggering, its special brand of peace is uniquely its own, and it tempts and tantalizes like a seductress, unlike some of the more flamboyant places in the world, which lay you liked practiced whores. It would do me good to spend some time there.

Having decided that my intentions for the next few days were good ones, we hung up and I called Dorothy Denton.

"Nice," she said when she heard my voice. "Very nice."

"Are you all right?"

"Very all right. A few cops are still hanging around, trying to get leads or something on the dead, but otherwise nothing. Well, not really nothing. I feel terrible, but I leave on a midnight plane for New York and a couple of days of talk shows and interviews. My agent thinks I'm eluding the public eye, and he wants to put me back in there."

It was good to hear her, the vibrant, confident voice rushing on, saying things as they came to her mind just because they happened to be there. She would make a terrible witness in a murder case where honesty was not completely desirable. I doubted her ability to lie about anything, or to be devious or indirect. That made three of the good, fine people: Hiram Rather, Cynthia Wallenstein, and Dorothy Denton.

"You don't mind that, do you?" I asked. "You like New York."

"Moderately. But I do want to see a new play which someone tells me someone else should buy for me. If I like it, I might even buy it myself. It sounds like something Jeanette MacDonald might have liked, but who knows."

"I didn't know you even knew Jeanette MacDonald, or knew about her, I mean. You're too young to have known her."

"Shows what you know! I'm a fan, idiot! I've cried through *Smiling Through* seven times, and I can give you back all her lines in *Love Parade*, and what else do you want to know? I even *think* of myself as the new Jeanette MacDonald. The trouble is, no one else sees me that way."

I could understand the problem. I didn't think of her that way myself.

"There's a catch." She was going to finish the thought. "I don't think Jeanette would have someone like you on her mind, now would she? She wouldn't be thinking it would be swell if I were there or you were here. I don't suppose she screwed around much, do you? She seemed to spend most of the time singing to Gable or Chevalier and being brave. Those were the days, David, weren't they?"

I never did get to answer that one, because there was a discreet rap at the door and I excused myself to open it. It was the bellhop, who handed me an envelope with one hand, extended his other for payment. I paid and went back to the phone.

"I'm keeping you," Dorothy said.

"Not at all. I've finished my business here and I'm starting back by way of Santa Cruz sometime today."

"Any chance you'll be coming to New York?"

"You never know, and I really mean that: you never know. Where will you be if I do come?"

"I don't know. Call my agent, Abe Lansing, at MCE. That's one thing the fathead always knows, where to find me, and that's because I'm very good about telling him. But get me a job? Forget it."

"Bitter."

"Very. I'll call you or you call me. Okay?"

I said it would certainly be okay, and I thought that I might very well decide to check on things at home and then fly to New York. I realized I was getting a little too secure professionally and not paying enough attention to my contacts in New York.

I was beginning to crawl back into a state of good spirits. The only thing troubling me at that moment was a slight matter of time. It was early in the afternoon and I had to decide what to do with the rest of the day: take a nap, see a few friends, cut out right then and go on down to Jay Summerhill's?

While making up my mind, I looked at the envelope delivered by the bellhop and noticed for the first time that it was elaborately addressed in a heavy Elizabethan script, and read: *Mr. David McEndree, Esq., Waterford Court Hotel, San Francisco, Deliver by hand.* For another thing, the envelope itself was made of a canvaslike parchment paper, like nothing I had ever seen before; it must have cost a fortune.

I opened the envelope, pulled out the enclosed note, which was made of the same parchment, and read:

Please come to a bazaar of natural wonders.
Enjoy cocktails, viands.
Time: Five until the last guest leaves.
Date: Today
Dress: Casual

A separate enclosure listed an address in Mill Valley, which is an exclusive rural area north of San Francisco.

The thing that attracted me about the invitation was the anonymity. I had been trying to think of satisfying ways to pass the hours left to me in the day. A way had been presented to me. My problem was solved. I had always been curious.

As I left the hotel, I told the desk clerk I would be checking out in the morning, waited briefly for a rented car to wheel up before me, and took off.

There is nothing I can think of that equals an unhurried drive through the Mill Valley region of San Francisco. Every road is a new experience, winding up out of or down into arroyos banked with trees and festive with ferns. You never see a house straight on; they always peer out at you, like sedate ladies who are too polite to let you know you'd caught them in an unguarded moment. The cries and shrieks of children are musical, and barkings of dogs sound rude and intrusive.

It was close to an hour before I found the road I was looking for. I turned off a main artery to bump and lurch down a paved but rutted lane that was aimed like a shattered arrow into a pocket of forest. The late-afternoon sunlight vanished and I turned on the headlights for several rough minutes. Then the sun blasted through again, and I found myself on the rim of a small valley, looking down on an octagonal house that was made of redwood.

It was the house in the forest that many people dream of—isolated, serene, protected, unself-conscious. The redwood itself was a warmth, bright and alive with the force of the sun; it threw off glints of energy. The glass facings of its eight sides, all of them ceiling to floor, reflected the tones of the sun like prisms. It was an enchanting sight.

Encircling the entire house was a veranda, also redwood, and filled with plants and flowers and small trees. That tiny and oddly shaped forest extended at one point into a larger area, and it was here I found the swimming pool, so artfully situated that it was part of the terrain. No chrome tables and deck chairs there, only smooth rocks decorated with pads that blossomed with vivid colors in startling contrast to the browns and greens: hot orange, vermillion, bright yellow.

I was cheered by the sight of the place, and yet mystified to see no sign of life, no indication that I was about to attend a party. I drove down to the house, circled into a generous parking area, and with a sudden and odd rush of suspicion, left my car in such a position that I could leave the area straight on, without maneuvering.

The door to the house was open, and I walked directly into its main room. I saw instantly that it embraced four sides of the octagon, that one of the sides was already open and led to the pool, that the room itself was riotous with colors, most of which appeared to be flower tones. In addition to all that, I caught a glimpse of a huge stone fireplace, dancing and glowing with a burning fire.

I saw nothing else about the house, because I saw Anna!

She was standing toward the back of the room, near a table that was already crowded with bottles, glasses, plates of food, a bucket of ice. The pose might have been deliberate; she held a glass in one hand, ice tongs in the other, as though the party had already begun and she was just about to fill the order of a guest.

It was Anna, all right. She was dressed in a sheer white blouse with, quite obviously, nothing underneath; a pair of suede slacks that clung to her as though they would never leave; bare feet;

no ornamentation of any kind. I stared at her. She was much more comfortable with me.

"I have a couple of drinks left in a bottle of tequila," she said, "and I can rustle up some salt and a couple of sad limes. If you don't want that, how about Scotch, or maybe it's gin you drink."

I said, "I'd rather have the tequila and sad lime first time around."

"You're sentimental."

"Yes."

"Second time around?"

"Scotch on one cube of ice, no water. Lots of Scotch."

"Sit down. Would you rather go outside?"

"Outside."

Acting on that, I went out to the pool area. I needed those few minutes to myself. She was so casual I felt disconcerted, and I was determined not to let her know ever again how deeply I felt before, after, during, in between. Anna dredged up my vulnerability like a laborer, and the experience was painful. I decided it would be wise to lie low for a while.

I thought it was curious that we had not exchanged greetings; we might have seen each other barely an hour or a day or so ago, for all the amenities we had observed. But that was just as well, because it kept our meeting sane and casual.

She came out carrying a tray that held an ancient bottle of tequila, a fair amount of salt, and two limes that looked as tired and wrinkled as old whores. We drank our drinks silently, downing the tequila, licking the salt, refreshing our mouths with what was left of the limes.

"So much for that ceremony," Anna said, and smiled. "I'm glad you did that."

"You're as sentimental as I am."

"Something like that. I don't like to be the first to make such an admission, that's all."

"I'm not sentimental often enough to be ashamed of it. Now, how about that real drink?"

"And some food? It's all ours, you know. This is the party."

She spread her arms wide to indicate the small portion of the world that was exclusively ours, to do with as we liked. It was an expansive gesture, and I could see she delighted in making it.

"No food now," I said. "I take it you're not rushing me."

"You read the invitation?"

I nodded.

"Then you know the answer to that one."

"I didn't plan on staying here any length of time. I didn't bring a change of clothing with me."

"I'm sure we'll find something suitable for you in one of the closets. Don't worry about it." She went for my drink.

The invitation had said until the last guest left. It was all mine, a decision I alone would make. I intended to take my time about making it.

When she returned with the drinks—one for herself as well as the one for me—I watched her carefully as she walked from the house, bent to give me the glass, then moved away to find a seat near me. Her movements were astonishing, as elegant and as poised as those of some superb animal sure of its body and familiar with its responses. She didn't have to think about what she did; she acted out of some primitive knowledge that, I was sure, had never failed her. I had never known anyone like her, certainly no one who was so consistently superior and unique.

"You look fine," she said. "A little thinner, maybe, but fine. Have you been well?"

"Very well," I said, "physically. I've had some bad moments inside my head."

"Anything you want to talk about?"

"Not now. If we get around to it."

"You not only look fine, you look extra spiffy."

I grinned. If she said so, it was so.

"I didn't know what I was getting into," I said, "so I played it safe."

"I played a long shot. I was counting on your journalistic curiosity. Journalists *are* curious, aren't they? Or is that part of their mystique and I'm taken in by it along with everyone else? I hate the word 'mystique,' by the way. Why do we all use it?"

"It's convenient. It's like heating up a TV dinner instead of starting from scratch."

"Is *that* what it is!" She laughed. "I hate TV dinners, too. I want you to know that everything you're having here tonight is strictly from scratch. I did it all myself, which is a side of me you know nothing about."

"I'm eager to learn."

"I don't have many more surprises."

"You're forgetting one. How did you know how to reach me?"

She studied me for a moment, then smiled that teasing smile I had seen a few times before. It indicated that she was not prepared to tell me what I wanted to know. My satisfaction was going to be delayed.

"It's still lovely," she said. "In another hour the sun will be down and it'll be cold in this valley. Would you like a swim?"

"Anything to get out of giving me an answer?"

"Something like that. I have a feeling a lot of questions are going to be asked, and not just by you. I think it's too soon for questions."

With that, she rose to her feet, stripped off her shirt and pants, and stood quietly waiting for me. I could do one of two things: stare at her, which is what I wanted to do, or break the strangeness of the confrontation by following her example. I did both.

We swam for a longer time than I expected to, playing on occasion as youngsters play in water, but generally swimming easily, aware of one another but having no need to break the quietness around us with talk.

I followed Anna's lead, leaving the pool when she left it, taking the towel she handed me to dry off with, going after her into the house, where she indicated I should sit on the huge couch that flanked the fireplace. She provided a robe for me, one that was both warm and colorful, but again I followed her lead and remained naked.

"I'll fix another drink," she said. "You just sit there and enjoy the fire. I told you it gets cold here."

She gave me the fresh drink and sat at my feet, leaning against my knee and looking with me into the fire. Her hand moved to my ankle, then made its smooth way up my leg to my knee, down again, up again. She shifted position, moving back against the couch so that her hand could roam freely, over my knee, up my thigh. It was simple, very simple. It was gentle and ingenuous, as subtle as light breezes flowing through grass. It was erotic, as it had never been erotic before. She gripped me tenderly and firmly, moving her hand to know every inch of me.

"I'll move my hands on you," she said quietly. "We'll see where we go from there. Lie back."

I lay back, my breath caught in my throat, feeling the pounding of my heart, and seeing its movement in my chest.

I thought it would never be like that again.

We lay on the sofa, heads propped up on pillows at opposite ends. Dinner was an hour behind us. Before that, we had made love, rediscovered each other physically, going about it slowly and deliberately, making certain no pleasure was overlooked.

I concluded time and again that I didn't know who Anna was. I would get a fix on her personality, and would then be diverted, set off in a direction totally unfamiliar to me; and I would land in a territory where I had never been before. She *was,* to put it at its simplest, and I doubted that even she could tell me *who* she was.

She said into the silence that lay between us, "When you think, everything goes to work inside you. I never knew a man like that before."

"Or a woman?"

"I don't think much about women, if ever."

"What do you mean, everything goes to work?"

"You throb. Not really; you know what I mean. It's something that happens to you."

"I was thinking."

"I wasn't going to ask you about what. Maybe I don't want to know."

"I was thinking about having another drink. Can I fix one for you?"

"You fix the fire, I'll fix the drinks. More brandy, or something else?"

I said the brandy would do, and I got up to throw logs on the fire and poke at the embers. I took longer than I needed, because I was, indeed, thinking. Anna had, after all, done nothing but take a plane for San Francisco instead of stopping off in Los Angeles. You don't hang a person for something like that. But the fact that kept staring at me, ugly and indelible, was that my suspicions of Anna really came out of von Kleinschmidt and Colin Davenport, a devilish set of twins if there ever was one, and I felt compelled to act on what they had said or implied.

I said, after we had rearranged ourselves on the couch, snifters warming in our hands, heads back as they had been before, "I had a surprise visit from von Kleinschmidt and Colin since I saw you last."

There was no word from her, no movement.

"Are you there?" I asked.

"I'm here."

"I said I saw von Kleinschmidt and his little pal."

"They turn up in unlikely places."

I felt her move, then heard the faint sound of her sucking at the snifter, taking in a mouthful of brandy. It was a pleasant sound, a kissing sound.

"I wasn't overjoyed to see them. I didn't mind much, either, I guess, not at first."

"At second you minded."

"Yes, I minded because they accused you of being a thief and said you were a liar."

"That's all?"

"No; they also said you were dead. I could ignore the other two. That one got to me."

"I'm the healthiest corpse you'll ever see."

"There seemed to be no doubt in their minds."

"Which says something about their minds."

She was not flippant; she was indifferent. There was a politeness about that exchange. I couldn't understand it.

"It was very disturbing to me to hear you'd been killed."

"As you can see . . ."

"I didn't see you then. There was an accident; there was also an unidentified woman killed. I took the trouble to find out."

She said, "I don't mean to sound as though I didn't care what you felt or thought. I don't care what *they* felt or thought, about anything."

"They don't mean a thing to you."

"How could they? I only knew them three months, and that's too short to really get to know anybody."

"They said they'd known you three years."

"That's tiresome. It's just not true."

Three days. Three months. Three years.

"I don't know what gave me the impression," I said carefully, "that you'd only known them three days."

"I might have said that. I'm very weird with time."

"I live with time. Minutes, hours, days, weeks. Bells go off. I was like that before I faced my first deadline."

"I never faced a deadline in my life."

I'm naturally dogged, so I continued, "Among the other things your boyfriends told me was that you'd stolen the snake necklace you wore at that party. They didn't seem to be kidding when they told me, either. I'd say they were goddamn serious, Anna."

She laughed, and I remembered that laugh from before. It was filled with merriment that choked up out of her before it broke free and became round and vibrant. "Oh, my," she said. "Oh, dear."

"I told you a good one."

"Indeed you did, darling. A very good one. Will you excuse me while I go to the john? I've been wanting to for two hours."

She returned dressed in a flannel nightgown, ruffled at the neck and wrists, white as clouds, decorated with tiny roses. It should have looked absurd on her, and it did not. It was just right, it was elegant, it was so feminine that it excited me more than her nakedness.

"Now, you just hold it," she said. "I'm going to say something and then I'm not going to say anything more."

She sat beside me, her hands held primly in her lap, her head bent to me so that the black hair fell forward, concealing half her face and giving her beauty an Oriental quality I had never seen before. The firelight had something to do with that, leaping out at us, touching her skin with colors that would never be there in ordinary light.

"God, you're beautiful," I said.

"Tell me that later. Let me talk now."

She took my hand with its brandy snifter and lifted it gently to my face. She was not only telling me to shut up; she was seeing to it that I did.

"I did not steal the snake necklace," she said. "I know how you must have felt when you heard that. You like me, and I like you. It hurts to hear things like that about someone you like. If I heard you used a ghost writer, I'd be destroyed. No, not destroyed; I hate that kind of exaggeration. But I'd be terribly hurt.

"I did not steal the necklace. The necklace is a copy, and it isn't even gold. I don't have a single piece of real jewelry. It's all fake, even my pearls, which are only cultured. That isn't really fake, but you know what I mean. My necklace—I have it here and I'll show you—is made of an alloy, and it's mine, I bought it in New York. Twenty-four dollars and ninety-five cents. I even have the sales slip. There *are* gold copies; I saw one in Marshall Field's in Chicago, another one in Bonwit's in New York. I wouldn't buy a gold one if I could afford it. I'm too careless, and yes, I'm too indifferent. I'm very sloppy in some ways, you'll see.

"Carl and Colin are mad at me. All those people they have around them are there because they're good in bed, good audiences, fun to be with, or couriers. I was supposed to be a courier. I wouldn't go to bed with any of them, I didn't find them amusing, I'm not amusing, so I was destined to be a courier. Courier means smuggler, David; let's make that clear. Usually it's jewelry for the Klein shops; Carl prides himself on never having paid duty on anything. I don't know how proud his father would be of that, but then I've never met his father and maybe he thinks the same way: 'Let's see what we can get by with.' Sometimes it's drugs—little amounts of coke, bigger amounts of grass; nothing really big.

"I was supposed to be a courier. When I went with you to Los Angeles, I was supposed to pick up a Fabergé brooch from a destitute Russian countess or her destitute child or something. I never believed in that countess and destitute crap and it made me very nervous. I was to get the brooch, smuggle it back into Mexico, and it was to be sold to some wealthy rancher in the state of Chihuahua, some dude who collects junk like that. My feeling was I was getting into something crooked. I thought the brooch was legitimate, but I also thought I was getting it from a thief. My instincts gave me a bad time on the flight back to Los Angeles, and I cut out and came back here.

"So much for Carl and Colin. I guess they were a little put out. Carl doesn't like losing. It gets him in his ego."

She took the snifter from me and drank from it, making that kissing sound I found so attractive.

"I'm going to bed," she said, giving the glass back to me. "You stay here and think. I think you want to do a little thinking. And I want to be asleep when you come to bed. When I wake up, whenever I do, I want to find you there. I like surprises."

She left me, and I started thinking.

She had explained everything—and nothing. There was no clue she had given me to the mysteries that still bothered me. I didn't know why Carl had been so angry. There was still no explanation for my hanged animals. The beating given Dorothy made less sense than before. I continued to wonder why it was so hard to find any information about von Kleinschmidt's whereabouts.

I accepted as true everything Anna had told me.

I awakened when she started to mount me. Her movements were languorous as she savored the experience, carefully made so there would be shared enjoyment. It was one of those moments when her selfishness became a gift that was given without reservation. She was thinking of herself, but she was not forgetting me.

I did as little as possible. It became a double pleasure for me, because my mind was as involved as my body. I was watching Anna, seeing the tension in her face, that marvelous parting of her mouth which meant ecstasy was getting close to agony. Then, without warning, she bent forward in a convulsive movement of her body that brought her breasts to my chest, her mouth to my mouth. Her mouth fastened on mine, wet and devouring.

There was no lingering time between our climax, which was hit like singers making it to the high note together, and the next thing we did. Anna pulled off me and dashed from the room and through the living room, out the door to that rippleless swimming pool. I was close behind her.

She said to me at breakfast, "What, of all the great things we could do, would you like to do? I mean things like horsebackriding, swimming in the ocean, picking berries, looking for antiques. Things like that."

"Why not start out doing one thing at a time? Let's pile into my car, set out, and let the world find us."

That is what we did. We traveled, going where our whims lay, following the pulse of the car and responding to the names of road markers. We ended at the beach, driving into an attractive old whaling center that was just beginning to spoil from the heat of popularity. We agreed that we had reached it just in time.

We had lunch there, and later in the afternoon went antique hunting in the countryside around Santa Rosa. I found a correct moment in which to ask her about the house.

"It belongs to the Neilsens," she said. "The Neilsens are old friends. I went to school with Noreen and was a bridesmaid, that sort of thing. Her husband's an architect and he built that house for their own use. There was an awful murder just a few miles away and Noreen was so frightened, she swore she'd never stay in the place alone. They bought a condominium in San Francisco and use the house only on weekends and holidays, when Jack can be with Noreen. They're in Europe now, and I have the place for as long as I want."

"How long will that be?"

"You mean how long am I going to hang around? You can come right out and ask, David. I haven't thought about it, I really haven't. What about you? How long are you going to hang around?"

"I have all the time in the world for my next assignment. I guess I'll hang around as long as you'll have me."

Her hand snaked out and caught my arm. She tugged at me, and I turned to see her face was dark and frowning.

"Don't say that," she said. "Don't you ever say anything like that to anyone!"

I was astonished. "Like what?"

" 'As long as you'll have me.' "

"It's what I meant."

"What about how long you'll have me?"

"Never gave it a thought."

"I really don't like it, David." She shook her head emphatically. "I don't have any control over you, and I don't want to have."

"That's not what I had in mind."

"What then?"

I tried to think of what it was I had in mind, and I was unable to come up with anything but the truth. All I knew was that I had a passion for her, to be with her sexually, physically, socially, all the ways there are.

"What I had in mind," I said finally, "is that I like you very much. I like being with you. Now, is that so bad?"

"It's not bad," she said, "it's a heavy load. I can't carry it all; I never could."

She terminated the conversation. Something attracted her attention along the road we were traveling, and she asked me to stop. If there was something to look at, I didn't see it. I had retreated into my mind, and I was remembering that day some weeks back when she left me at the Los Angeles airport and headed for San Francisco. It was happening again; I could feel it coming.

I wanted to make the break this time, and I intended to do it as soon as possible. I didn't mind letting her have the lead in most things; I refused to let her have it in all.

I was fully and cautiously aware of her for the rest of that day and into the next. On the afternoon of the third day, I decided it was time to go.

My decision made, I found no difficulty in maintaining the mood of the day. Anna and I swam in the late afternoon, made a kind of caramel love out on the sun deck, showered and got dressed in slacks and sweaters, then sat down to a slow dinner. Our comfort was as thick and creamy as I had ever known it to be.

I said at one point, "People are always saying how one thing reminds them of another. Tonight reminds me of no other night I ever spent in my life."

"That's a very nice thing to say." Anna was propped up in a corner of the couch, her face directed toward the fireplace and its burning logs. There was an unearthly quality about her, a contrasting whiteness and darkness, an impenetrable serenity that I had never seen before. It put her completely out of my reach.

"I'm not used to all this calm," I said. "Now that I think about it, it's a whole new way of life."

"Maybe you'll get used to it."

"I wouldn't want to. I wouldn't enjoy it in quantity; I'm too perverse."

"I haven't seen that in you. There're times I've thought you were a little too straight. You can get hurt that way."

"Is that a warning?"

"Now you *are* being perverse."

She shifted on the couch, and it seemed to me she did it uneasily, as a way of doing something that would change the atmosphere. "When I was a little girl," she said, "I always wanted each day to last forever."

It was not what I would have expected her to say.

She said, "I wanted each day to last forever because each day was perfect, and I thought there would never be another like it. I guess that was because I was born into love and I was surrounded by it for all of my childhood."

Was she now? I tried not to stare at her, but I wanted to see if she was preparing more surprises for me. I couldn't detect any sign of mockery or malice in her face.

"I always thought your young life was on the grim side," I said.

"Whatever gave you that idea?"

"I guess something you said."

"I dramatize myself. It's a nasty habit. I don't know why I do it, unless it's because I feel dull otherwise."

I let that one go by, and said, "So you were a happy, lovable child."

"You don't believe me."

"Every word."

"I doubt that. What about a drink?"

She didn't wait for the answer. In a matter of minutes, I was nursing a large load of brandy, enjoying the taste of it and its slow passage through my body.

"Tell me more about yourself," I said.

"I don't want to repeat what you've already heard."

"I'll stop you."

She thought a moment, and said, "I got into modeling because I didn't want the loving to end. Mother died when I was fifteen, horribly—I mean she died horribly, not that I was fifteen horribly." She chuckled at her little joke, and continued, "There were just Dad and myself. He was terribly good to me, really good. He gave me self-confidence and taught me to be self-reliant. I was just short of twenty when he was killed; it was exactly one week before my twentieth birthday. I got through that, and all I had to do was use everything he'd ever taught me. I found I was strong enough to survive, and I started surviving on the day of his funeral."

She lapsed into silence quite suddenly, uncoiled herself from the couch, and left the room. I was sorry to see her go, but I wasn't sorry she had stopped talking. The absurdity of her heart-rending story had made it a good deal less than rending. It was certainly puzzling, and perhaps that was all it was intended to be.

I swallowed my drink, fixed another, and lay down before the fire. I stared into it, listening for her, hearing no sound. I started to go over the lines I would use tomorrow, the it's-about-time-I-got-on-my-way lines. I thought about how important she had become to me, and how smart I was to cut out now, before I couldn't handle the importance.

I fell asleep.

I awakened to find myself on the floor, the fireplace dead, the room soft with sunlight, my shoulders and arms and legs stiff with the rigidity of my sleep. I also found a note that was lying within inches of my hand, a scrawl that showed all the signs of haste as well as a poverty of ideas. It read: *I believe in going just so far and no farther. I hope you feel the same way.*

There was no salutation, no signature. It was the kind of kiss-my-ass note that I might possibly send to someone I thought very little of. I hated it.

I lay there for a while, thinking about it all, and coming to the conclusion that I had indeed been had. What bothered me most of all was my sense of self-betrayal. I had had the premonitions, I had sensed it coming, and yet I had let her get away with it after all.

I made a tour of the house. She had come and gone, that much was clear. I don't know how she managed it, but there was no trace of her. There were, to be sure, traces of the two of us: unwashed dishes, used bath towels, a Kleenex she had used to wipe her mouth clear of lipstick, signs and smells in the bathroom we had used together. Otherwise, nothing. She had even gone so far as to make the bed, assuming, of course, that she had slept in it. I had no idea when she left; it could have been as soon as I had fallen asleep.

After making coffee, I showered and shaved and dressed, and took one last look around. The doors were shut, the windows tight, the gas and electricity off. It was all closed up, and I included

Jay continued talking about that case and others. I was a good audience and he made the most of me. It was pleasant to be on the porch of that old-fashioned house in Santa Cruz, drinking straight Scotch on the rocks, and very good Scotch at that, listening to an old friend talking about himself and his business. There was meaning to life when friends gave it continuity and had an inflexible interest in you. Jay was such a friend, and we had maintained our friendship in spite of his wife, who was a terror and deserves no mention here.

I stayed in Santa Cruz that first night and into the next day. Then Mrs. Summerhill (I always thought of her that way) became too much for me, badgering Jay and belaboring me with local gossip, and I made my excuses, claiming business pressure. I invited Jay to Los Angeles for as long as he cared to be my houseguest, and took off for home, where I'd find the peace and quiet in which to do the thinking I had to do.

When I reached the airport, I called Hiram and Dorothy, announced I was on my way, and promised to call them at my first opportunity.

That night, Dorothy Denton came for me at eight o'clock precisely. I hadn't asked her to come, I hadn't known she would come, and certainly I didn't know her reason for coming. There she was, standing on my doorstep, the spectacular blonde who was almost as familiar to the world as she was to me: unforgettable, sensual face, the splash of white-blond hair, the figure that was said to have no rival, the attitude that was a little hard and perhaps more than a little knowing. It was good to see her.

"This beats all, doesn't it?" she said. "Dorothy Denton comes to pick up a man."

"You look great," I said, and reached for her.

She eluded me long enough to tell me, "I just learned this

afternoon it's Hiram's birthday and the party's on me. Now, how about that?"

Then she kissed me with energy, grabbed my arms, stepped back from me, and said, "Let mother see how you look." She kissed me again, with considerably more energy, and drew back again to say, "Would it be unladylike if I were to say I'd like to screw right now?"

I started to pull off the slacks I'd just put on.

"I never did like a pushover," she said. She watched me undress and seemed pleased with what she saw. She could, indeed, see everything but the twinge of guilt that shot into me at the thought that I'd been with Anna just a few days ago. On the other hand, it wasn't as though I were depriving either of them of something. I didn't ask them what they were doing in between times, and I didn't expect them to ask me. As a matter of fact, neither of them had ever questioned me about a possible other life. What was my attack of conscience all about?

It was great to be with Dorothy again, totally unlike being with Anna. Dorothy was a mechanic; she knew precisely what to do and when to do it. Anna was an artist, putting all of herself into making love as though it were something that had to be created and not merely set into motion like a machine. I had no complaints about either technique.

We were almost an hour late in picking up Hiram and Cynthia Wallenstein. I knew how pleased I would be to see Hiram, but I was not prepared for the lift it gave me to see Cynthia. Her angularity and no-nonsense approach to life were an unusual joy, a decided contrast to Hiram's roundness.

We had dinner at Pepino's, a very elegant and very expensive restaurant on the edge of downtown Los Angeles. With our first drink, I suggested we toast Hiram's birthday first, and then something very important to each of us at that moment.

Hiram spoke up: "My ministry, which is growing fast enough to demand a new church."

Cynthia: "Building Hiram's church, which is going to be my project."

Dorothy hesitated, then said: "I have a project, but I can't talk about it. Will you pass me?"

Something was coming from her to me, but I couldn't read what it was. I said: "It's hard to put into words. The best I can do is . . . getting out of the woods and into the clearing. Being here with people I love and respect."

Dorothy said, "That's two. I didn't even have one."

"I had one for you," I said.

We ate. A superb dinner of caviar, veal piccata, gnocchi, delicate salad, mousse. It was a feast, and made better, as it had been once before, by the marvelous spirit of belonging and enjoying that the four of us shared.

When dinner was over, Hiram announced grandly that it being his birthday, he got to say what we would do next. What we would do would be to return to his house, settle ourselves comfortably with brandy or whatever, and listen to music on his stereo system. I'm not that familiar with good music, and I knew it was a total mystery to Dorothy, but we became addicted to it that night. We listened for two hours, our mouths shut and our heads receptive to sound, and the feast was continued. It was sharing as I had never experienced it before with another person, let alone three others.

The mood was still upon us when we separated for the night and Dorothy and I got into her car for the ride home to my house. Neither of us wanted to interrupt the sensations that were still moving around inside us. Dorothy made the break finally.

"I would like to stay with you tonight," she said quietly. "It's Saturday and I have nothing to do until Monday at ten."

"Okay. I'd like that."

"What's your schedule?"

"Yours."

"That's very nice, you know it is. I'm just barging in."

"No. You just said it first."

"What *is* your schedule?"

"I leave for Texas on Tuesday or Wednesday. I have to start my research."

"How long will you be gone?"

"I'll be in and out as I gather material and start putting it together."

"I think I could stand that."

"It'll take me at least a month to get it all together."

"I'll be ass deep in a picture by then."

"I'll wait."

"And I'll wait."

"What's the shooting schedule?"

"Eight weeks."

"Swell. I mean really swell."

I gave her a glance and I saw she was smiling. It was a childlike smile which meant she knew everything was going to be all right.

"We'll do anything you want this weekend," I said. "It's all yours."

"I'll make a list. Let's start it off by getting to bed as soon as we reach your place."

"You make me feel wanted."

"You are! You are!"

We started into the hills, wound through the canyon, and finally made our grinding way up my street. My house is hidden from street view, and you come upon it suddenly by making a sharp turn into an ascending driveway. I made the turn and I gave a gasp.

The only thing I could say was, "Sonofabitch!"

All lights in the house, grounds, and garage were blazing like a Mexican festival!

"Jesus!" Dorothy said. "You didn't leave all those lights on, did you? Or did you?"

I started a slow crawl up the driveway. I didn't like any of it, and I looked quickly for things that would represent normalcy to me: my car, which was safe and still in the carport; the front door, which was closed and presumably locked; the windows, all of which were closed, with panes of glass intact. All perfectly normal except for the lights!

I rounded the car into the parking space in front of my house, and then I saw the first of it: There were dark spots going up the front steps, patches of glistening wet darkness that were so regularly spaced they looked as though they had been painted there. I followed them with my eyes, and I saw they came from the carport. Then, with a start of realization, I knew they had originated in the car and had dribbled from the carport to the house. Swell!

I said to Dorothy, "Why don't you take your car and get the hell out of here?"

"I knew you were going to say that," she said. "Would it break your heart if I said no?"

"I knew you'd say *that.* You've got a lot of guts."

"I've got a lot of something," she said, "and it has a lot to do with you. Shall we go face the bogeyman?"

I laughed, finding the use of that word a throwback to my childhood. Only, in my childhood, blood came from your nose or your finger, and it never formed spots as large as those leading into my house.

I said, "I hope we face a bogeyman. I could stand that. I don't know what I'm going to do if we find a real live person."

We got out of the car, walked up the steps, entered the house. Dorothy rattled in her throat with alarm. I handed it to her. She didn't scream, though she had a perfect right to.

We didn't find a real live person. We found a real dead one.

He was blond, sitting absurdly and comfortably in an easy chair, stark naked, a hole drilled into his forehead. I noticed instantly that his face was masklike but not unpleasant to look at. He must have been shot when he was at ease with himself and the world around him. His composure in death was, I decided, obscene.

"He's like the other one," Dorothy said softly, marveling. She looked at me, trying to communicate her sense of wonderment. "The dead one on the beach."

I was trying to figure out the conventional thing to do with a corpse found lounging in your living room. In a curious way, his nakedness was an affront. Fuck you, he seemed to be saying; if you don't like it you can lump it. I never did understand what that meant, to lump it, but that's what the blond seemed to be saying, all right.

"Did you hear me, David?" Dorothy said. "I said he's like the other one. Not twins exactly, but dead ringers or something. They're even built alike." She thought about that for a second and said, "Well, as far as I know, they're built alike. The other one wasn't quite as altogether as this one, if you know what I mean."

Her giggle brought me to, and I began to listen to her. In thinking back, I had indeed heard everything she said. She was telling me without putting it into so many words, that a pattern was forming, and it got uglier the larger and clearer it got.

I started to be sensible. "Now, Dorothy, I'll tell you what I think we ought to do. You get back in your car and you get the hell out of here. No arguments. I don't want you involved in this and you're not going to be."

"You've just hit a large area of resistance," Dorothy said. "What's your next idea, and we'll see how I get along with it."

"I'm not joking," I said. "You get out of here. When I hear your car heading down the hill, I'll call the police and I'll take it from there."

"I'm a witness—your only one."

"I sent you home before I made the discovery."

She was scornful. "You sent Dorothy Denton home? Now, who in Christ's name is going to believe that?"

That made me laugh when I didn't want to. "I have a reputation for being a little crazy," I said, "particularly with the police department. They'll accept anything from me."

"I don't like it, David." She was very serious and beyond further jokes. "You think it's going to be simple, and it's not."

"Miss Denton is right," a voice said from behind us. "It's not quite that simple, David."

As we turned to the sound, Dorothy edged closer to me and grabbed my wrist.

Carl von Kleinschmidt and Colin Davenport were standing

there, just inside the door. They might have been two charming, highly desirable guests arriving for a party. Their elegance was carried to limits I had never seen before: Both wore dark suits, white-on-white shirts, vivid ties; their hair was suitably styled, their faces fresh and shining; and their immaculate shoes could easily have mirrored their faces. I wasn't happy to see them.

"May we come in?" von Kleinschmidt asked.

"By all means," I said. "You arrived just in time." When Dorothy moved uneasily at my side, I said, "You know Dorothy Denton, of course."

"Of course," von Kleinschmidt agreed. "It's a great pleasure, Miss Denton."

"A pleasure, you know," Colin Davenport said, and gave a little bow.

"It's marvelous meeting my fans," Dorothy said.

"They didn't say they were your fans, Dorothy," I said. "They're my fans. Aren't you, boys?"

"Our pleasure," von Kleinschmidt said, and he came farther into the room, Colin following him like an echo.

"Drink?" Dorothy asked. She was being the perfect hostess, composed and gracious. I knew her well enough to know she was filled with tension and hostility. She had taken an immediate dislike to them.

"No, thank you, Miss Denton," Colin said. "You know, you really don't like us, do you?"

"Aw, come on!" she said, and moved from me restlessly. "Don't lay that on me. I like you just fine."

Dorothy was taking it well. She was, after all, a highly competent actress and it was just possible she was creating a scene for herself out of that strange circumstance. I felt easy about her. We were both doing pretty well.

I said to von Kleinschmidt and Colin, "I know you didn't make a timely arrival. Do you mind telling me why you timed your arrival?"

"A fair question," von Kleinschmidt said. "I think I will take that drink. Dorian?"

"If you're having one," Colin said. I wondered if he ever did anything entirely on his own. "We'll both have Scotch on the rocks."

Dorothy moved to fill their request like a fat lady to food, happy to have something to do. As she mixed the drinks, I looked at my visitors, at their elegance and finesse, as neatly conceived as varnish brushed over a beautiful canvas. They were unreal. My father and mother would have called them "collar ads," because they were both so impossibly good looking and well put together. That description didn't cover everything. There was another quality, so hidden and insidious that it kept eluding me. It would take more perception than I had to determine what sickness was at the core of those two men.

"I'd ask you to sit down in my best chair," I said to von Kleinschmidt, "but it's occupied."

"Maybe one of them wouldn't mind sitting in its lap," Dorothy said brightly, and handed out the drinks. She said to me, "I didn't fix you one, David. Maybe another time."

"It's not my night for heavy drinking," I said.

"Keep your wits about you and all that, you know?" Colin said. He smiled sweetly, the pretty face almost beatific as the brilliant teeth came into view.

"Something like that," I said. "Now, if you don't mind, I'll call the police."

"Let's talk first," von Kleinschmidt said. "Nothing very serious; just a little clarification."

Again I said to Dorothy, "Why don't you go? There's no reason for your staying."

"There's every reason," von Kleinschmidt said. "We never expected to catch Miss Denton. She's our bonus, and we like that very much, don't we, Dorian?"

Colin smiled his approval, as though something fabulously witty had been said. I was beginning to hate his display of perfect teeth and thought about kicking them all out.

"Are you telling me"—I was being very slow and deliberate, making every effort to keep things clear—"that you don't want me to call the police at this time? This precise moment?"

"Something like that," von Kleinschmidt said. "As a matter

of fact, that's exactly what I'm asking you to do. I'm asking you to not call the police."

"Very well put," I said, and the artificial things I was saying came back at me, sounding stilted and phony, as though I were doing a scene in a dreadful play. "I'll leave it up to you. What should we discuss?"

"The options," von Kleinschmidt said.

"Your options, you know," Colin said.

"I get a choice of things I can do," I stated. "That's very reassuring."

"We want you to be reassured, you know," Colin said. "We don't like ugliness any more than you do."

Dorothy came to me again, attaching herself to my side as though it were safe there, taking my hand in hers and holding it in a strong, dry grip. I pulled her with me as I sat down in a chair closest to us.

"Sit down," I said. "I guess this is going to take a little time."

"As little as possible," von Kleinschmidt said. "We just want to tell you what we're about."

He sat on the sofa, with Colin next to him.

"You should listen to Carl, you know," Colin said. "He's going to be very precise, you know, aren't you, Carl? You should hear him out carefully."

I was being warned, and I didn't like it.

"There are three things you can do," von Kleinschmidt said. "You can let us handle this. . . ." He indicated the corpse, who now, in the circumstances, had begun to look like a rather racy guest who had forgotten his manners. "That's what I would like to suggest that you do. Let me handle the body and the mess."

"Did you know him?" Dorothy asked.

Von Kleinschmidt stared at her, then smiled a rather mocking smile, and said, "What an odd question."

"I thought so, too," Dorothy said. "And that isn't an answer, either."

Von Kleinschmidt turned back to me, and said, "Or you can call the police as you wanted to do. We'll see what happens after that, when we get to the third thing."

I said, "I'm not used to having dead bodies in my living room."

"One gets used to it," von Kleinschmidt said, "or can get used to it in proper circumstances. But you suit yourself."

I went to the phone and dialed the operator. "Give me the police, please. I guess that would be the Hollywood station." When the connection was made, I said, "I want to report a murder," and I gave my name and address. Then I went back and sat down next to Dorothy.

Von Kleinschmidt got to his feet, saying, "May I use your phone? I really don't need to, but I'd prefer to."

"Help yourself."

He dialed, listened for an instant, and said, "Carl here. Thank you."

I looked at Dorothy and managed a smile. "It's all very routine, isn't it? Killing isn't as difficult as we think."

A squad car manned by two officers was the first to arrive. They were followed by a lieutenant of detectives; he by a police technician and a photographer; and after them came a medical examiner; finally an ambulance and two attendants.

The efficiency of that small group of men was admirable. All went about their business with a total disregard for the circumstances or environment in which they found themselves. They asked what questions needed to be asked, recorded the answers or not, according to their individual needs, and left as soon as they had accomplished what they had been sent there to do.

The lieutenant lingered longest and asked the most questions. He showed no interest in any of us and permitted himself the luxury of a reaction only when he at last recognized Dorothy and acknowledged her place in that sordid production. When he was finished, he left as had the others, thanking us quietly and suggesting that we hold ourselves available for further questioning. I was sorry to see him go.

I did ordinary things to fill the vacuum left by the departure of the police officers. I turned off all outside lights, cut down the number of them burning in the house, set a pot of coffee to brew with Dorothy's help and suggested it might be time, as well as a good idea, to hustle up some bacon and eggs. I did all that without making acknowledgment of the fact that von Kleinschmidt and Colin were still there, still sitting on the sofa, as they had been before, during, and now after the police investigation. They were as dignified and expressionless as penguins.

When they didn't go away, I hit them head on.

"Why don't you get the hell out of here before I throw you out?"

"We'll go when we finish our business with you," von Kleinschmidt said.

"I have no business with you."

"You should think, you know, about that," Colin said.

"We have something in mind," von Kleinschmidt said, "and we want you to cooperate with us. It would be better for you if you did cooperate."

"Don't be a hardhead," Colin said. "That's what Carl calls you, you know."

"Clever."

"Not really clever, you know, but an exact description." Colin addressed himself to von Kleinschmidt and gave him a reassuring wink that seemed to say: Everything is going fine; now's the time to give it to him.

Von Kleinschmidt faced me again, and I saw that the handsome, tanned face was drawn and white enough to be considered tense. There were lines around his eyes and mouth that I had never seen before, and they showed up against the tinted skin like brown furrows drawn into place by some sharp instrument. For one of the few times in my life, I was glad that my passable face with its marks and lines was honestly come by. It would never be corrupted into the handsome-ugly mask that von Kleinschmidt was showing to me then.

He said, "Let's go over a few things, David." He considered those things for a moment, then said, "What do you think about your phone call to the police? Did you notice there were no press people here?"

I had noticed that, had even been surprised by it. I made no answer.

"You're an honorable man with a great deal of courage. We thought you'd do what you did, so we made arrangements in advance."

"You know people in high places," I said.

Von Kleinschmidt nodded agreeably. "Quite a few; most of them corrupt and easily persuaded, one way or another."

"I don't believe that."

"I think you do. You've been around too long and in too many places not to believe it."

He had me there. I had known more than a few people in high places myself, and most of them revealed an amazing lack of integrity. It had been proved to me more than once that positions of power usually gave rise to expedient behavior: what is mine is mine, and now I want more no matter what the cost to anyone else.

"No comment?" von Kleinschmidt asked.

Again I said nothing. I looked at Dorothy and saw her face was anguished. Her control was slipping away and her mouth was twisting with the violence of her thoughts. She was beginning to tremble, and she clasped her hands tightly in her lap in an effort to keep the tremor from becoming visible.

"I don't believe this," she said. "I just don't believe it."

"You'd better believe it," Colin said amiably. "It's all happening, you know."

She turned to me for reassurance. "David?"

I had nothing to say to her, and I turned back to von Kleinschmidt. "Get on with it."

"Gladly." He was more at ease now, looked less malevolent. "I was saying, we made our arrangements before coming here. You have nothing to worry about for the time being. Now mark that: for the time being."

"When should we start worrying?"

"When you refuse to do what we want you to do."

"And that is?"

"Not so fast." He held up his hand to warn me against going on. "We want you to be perfectly clear as to what your position is, and I mean both you and Miss Denton." He looked at her without seeming to see her, and she returned the look with a grimace of pure outrage and disgust. He saw that, all right, and said, "You could kill us, Miss Denton, I know."

"Happily."

"Leave the killing to us. I should say, leave it to the people who do it for us. Dorian and I don't get involved in such things, and we don't authorize it unless we feel it's necessary."

It was a strange word to use, "authorize," and he caught my reaction to it.

"Authorize is what I meant, David. We're very well organized and we rarely do anything without thinking it over carefully. The young man who was carted out of here drank too much and talked too much when he drank. We can't have that, you know."

"Oh, no," Colin echoed him, "we can't have that. The same goes for the young man who washed up on your beach, Miss Denton. He was talking about his encounter with you, very indiscreet, you know, and we couldn't have that, either."

"Why was it my beach?" Dorothy asked.

"It seemed an amusing idea at the time, kind of like rounding everything off perfectly. You know?"

"Jesus!" The enormity of the admission was too much for her to accept.

"You think we're terrible." The little man smiled beatifically, as though our thinking they were monstrous was the finest compliment.

Von Kleinschmidt got down to business. "When Miss Denton picked you up this evening, David, you were careless enough to make love immediately. I'm putting the best possible construction on what you did, because your hunger was something to see, wasn't it, Dorian? Not that we were actually here and saw you; you mustn't think that. But we have excellent photographs of what went on. We've seen those, and we should thank you for leaving the lights on. Nothing left to the imagination.

"Then . . ." He settled himself against the sofa and crossed his legs, taking care to preserve the crease in his pants. "Then when you went off for your birthday dinner with Miss Wallenstein and Hiram Rather, we had pictures taken of the young man, who was very much alive then, and matched them against the pictures taken of you. I mean positioning him properly, things like that. You understand?"

I understood, and I knew Dorothy understood. I wanted to look at her to see how she was taking it, and knew I couldn't. The nature of the betrayal was worse than anything I had ever experienced before, and I was flailing around inside myself, trying to find a proper way to react to it.

Von Kleinschmidt went on, "The photographs should be quite sensational when they're doctored the way we want them." He was looking at me now. "You're very original, David, and we'll try to make the young man look just as good." He pressed his hands together with satisfaction. "So, that takes care of one thing more. We have the murder, which will not appear on the books and will get no publicity until it's needed. And we have a set of photographs, which will be nothing short of spectacular. That's a nice combination right there. But time passes, and things grow dim in the public mind, so we've come up with something else." He was looking at me with great intensity now, the blue eyes fixed upon me with a riveting gaze. "You see, David, all of this is in the interests of your doing what we want you to do. Make no mistake. You're going to do what we want, because you're going to see you have no choice. And Miss Denton has no choice, either."

"I understand," I said.

"I don't!" Dorothy interrupted, and her voice was whore hard, as grating and belligerent as I had ever heard a woman's voice to be. She was so furious that her body was now visibly shaking. "You're not going to scare me with a bunch of phony pictures and a dead man I had nothing to do with." She came to me and sat near me, her defiance gone, the act of rebellion at an end. She turned to me for support. "Tell them, David."

I said, "They're telling us, Dorothy. I don't have much to say to them." Then I said to von Kleinschmidt, "I think you'd better tell us what else you had in mind."

"Of course." He crossed his legs the other way, taking an equal amount of care. "If you don't think the photos and the dead man are enough, we can arrange for something else. We would not want to invade the privacy of Miss Denton's house any more than we already have, but if you force us, we can work out another murder or two, in Miss Denton's house, and we won't show up to lend a hand next time. It will just happen, and that will be the end of it, with, of course, suspicion pointing in the right direction. We never lack for bodies, because people are human and make guilty mistakes."

"We can't have mistakes," Colin said, "you know?"

"You said something like that once before," I said.

"It bears repeating."

Von Kleinschmidt got to his feet and Colin took up a position beside him. They were incredible: elegant, groomed, well-mannered, frightening. I could feel my hands opening and closing at my sides.

"What do you want me to do?" I asked.

"You see the picture clearly now," von Kleinschmidt announced. "I'm glad." He started for the door, Colin following him. "There's nothing to do at this exact moment. We'll call you in good time. And, David, you won't try to play fast and loose with us, will you?" He turned at the door to fix me again with that wide-eyed look. "No, I'm sure you won't. And I'm sure you won't do something really foolish, like trying to think of a way to get rid of us. That would be very hard to do, David, if not impossible. Colin and I have too much going for us to be careless about ourselves, and don't you ever forget it."

He nodded to Dorothy then, gave me a sly smile. As he passed through the door, Colin turned to me and said, "By the way, in case anyone should ask you, you know the dead man, you know. You met him on the plane going to the party in Baja California. In case you've forgotten, his name was Caddy. You know?"

Yes, I knew. Now I knew.

Dorothy slept in my arms the rest of that night, "getting back my sanity," as she put it.

I was unable to sleep. I stared at the dark ceiling and into the outer darkness as though there would be a solution in one or the other place. I watched the struggle of the night against the sun, glad that the night was ending.

I thought, always with my writer's mind, of what was and what could be. There were facts I could not escape. One was the dead man found in my living room, the man I had met once, had said hello to, and had never seen again. Another was his nakedness and my nakedness with Dorothy and the fact that I would never be able to dispute the pictures taken; I had seen doctored pictures and knew they could be made to spell out something other than the truth of them.

It was a dilemma beyond question of doubt, and it was damnable.

When the dawn was in its implacable position, not to be denied, I pulled away from Dorothy, closed the door on her deep sleep, and got myself washed and shaved and together. I put coffee on the stove, laid out food for our breakfast, and then did a curious thing. Like a Dutch housewife, I got pail, water, and lye soap, and I attacked those brown-darkening-to-black spots of blood. There was no problem with the steps and the sidewalk; but I worked harder to erase them from the living room carpet and the upholstery of my car. I rubbed at them furiously, and with each movement of hand I seemed to be rubbing the fur of my fury the wrong way. I was astonished by the intensity of my hatred for von Kleinschmidt (Colin Davenport was a lesser matter), and my disgust with myself.

I had no idea what steps to take from that point forward, until I saw by the clock that it was exactly nine of a fine morning. Businesses would be closed and people would just be getting out of bed. I began to make phone calls, placing the first one to Jay Summerhill.

He was in at home, as I expected him to be, grousing because it was a dull, inactive day. He told me he was holding me to my invitation, which he expected to take advantage of within the next couple of months, and then asked me if I had anything special on my mind.

I said, "I'd like to give you three names, and I'd appreciate anything you can find out about any one of the three, preferably all of them. Carl von Kleinschmidt, Colin Davenport, H. V. Klein. As far as I know, only one of them lives in San Francisco or the Bay area: that's H. V. Klein. About the other two, I can't give you much to go on. I hate asking a favor like this; it must be a damned nuisance."

"Anything for a friend," Jay said, which I expected to hear from him, and he promised to get back to me no later than the following day. As I hung up the phone, I realized I had started to ask him about Anna. I didn't for a very simple reason: She had never bothered to give me her last name, and I had never bothered to ask for it.

My second phone call went to the home of an assistant D.A. in the Los Angeles office. He was an old college chum of mine, Blake Atkins, the sort of man you pal around with in school and rarely see after graduation, when the grim facts of life change relationships.

"Long time no see," Blake said pleasantly; he always felt most comfortable when he said the things you expected him to say.

"We'll change that soon enough," I said, "but now I'm calling you for your help."

"How've you been?"

It was going to be like that, and I went along with it. I told him how I had been, and he told me how he had been, and his wife and his five children. I gave him the three names I had given Jay Summerhill, asked if he could give me any information about them, and was told I would hear from him no later than the following day.

I called Hiram, expecting to haul him out of bed, but I found him up and about and ready for whatever I had to say. I felt some sense of relaxation for the first time in hours, and I was able to fill him in on the events leading up to my phone call.

The silence peculiar to Hiram when he thinks deeply and carefully was uncomfortable, but I bore with it, listening to his breathing as it pulsated over the wire and into my head. That was a good, deep thought, all right, because it was a full three minutes before Hiram allowed himself to speak.

"What are you doing today?" he asked.

"Nothing. Brooding, maybe. Dorothy's with me and she's a likely candidate for some brooding herself."

"That's what I thought," Hiram said. "Hold it a minute. Cynthia's here and I want to ask her something."

Hiram came back and said, "Cynthia suggests we have a late lunch at her place. It's easier than here, and God knows a lot better than going to your place. We'll be alone, and she'll see that no one bothers us."

I thought it was a capital idea, and said so. Dorothy might have other thoughts when she awakened, but I didn't anticipate her raising any serious objections.

On the contrary, she raised neither objections nor her voice. A depression had engulfed her, shadowing that famous face with a sadness and withdrawal I had never seen before. She tried desperately to muster a smile for me, but it came to her face lamely and was never there long enough to make its mark. I knew she was verging on tears; I even encouraged her to let them come if she thought they would make her feel better. She shook her head at that, turned her face from me, and did some little thing to distract both of us from the subject. It was a good performance, and I knew it came from Marie Stark and not from Dorothy Denton.

I couldn't shake her from her melancholy, and it seemed to deepen as we drove to Cynthia's Bel Air mansion, said our hellos, and allowed ourselves to be taken in hand by Hiram and Cynthia. As we sat down to lunch, we wasted no time in getting into the subject at hand.

"I've been thinking," Dorothy said, "and I know what I think:

Are a couple of creepy killers going to ruin everything I've worked so hard for? Are they? Is that what it's going to come down to?"

She put her fork on her plate, placing it carefully as though something important were involved in that small piece of action. Then she put her hands to her eyes, and she was crying. There was no sound from her and no movement.

"Have you got an answer for that?" Cynthia asked me, and the question was put without accusation.

"That very thing has been in my mind since the boys left the house. If this gets publicized, it's going to do more damage to Dorothy than it ever will to me. Writers are expected to be a little silly or strange, and certainly irresponsible. Dorothy means something special to a whole world—she's what every red-blooded girl wants to make of herself."

I looked at Dorothy, who was still crying, surrendering completely to her fright and unhappiness. I had come to rely upon her wisecracking and indifferent attitude, but those qualities vanished when the fork went down on the plate and the hands flew up to shelter her eyes. She had become a vulnerable female.

"Let's get off the subject," Cynthia said testily. "How can the world be so lousy on such a beautiful day?"

She indicated to one of her servants that the table could be cleared; it was time for dessert and coffee. At that same instant Dorothy raised her head and let her hands drop to her lap. She looked at all of us, one at a time, saving me for last. I was uncomfortable, not because of what she did but because of what she hadn't said.

As she turned to me, she asked, "I don't mind being in love with you, but why does it have to cost so much?"

There it was, out in the open, confronting me as any accusation would.

"I had to say that, David," Dorothy said, "because that's what I was crying about. Why does something I enjoy so much have to turn out to be so lousy? That's what I have in my mind."

I said, "I don't have an answer, Dorothy. I have to cop out.

Let's give all the pieces to Hiram and see if he can put them together."

We looked at Hiram, who had been silent through most of the meal. I had recognized the signs of his retreating into his mind and searching it for answers.

"It took no genius for me to come to one conclusion," he said, speaking carefully. "You're in an untenable position and your opponent has all the strength."

"I get sick thinking about them," Dorothy said. She had gone through her misery and worn it out; I could see the nervy girl coming back again. "Well, not sick exactly; I don't want to puke or anything. Let's put it this way: If I were a lady at the turn of the century, I'd swoon with alarm." She turned to me and asked, "Now, how would you put that into English?"

"You did just fine," I said, and laughed.

"I hate to say it," Hiram said, "but they have you by the balls. It beats me."

"They have," I said, "and it hurts. They can push me into any shape they want."

Hiram said, "Do you have any strength at all, and if you have, what do you intend to do with it?"

That took very little thinking. It seemed to me perfectly clear what I could do, so I said, "My only strength is, they don't know me and they can't anticipate my next move."

"Where does that lead you?" Cynthia asked.

"To them," I said. "I'm going to agree to do what they want me to. At least, I'm going to appear to agree, if you get what I mean."

They got what I meant, and Dorothy said, "David, do you really honestly believe you won't hear from the police or the newspapers or anything?"

"I really honestly believe that," I told her. "And I honestly believe you won't be involved in any way as long as I agree to do what they want me to do."

"You must be curious," Hiram said. "You must be wondering where all this is going to lead."

I grinned. "You know something, Hiram? I really, honestly am."

We went our separate ways at the end of that afternoon. Dorothy promised to call me when she could, which was problematical in view of the picture she was about to start; and Hiram and Cynthia said to keep in touch. As for myself, I went home to work it all out as best I could.

I got a call from Blake Atkins late the next day.

He said, "How's the boy?" I said the boy was just fine, and I asked how he was. He said he was fine and he thought he'd call and give me what information he'd managed to get together.

"Nothing whatsoever on Colin Davenport," he said. That didn't surprise me. "Not a great deal on H. V. Klein. He owns a jewelry shop in the Beverly West and comes here once in a while to look into things, but he never stays more than overnight, then goes home. Home's San Francisco. If you need anything more, I'd suggest you try someone up there."

I told Blake I would try someone there, and asked, "Anything on Carl von Kleinschmidt?"

"Yes," he said, "but not much. He's very social, Dave, photographed with the mayor and with some of the toniest people in L.A. society. Big industrialists, philanthropists—that sort of thing. Rarely seen with any of the movie crowd, which is pretty odd considering he registers strongly as a playboy. When he does show with the movie big shots, it's always with the biggest, and I mean *big.* Lots of speculation about him because he has no known source of income but is very lavish with money. Apparently has a big hard-on about charities and gives generously. But his name is never used on lists of sponsors or anything like that, which is another funny one."

I agreed; that was a funny one, all right. Then I asked, "Any word as to where he stays when he's in town?"

"Got one lead," Blake said, "and one lead only. Never registers in a hotel, always seems to stay with friends or something. You might check the Westwood Summit, where he's been seen a couple of times."

"That's very good," I said, even though I was disappointed; it didn't give me a hell of a lot to go on. "If I should need to get into the apartment or whatever it is at the Westwood Summit, can you give me a hand?"

Blake chuckled indulgently. "You up to something illegal, Dave?" he asked, and added hastily, "Don't answer that! I don't want to know about it if it's illegal."

"Just a little illegal," I said. "I wouldn't involve you, you know that."

He knew that, he said, and we again agreed that we'd meet very soon. I honestly hoped we would, because Blake was trying very hard for me and I appreciated his efforts. But the way things were shaping up, I didn't expect to have informal, chatty evenings with friends for a long time to come.

The call from Jay Summerhill came late at night, after I had gone to bed for a two- or three-hour session of stark, staring wakefulness before I fell asleep. I was alert for his call and pleased to hear from him, as always.

"Nothing on Colin Davenport," Jay said, "only his relationship with von Kleinschmidt, which lifts a few eyebrows here and there, judging from what I hear from my boys."

"Boys?"

Jay laughed. "The boys I called for the information. It takes all kinds in this business, Dave. Now you figure that one out."

I didn't know what he was talking about and asked about Klein.

"There's a great deal more on him. There seems to be some connection between him and von Kleinschmidt, but no one was able to tell me what."

"Father and son," I said.

"Sonofabitch!" Jay said. "Never occurred to me. That only makes it all the more peculiar. Klein is a respected Frisco businessman but not well known and not well liked. Keeps to himself, seems to live in the fourth-floor apartment of his store. Now, that's a hell of a strange thing, Dave. He has a home in Burlingame, a big one—walls, electric gates, guard, the works. He never goes there, near as I could learn. The place is lived in by *Mrs.* Klein, who is never seen, never stirs outside, no visitors."

"That's a surprise to me," I said. "I knew about papa but never even heard mention of mama. Anything more?"

"On Klein, yes. He's German, as you may have guessed, but maybe you didn't guess he's not Jewish."

I didn't bother to tell Jay that his news was no news.

Jay went on, "Klein was involved in the Nazi party but was strictly a no-weight. I mean he was a party member but on the lowest echelon. According to my information, he was a border guard. Small-town stuff all the way. Then suddenly he shows up in the U.S. with money and a lot of the crap he sells in his store. Not the same stuff, I'm sure, but like it, if you get what I mean."

I got what he meant, and asked him about von Kleinschmidt.

"Social lion," Jay said, which was getting to be like a repeated refrain. "Keeps himself out of the papers as much as possible, but known to make lots of time with the big numbers up here in the bay region."

"Any clue as to where he lives?"

"Hard to pin that one down. He seems to favor a number of apartment buildings, all on the plush side, and what I mean, he seems to have been seen in these places and sometimes he stays overnight, but who doesn't?"

"Who doesn't what?"

"Stay overnight *some* place. I think everyone should have a good time. Anyway, there are, at least as far as I've been able to go, no real home connections between von Kleinschmidt and Frisco. The only one I could come up with is a house he owns out in Mill Valley."

"Mill Valley?" I asked, alerted.

"That's right. It's apparently quite a nice place in a good section and worth a modest bundle. I have the address, if you want it."

I wanted it. It was the address of the house in which Anna and I had spent our idyllic few days. I was instantly struck by how unidyllic a few days could suddenly become.

"So far, very good," I said, which was the first thing I could think of to say.

"That's just about it," Jay said. "I tried to pin down a source of income for von Kleinschmidt, with no luck. No known source of income, but the assumption is that money comes from papa, maybe mama. I checked out Klein's bank and got nowhere. One of the bank employees with a big mouth and a strong taste for hard drink thinks Klein only keeps a business and small personal account in Frisco. He gets the impression the big money goes elsewhere, maybe other cities, maybe Switzerland, or who the fuck knows? Nothing on mama, by the way. All household expenses for the Burlingame place are paid out of the business account, including servants. She keeps a staff of four, if that means anything to you."

Everything meant something to me, but I wasn't exactly sure what, at that precise moment. I thanked Jay, who had been more than his efficient self, and was about to hang up, when he said abruptly, "Oh, Dave, remember that couple, burned in the Santa Cruz Mountains, Rolls ripped to pieces?"

"I remember."

"Came to a fucking dead end. Cold, stone dead. I shouldn't be shooting off my big mouth, but when I tried to keep goin' on it, I was told to lay off, and what's more, consider the case closed. So I laid off and it's closed. Who the fuck cares anyway?"

"You do," I said.

"Yeah, it gripes my ass. Anyway, be seein' yah." He hung up.

I didn't spend much time thinking about the information Jay gave me because it obviously added up to next to nothing. I have rarely been as confused and apprehensive as I was at that time. I seemed to be traveling endless roads, all of which went in various directions and none of which came to a destination. I was glad the case of McEndree versus von Kleinschmidt had not been given me as an assignment. It was one thing to be involved in its coils like some hapless rabbit; it would have been another thing to examine its maddening complications and be forced to make sense out of it. I was glad I only had to find my way out, and not explain it, to myself or anyone else.

I have little patience for the waiting game, and I had to do something. I went to the Westwood Summit the following day and I parked outside the building and stared at it, scanning the floors carefully, having no idea what I would get from my scrutiny. I had been there once, to a party given by a rich fat lady who looked like a female impersonator and had delusions of becoming one of the great entertainers of all time if only she could get someone to recognize her talent. It was a sad affair, and I wondered, assuming this was indeed the place that von Kleinschmidt and Colin Davenport called home when in Los Angeles, if it would house sadder affairs yet to come. I was, I knew, slipping into angry depression. It was time to go.

I drove home nervously, pressing my luck more than once as I tailgated, switched lanes, leaned heavily on my horn. It suddenly occurred to me that I was busy making business. I was very much like the fly in the web, struggling to get free and getting more enmeshed in stickiness as I fought against the insanity of my predicament. I was loathing Carl von Kleinschmidt and Colin Davenport for what they had done to me, but more than anything else, I was loathing myself for letting them do it to me. It was a bad feeling.

The bad feeling became rotten when I reached home in time to intercept a phone call from my New York agent. He was furious, so beside himself with rage, in fact, that it took him no more than a minute to get it all out: What in Christ's name was wrong with me, he wanted to know, what made me such a fucking idiot that I would cancel out on my university assignment without letting him know? Why did I take it upon myself to call the heads of four universities and curtly let them know I wasn't interested in the project, how about getting someone else to do it? I could go fuck myself, that's what I could do.

He hung up without hearing a word out of me. He would never know that I was unable to say anything, in any case.

I had made no such phone calls, I had said no such things. I did, however, know beyond doubt who *had* made the phone calls.

I decided to get drunk, but I was too bone weary, too abysmally discouraged, to do more than break open a can of Coke. I was stone sober when the call came from von Kleinschmidt.

"David?" There was no mistaking that inflected voice. It would have been too much if he had called me "hardhead."

"Yes." I kept my voice clean and clear.

"Are we in sync?"

"No doubt about it."

"I'm calling from New York. Can you hear me all right?"

"Perfectly."

"You sound in good humor."

"Perfect."

There was a chuckle, then: "That's the way we want you. That's to say, that's the way it should be. Everything working out the best for everyone."

"I wouldn't want it any other way." The tone was still clean and clear, but I knew it would thicken if we didn't finish with the amenities very soon.

"Have you got your business in hand?"

That was a curious way to put whatever he had in mind, and I said, "Would you say that again?"

"Are you all set to come with us?" The chuckle came again, but he wasn't letting me in on the joke. "We're ready for you, if you're ready for us."

"I'm looking forward to it."

"I hope you mean that, David. If you really *are* ready, there'll be a first-class ticket for you at TWA on any flight. Try to make it within the next few days. We'll leave it up to you, and we don't want to pressure you, you know. By the way, Colin's here, and he sends you his best."

"Right back to him," I said amiably. The conversation was so grotesque, so at odds with what had happened to me, that I was perversely inclined to laugh at all of it. "By the way, I want to thank you for canceling my assignment, you know, the one with the universities."

"Nothing to it," von Kleinschmidt said. "Your agent is a very chatty fellow, and we happened to find out what your schedule was and it conflicted with ours, so we thought it would be in the best interests of all of us to cancel. We found a marvelous replacement for you, so don't you worry."

"Wouldn't think of it," I said. "Now, after I get on my flight and reach New York, then what?"

"There's a suite waiting for you at the Wellington Towers. Everything has been taken care of, and we'll know when you arrive. Okay? Now, David, be sure to hold Saturday night open for us. That's very important. Saturday night. Does that suit you?"

"Just fine." I imagined it suited von Kleinschmidt and Colin even finer.

"That's all, then. Until we see you?"

"Let's hear it for Archie!" I said as my parting shot.

The phone clicked off in my ear.

My leavetaking to New York should go down in history as one of the gloomiest ever to be held in Los Angeles International Airport.

I said goodbye to Dorothy on the set of her latest motion picture. There were no tears and no unnecessary well-wishes. We held each other for a moment, kissed each other; I said I hoped her picture went well, and she said she hoped I had a nice trip. That was it.

It was somewhat different with Hiram and Cynthia, who took me to the airport. Hiram was reflective, talking only as he extracted more information from me about what had happened on this or that occasion. "It's interesting," he said, "that neither of them seems to have a shred of belief in the innate decency of human beings."

That set Cynthia off, and her ultrarefined face flushed an angry pink as she said, "You poor darling! You salute human beings as though they really were innately decent."

"I'm a minister," Hiram said, quietly. "It's something you'll have to face."

"I'll stay out of this one," I said.

Cynthia flushed again, with embarrassment, and said, "That's really too bad of me, it really is. But I'm honestly terribly worried about you, David, and I know Hiram is. He won't say it, but he is. And by 'you,' I mean Dorothy and you, of course; she's as much in it as you are. Only you're doing the dirty work. Dorothy's threatened with burning, but you're in the fire."

"Nicely put," Hiram said. He turned to me and grabbed my arm. "I worry terribly, and I'm sick with frustration. I want to help, but I can only think, sort of mull it over in hopes I can find a solution."

"Your mulling over is better than any other man's effort," I said. "I'll settle for that, Hiram; it gives me a good feeling."

"We love you," Cynthia said.

I was uncomfortable in the face of that and glad to hear the announcement of the plane's departure. We said nothing more, but we exchanged looks that left nothing unsaid. I was off to whatever the future held for me, and not very damned happy about it, either.

I thought often of the plane falling out of the sky, because it seemed an appropriate time to look for easy outs. But the plane stayed up there, we reached New York without incident, and I was soon in my suite at the Wellington Towers, looking out at the Manhattan skyline with no anticipation and no appreciation for its magnificence.

Even if I had tried, I would have been unable to complain about the accommodations provided for me by von Kleinschmidt. The suite was baronial, and I was frankly overwhelmed by it. The bellhop verified my impression that it had been newly decorated, and it gave me no satisfaction that he told me about the redecoration while eyeing me with obvious respect. He didn't know I was sailing a rough sea under false colors, and I wasn't about to tell him so. I did, however, extend myself in handing him an overgenerous tip.

I took a tour of the place, locating the two bedrooms and two baths on an upper floor, exploring the downstairs, which consisted of a living room, den, dining room, kitchen, and guest bathroom. All of it was colorful, all of it was elegant. I was not completely at ease in the welter of dark woods, tapestries, satins, and silks;

and I was distinctly put off by the deliberate touches in books, records, art objects, and paintings, all of which couldn't have been more obvious. It wasn't my home, however, so the hell with it! I was only a prisoner there.

After I had got myself organized in the place, more or less, I called the desk for messages, and there were none. I reacted to that news with impatience, then remembered I was not definitely expected until Saturday, and this was only Thursday evening. There would be time to get myself together, to become oriented to my strange surroundings. I tried to suppress it, but I suddenly found myself responding to a vestigial excitement. Something very odd and very dangerous was happening in the atmosphere around me, and it was beginning to translate itself into an almost pleasurable sensation inside myself.

I debated having dinner in my room or going out, and opted for going out. I hadn't been to New York for several years and I welcomed the opportunity to reacquaint myself with the city.

I believe I have New York where it belongs. A wag once said it was a nice place to visit but he wouldn't want to live there. That's good enough as far as it goes. In my opinion, New York is an absurdity. It has something for everyone in elaborate profusion, but you have to know when enjoyment stops and endurance begins. I've always enjoyed New York because I've always known when the time has come to leave the place.

I started out into it happily enough, taking the long downward cruise in the elevator, striding out across the lobby as I headed for Park Avenue. I was almost to the revolving doors when an assistant manager intercepted me, calling me by name, and deferentially asked me to come with him to the manager's office. I followed him with some annoyance, wondering if these things would always be happening to me: being recognized without my knowing why, being followed without my knowing it, having my moves anticipated as though I were under constant surveillance. It was unnerving, and I had yet to find a way to deal with it.

The manager was a fat and charming man, well colored by alcohol, who approached me directly and without the hand-wringing obsequiousness that seems to be bred into the breed.

He introduced himself as Mr. Ballantine, which was rather a

bad joke on his complexion, and said, "I just want you to know your letter of credit was received half an hour ago. All the formalities have been concluded and it's yours to draw on as you wish."

I took that in stride, and muttered something about the amount.

"Ten thousand," Mr. Ballantine answered. "Isn't that what you arranged for?"

"Of course," I said. "Of course."

"We'll notify the bank as soon as it reaches the two thousand mark," Mr. Ballantine said. "You can count on us."

I said I was sure I could, and I continued on into the Manhattan night, infinitely richer than I have ever been and more than ever uncomfortable with my new position in life.

New York softened the sting of my new reality. My dinner at Chantal was superlative, my after-dinner brandy was ageless, and the night air I came out into was heavy with an unaccustomed mist. I walked to the United Nations building and circled back along the East River. I owned the city and the city owned me, and I could almost forget the circumstances that had brought me there.

Then, within a block of the Wellington Towers, I was accosted by a whore who was a far cry from the average streetwalker. She was a smasher such as I have seen only in London and Paris, and I say that without meaning to do a disservice to the whores of the evening. She had white, white skin, dark hair and eyes, a luscious and insinuating mouth, and carried her great body so well I could only compare her to one other person. Anna, of course.

She asked if I was busy for the evening, and I said, "Why this way? Why sell it when you can promote it?"

"Oh, God!" she protested. "Don't tell me I walked into a lecture!"

"Not bloody likely. I just think you're putting yourself down."

"Why not do it instead of talking about it?"

"I don't want to fuck you," I said coldly. "I've already fucked you. I was just curious about your selling it on the streets."

"I'm getting even with my pimp. He doesn't think I'll do it. How does that grab you?"

"Right in the stomach," I said, "like American apple pie."

be expected to know everyone. Most of the people coming don't care who's giving the party; they only care that there *is* a party and it's here, in this suite of the Wellington Towers. This is the Presidential Suite, David, did you know that?"

"I didn't know that," I said, "but it makes me feel a great deal better. I don't like staying just anywhere."

"Of course." I seemed to have said something reasonable, and von Kleinschmidt went on, "Anna will be your hostess, and that should get you over any rough spots."

"Nice," I said, and I looked at her, wondering what I would see.

She was looking at me pleasantly, which was the most to be said about it. There was no speculation in her eyes, certainly no appraisal. She wasn't wondering what I was thinking, how I was feeling; at least, that was the impression she gave me. I could have been anyone met yesterday, or a month ago, or a year ago. It didn't matter to her, because, it seemed to me, nothing mattered to her above and beyond looking beautiful and being where she apparently wanted to be.

"I've met most of the people who'll be here," she said—and that rounded, very caressing voice did to me what it had always done—"at least casually. I can fake it with those I don't know."

"I'm sure you will," I said, and I meant it exactly the way the sarcasm came out.

"You can count on me." She smiled again, that same smile.

"I will."

"Then there's nothing more," von Kleinschmidt said. He got to his feet, turned to help Anna, who was already unwinding from her chair. "Colin? Is there anything you can think of?"

Colin was downing his drink, and as he put the glass back on the bar, he shot me a look that was not pleasant to see. It came out of his sullenness, his sense of pique and hurt. I have seen something like that before: the beautiful face that loses its composure and begins to reflect bad thoughts. I would never know how bad the thoughts were in Colin's head, but I did know his face had become heavy and disagreeable with hostility.

"You know, David," he said, his voice light and breathy, "I

don't think you respect me. I think you should try to respect me more than you do, you know."

He exited, von Kleinschmidt and Anna following silently.

Colin was right. I didn't respect him, and I doubted I ever would.

I received the invitation list for the party with my morning coffee. It reached me in a sealed envelope, and I threw it away without reading it. I figured if I was hosting a charade, I might as well make it interesting for myself by letting each guest come as a surprise to me. If I turned out to be shocked as well, so much the better.

I kept myself busy throughout the morning by calling Dorothy Denton, with whom I had a warm and insinuating conversation that took away a lot of the sting left by Anna's reappearance. We agreed we could be in a worse situation, and we decided we missed each other very much, so it was a good thing we were both busy. Not much of a conversation, but satisfying because we were in contact.

Then I called Hiram and asked him if he had any new ideas, and he said he had none, and added that it showed you what a piss ant he could be when faced with something of large proportions. I told him I didn't know about piss ants and we could discuss that later; all I wanted from him was his assurance that he felt I was doing the right thing so far. He seemed to feel I was, and assured me I was behaving admirably in a situation that would normally have me behaving like a madman.

Those phone calls gave me the sane contacts I needed to get back on balance for the rest of the day and into Saturday. I was ready for that evening when it finally lowered on me like a particularly vicious thunderhead.

Anna and von Kleinschmidt were the first to arrive, stunningly dressed as usual and as I expected them to be. Surprisingly, they arrived without Colin, a fact I chose not to comment upon, but he arrived soon after, looking so radiant and spiffy that he could have been taken for a lovely male impersonator. He turned up with a blond surfer type as well as a rather cunning girl who looked as though she had slipped away from a centerfold in order to enjoy a night on the town. It didn't surprise me at all that both blond and girl immediately revealed themselves to be void of either intelligence or sense.

Colin was amiable if not downright cordial. He took great pride in introducing me to his companions, who were presented to me as "Grad" and "Lacey," and told that I was one of the most famous writers working in the field of current events today. They were informed that it was a mark of distinction to be in the same room with me, not to mention being invited to a party I was giving, and if they were very good, I might be able to spend some time with them during the evening. Grad and Lacey were less than impressed, but Colin had made his point. The ax had been raised and lowered between us, and it was not destined to strike a blow.

They kept on coming, and I discovered it would have helped if I had gone over the list at least once.

I have interviewed heads of state, celebrities of all kinds from all over the world, highly controversial personalities—in short, the famous as well as the infamous. But I have never seen as distinguished a collection of national and international figures. There were too many to count, too many to register clearly in my mind or to be entirely recognizable. Those I did recognize, to name a few: The radiant socialite wife of a network president, famed for her beauty and her talent for wearing the freshly minted clothes that set style trends. A news analyst who was fabled for his haughtiness and disliked for his monumental egocentricity. The black mayor of a Southern city, a man of dignity and stature who could not conceal the contempt with which he viewed the world and its people. A vicious little man, a columnist, with the face of a corrupt angel and the croaking voice of a six-year-old child. The host of a talk show, a seemingly gregarious and jolly man who struck me as being artificial and mean.

There were others who do not deserve specific mention: a sprinkling of relatively well known show business people, one acknowledged star who was as great of mouth as she was of talent, a British actor who had won the past year's Tony Award and proved to be totally inarticulate. There were writers in addition to the freakish one already mentioned, all of whom viewed me with suspicion, wondering how I was managing both the Presidential Suite and the party. And there were five world-renowned musicians including a flouncy conductor who set out to upstage everyone, several editors of publications, one publisher, and a nationally known decorator of bizarre toilet seats.

It was, in short, an exotic mixed bag, and I had seen nothing yet.

The man who was meant to be the hub of that gathering, the man who was destined to be bound to me with the umbilical cord of mutual need, arrived an hour late, when the other guests were already on the way with silly chatter and too many drinks. He arrived with two secret service men.

I recognized him instantly because of his wildly red hair, the lean, saturnine, and florid face, the indelibly Irish look of wit and cunning. He was Vincent Moriarity, adviser to the President and the State Department.

I had never been able to form an opinion of the man from all the news accounts I had read of him, or from his thoroughly publicized exploits in the fields of diplomacy and foreign and domestic policy, or even from his official biography, which I had read with interest but without conviction. I knew he had been discovered in a "think tank" somewhere in the north Midwest, I knew he had published, I had more than once crossed paths he had blazed over the world as representative of two presidential administrations. But I had never thought I had the proper "fix" on the man, that I had ever been given information about what kind of person he was.

I was meeting him at last, and I began to see qualities in him that I could never have learned about from words put on paper. What I saw was a tough, possibly ruthless, certainly astronomically intelligent man who was sick with an apparent flaw. Vincent

Moriarity was, I perceived instantly, both highly emotional and excruciatingly sensitive. With a combination like that, I wondered at his ability to have stayed alive to the advanced age of forty-three.

His large, freckled hand enfolded mine and threatened to crush it. I crushed back, and we both grinned, knowing we were playing a certain kind of game. It's called In the Same Boat Together.

"Mr. McEndree," he said, that smooth, resonant voice laving me like soap, "it was good of you to ask me."

"Mr. Moriarity," I answered, "it was more than good of you to come."

We crushed hands again, grinned again, and he drifted away, his secret service cronies taking off with him.

"I think you like each other," Anna said. It was the first thing she had said to me that evening. I had said nothing to her, because there was nothing to say.

"You're more astute than I," I said. "You know, I'm fucking sick and tired of standing in this foyer saying stupid hellos to people I don't know and don't care to know. What a noxious group!"

Anna was looking at me closely, demanding that I look at her. I did, and I immediately fell into those eyes, seeing as much depth in them, as much mystery, as I always had. It was hard to believe she was naturally so hateful.

"The world is noxious, David," Anna said carefully. "We all have options. You've decided you'll fight it and beat it at its own game—if you can. I decided to get through it as easily as possible, with little effort, and possibly as quickly as I can."

She left me then, moving off into the raucous crowd, talking, laughing, pirouetting, charming the bejesus out of everyone. I had to admit it: there was nothing she didn't know about charm and seduction.

I wandered into the crowd myself, not going toward anyone in any conscious sense, but circling around in an ever decreasing circle until I found myself near Moriarity. He was entertaining a couple of ravishing ladies, one of whom kept a hand in constant motion on the sleeve of his coat. He appeared to be enjoying himself, and yet be broke off the conversation within a minute of my appearance at his side, excused himself, and came to me.

"Where can we talk?" he asked.

"Upstairs. There are two bedrooms. One is more isolated than the other."

"There, then."

He said something to the secret service agents, and let me lead the way upstairs.

We sat in a corner of the room, lounging in deep armchairs, facing each other like a couple of pals who did that sort of thing quite often. He had his drink with him, and I also noticed that he smoked heavily; he didn't light one cigarette with the end of the other, but he might as well have done. I noticed then that the mellifluous voice was slightly husky from smoking and I had an anxious moment as I thought about the condition of his lungs. A curious and presumptive thought, but I found myself liking Vincent Moriarity.

"How did you get into this?" he asked. He drank from his drink and lit another cigarette.

"Blackmail." I knew it would be stupid to equivocate with the man. I was safe with him, and I would always be safe as long as I remained honest.

"Care to tell me about it?"

"Do you want specifics and details or a general outline?"

"However you care to tell it."

"As I said, blackmail. Minor crimes against my own house. Intimidation of a lady I've been close to and with. Murder, circumstances so incriminating to me that it could only mean the most disgusting kind of scandal if not trial and imprisonment."

He nodded, the florid face redder than it had been before. It was like watching a man go up in flames. I wondered when the explosion would occur and how much of him it would leave in one piece.

"A nasty business," I said, "altogether. It would be a little more bearable if I knew what they wanted. I don't."

"Nor I." He was thinking, and his eyes closed with the intensity of his thoughts. "Do you know what our connection is, you with me? Have they at least told you that?"

"No. Not even that we *are* connected."

"We are, all right. You're about to write my biography—didn't you know that? No, I see you didn't. Well, that's what you're about to do."

"I won't say no." It was hard for me to make light of the matter. In fact, I was actually flattered that we were to have a close association. "When do we start?"

"I haven't received word yet."

"You seem to know as little as I do."

"Possibly less."

"Can you tell me what you do know?"

"I ask only one thing. Don't ask me why I'm in this. Not yet. There's time enough."

"I respect that."

"I hoped you would."

"I'll let you take the lead."

He thought about that, and I saw his face relax a little, the redness receding until only its natural florid color remained. "Maybe we can think of a way out of this," he said. "I know you're very bright, because I've read most of the things you've written. You can't write that way without intelligence and perception. We got into this, maybe we can get out of it."

"I don't think intelligence is what got us here," I said.

"You're asking a lot. Maybe we can rely on our stupidity to find the way out."

At that, we locked in an exchange of glances and began to laugh. It was absurd, we knew it. Mature men roped, tied, and thrown, and by the likes of Carl von Kleinschmidt and Colin Davenport.

It didn't take us long to laugh ourselves out, and Moriarity said, "I've received official permission for you to travel with me, all in the interests of gathering material for my biography. You'll be subject to inconveniences from time to time, examination of your person and belongings, some surveillance—that sort of thing. In the interests of national security, not to mention mine as representative of the President and the U.S. In other words, you go where I go for however long we're told it will last."

"I'm beginning to get the glimmering of something," I said. "An idea is forming."

"Keep it to yourself until you're sure of it," he said. "I don't mean to be as rude as that sounds. I know myself, that's all: I work best with concrete facts; I'm not inclined to rely on instinct or intuition. I'll let you be the intuitive one."

"Fair enough." We were starting off on an equal basis, which was fair enough indeed. I could see we were going to get along just fine.

"I imagine we'll go as soon as they give us the green light," Moriarity said.

"Assuming the light is green. I don't believe those boys work according to established rules."

"Anything else?" he asked, getting to his feet.

"Nothing I can think of."

He told me how I could reach him at any hour of the day or night, and then he said, "I'm glad it's you. It could have been someone else, and I wouldn't have liked that worth shit."

I knew I wouldn't have, either.

Vincent Moriarity vanished half an hour after our conversation. He was followed by one or two others, and then I had to face the fact that my party which wasn't my party was a grand success. I hated everything about it and everyone in it, and decided I was free to leave if I so elected. I left.

It was a terrible night in New York, dank and lowering, but it was better than where I had been. I walked, striding out furiously, looking nowhere except straight ahead of me. It was, in a sense, a punishing walk, and I was laboring to catch my breath by the time I returned to the Wellington Towers. I avoided the desk and went instead to the house phones, where I asked for my suite. It was a long minute before the phone was answered, and I knew why instantly. Judging from the noise, my party was getting better by the hour. It was no place for me to be, and I slammed up the phone without saying a word.

I bought a morning paper, settled myself in a remote corner

of the lobby where I could observe the bank of elevators, and prepared for a vigil. I had no intention of returning to the suite until it had been cleared of the last of them.

Within the next hour, I saw seven recognizable celebrants leave. Ten unproductive minutes followed, and then another group vomited out of the elevators, screaming crazily at one another and promising to meet in a few minutes at some other place in the city. In another five minutes, Grad and Lacey, the beautiful children who had arrived with Colin, lurched drunkenly across the lobby, holding each other to keep themselves upright, giggling with pleasure at the silly state they were in.

I had waited long enough, and I went back upstairs. I stepped aside for two or three stragglers as they stumbled from my doorway, and I hoped that was the last of them.

The downstairs area of the apartment was indeed empty, except for hotel employees who were collecting the debris that had piled up during the party. I started to ask them to leave, and was approaching a man who appeared to be the authoritative head of the cleanup squad, when a torrent of invective exploded into the quietness of the place

"No, no, no!" a resonant male voice yelled. "You stupid sonofabitch, you were not suppopsm y4 leave them alone for a minute unless a recorder was on in the room with them. I wanted every word they said down on tape. I arranged for it, for Christ's sake, you fucking idiot! All you had to do was follow through."

I turned to the stairway that led to the upstairs bedrooms, and waited for more to come. The cleanup squad had paused with me, as startled as I, equally as interested. I motioned to them to leave, and they did so with a reluctance tinged with more than a little relief.

A voice came again, and I recognized it as Colin's: "I have to do everything, every fucking thing! What good are you? And you, too." The "you, too" was said to a third party, and it was laced with a petulance that I had come to expect from Colin. "I told you not to let Grad and Lacey get away. They were supposed to go home with me."

Somebody said something, this time in a deeper and softer

male voice, and Colin came back even more viciously. "I don't want your excuses. You know everything depends on this, every goddamn thing, and if any of it goes wrong, I'll have your ass, I guarantee that. Get away from me. Go on, both of you, get away from me." The last words screamed out of him: "Get out!"

Carl was the first one down the stairs, taking them three at a time with a sense of urgency that I could feel as well as see. His face was tormented with outrage, and his thoughts were so consuming that he failed to register me in his mind even though he looked directly at me.

Anna followed him, moving in her stately way with no measure of anger or anxiety. She noticed me as she reached the last step and turned toward the outer door, and although she saw me, there was no glint of recognition in her eyes. I could have been anyone standing in that room, certainly not the man who had been drawn into this dangerous and ugly charade because of her and his passion for her.

It took a minute for Colin to put in his appearance, and he came downstairs, then toward me with the calm of someone who knows he is supremely in command of himself and the situation he has created. He was smiling, and if I had not heard his shouted vilification, I would have thought him nothing more than an amiable and personable little man.

"How much did you hear?" he asked, managing to speak through that smile.

"How much was there?"

"About fifteen minutes' worth."

"Just the tail end."

"That was enough."

"I thought so."

"You didn't like what you heard?"

"It surprised me."

"I can imagine."

He turned from me and walked to the large picture window that framed the staggering vista of New York enshrouded in its winding sheet of fog and mist. I watched the little man as he positioned himself with his back to me, his hands clasped behind him in a posture that was at once defiant and self-satisfied. I was not used to him yet. This was another Colin Davenport, and I had never had a glimpse of him before.

"You know," I said with deliberation, "you seem different to me. You know?"

He turned back to me, the smile still fixed, but tense with the strain of keeping it there. "You're mocking me, and I wish you'd stop. I'm not your fool, David, or anyone else's. If I choose to play the fool, and I do sometimes, if I stammer and say too many 'you know's, I do it with reason. Had you ever thought there might be a reason?"

Of course, I had not thought any such thing, as he well knew. I remained silent.

"Come here, please," Colin said, and turned from me again.

I went to stand at his side, and looked out to see what I could see. I had no idea what he was looking at, or why. It was all New York, out there below us, a marvelous, exasperating, and often terrifying city that had no match anywhere in the world. And with its mysterious shifting cloud formations, moving now as the wind prompted them, it seemed a perfect place to contain the likes of Colin Davenport.

"Look there," he said, pointing to his right. "You'll see a building that's taller and thinner than any of the others around it. The one with a soft glow at its top. It looks as though it's floodlighted around the very tip, and it is."

"I see it. What is it?"

"It's the Action Building. That's spelled A-c-t-i-o-n."

"Impressive."

He looked at me quickly, staring up intently to see if I was being sardonic or disrespectful. I happened to be respectful, which is understandable because skyscrapers have always been a source of awe for me.

"It's fifty-four stories tall. The top floor is a penthouse. The next floor below is a series of smaller apartments and servants' quarters. There are only two ways of getting into the penthouse, and it can only be reached by using a combination of signals, either on the elevator or on the stairway that goes to the penthouse from the next-lower level."

I said, when he let that information fall into the room, "And you're going to tell me you own it."

"I do, and a lot more besides." The voice that had been so strident such a short time before had become soft and deep, with an almost sensual quality. "I live in that penthouse when I'm in New York. Half of it is covered by a transparent dome. There's nothing else like it in the world. I live there and the only people who ever come to visit me or stay with me are the ones I feel closest to. Except the servants, of course. I'm well taken care of."

He turned from the window, gave me another look, which was prideful and strangely triumphant, then strutted his way to the makeshift bar that had been set up for the party. He started to fix himself a drink, moving precisely yet delicately, as though everything would be perfect if he did it right. I had a fleeting thought of Napoleon, and wondered if he had ever acted in that exact manner.

His drink prepared to his liking, Colin faced me again and said, "Are you having anything?"

"Nothing; I've had all the booze I want this evening. Particularly the booze drunk by other people."

Colin laughed at that, sat down, and said, "I'll just stay long enough to finish this. I want you to get to know me, David. I think it's time you knew what I intend to tell you."

"I have no choice?"

"You don't want a choice. You want to hear what I have to say, don't you?"

"Yes. Yes, I do, Colin. I want to hear what you have to say."

I flopped into a chair opposite him, and I prepared to listen carefully. There was a hell of a lot at stake.

"Carl has never been in my penthouse," Colin said. "He's never been in the Action Building, and doesn't know I own it." He laid in a pause at that moment, making it weightier than it need have been. "I *own* Carl. Think about that for a while."

I didn't have to think about it for very long. The revelation hit me hard, not only because it violated every conclusion I had reached about the boys but because it introduced a sinister note I was not prepared for. I thought I had seen where the ball was coming from, and now it was being fielded from a totally opposite direction.

I said, "I guess I don't know you, Colin; I guess I don't know one frigging thing about you."

That pleased him, and he spoke through another broad smile. "No one does. No one ever did."

"What's so great about that?"

He was struggling with a thought, and I waited until he let it out: "I wanted *you* to know me." His smile was beatific. "I've never met anyone like you before."

"How could you not meet someone like me? Writers are just as hungry and greedy as other people. They just do something a lot of other people don't do, and most of them do it badly."

"I don't mean writers," he protested. "I know writers. I mean you."

"Why me?" I wasn't flattered.

"You're a human being. I know. We're all human beings, at least that's what they say. I mean you're a human human being." He reacted to the beginnings of a smile on my face, and said, "Don't laugh at me, David. I know that sounds funny, but I don't mean it funny." Then, more quietly, in earnest: "I want you to take me seriously."

He had my attention again, and he said, "I know lots about you. I personally know your last wife, and I must say you're well rid of her. I didn't bother about the other two. I figured if your judgment could be so bad on the third, the others weren't worth my time."

"Sonofabitch!" It was all I could think of to say.

"We don't have to talk about Dorothy Denton, do we? I know about Cynthia Wallenstein and Hiram Rather. If I were living in Los Angeles, I'd go to Mr. Rather's church. He sounds like a wonderful man."

"He is," I said, stifling the alarm I felt at being so exposed to view. Colin Davenport was winning my grudging respect very fast.

"I know about Jay Summervale—"

"Summerhill."

"Jay Summerhill. I also know about your visit with Mr. Klein in San Francisco and that you were asking about Carl and me."

"I was asking about Carl. At the time, I thought he was the one to be reckoned with."

Colin laughed wickedly at that, then said, "Mr. Klein hates me, and I hate Mr. Klein. He's petty, and I think it's hilarious that he thinks I'm a bad influence on Carl. Doesn't that make you laugh? A bad influence on Carl! The lap of luxury, that's what Carl is living in, and all due to me, let me tell you. He'd be living off some old crone, or even an old man, for that matter, if it weren't for me. There wouldn't be any H. V. Klein if I didn't let it be. Why don't you have a drink?"

I said maybe later and encouraged him to go on. His eyes were glazed with excitement, his lips were moist with the workings of his tongue, and his body had begun to jump with the intensity of his feelings. I thought whimsically of a Victorian drama in which one character says to another, "You're mad, mad, mad." Only Colin wasn't mad. He was stark, raving sane, which made him even more frightening.

He said, "I was always pretty, even when I was newborn. Do you know what it's like being pretty? No, you wouldn't know, David; you're not pretty. I really don't know what you are—strong-looking, maybe, which I wish I was. I was pretty. Pretty boy, pretty adolescent. My stepfather raped me when I was twelve, and I never got over that. It happened again in boarding school when I was fourteen, an older boy with three others holding me down. I said then I'd never let anyone touch me again, and no one ever has. I can buy it. I can pay to have it done for me. I can watch it, and it's the same thing. I almost feel it, and sometimes I do, especially when it gets a little cruel. You know what I mean?"

"You bet," I said.

"You're not taking me seriously," he complained, but this time he was pleading with me and not being rancorous.

"I'm not taking you any way," I said. "I can't identify with that, Colin. I've never been raped and I'm not a voyeur. If it makes you happy, swell, but don't ask me to understand it."

He decided against sulking, and said more calmly, "I wasn't strong, and I wanted a way to be stronger than anybody I'd ever meet. I didn't have to look far for the answer. Money. Lots of money.

"People love money, David, and that's another thing about you. You just want enough. I wasn't impressed by your bank account, I must say. I was even tempted to add a little, but I figured you hadn't earned it yet, and besides, we hadn't had this talk and maybe we never would."

"I don't want your contribution, Colin. I just want out of this."

He smiled sweetly, and said, "In time. In my time. Maybe soon, maybe later." He cocked his head at me, a caricature of a crafty ingénue.

"That kind of remark isn't going to make me love you," I said. "Don't play coy with me."

"I wasn't being coy," he said. "Don't mistake what I say because of the way I say it. Understand?"

He wanted an answer to that one, and I said, "I understand what you're saying. That's as far as I can go."

"It's far enough for now. You see, David, I like you and I want your respect and understanding, but I don't expect to get your friendship. I'm not even sure I want it."

"We've reached a point of agreement."

"I'm not a bad friend, you know."

"You haven't done anything that'd make me treasure you."

"I'm not talking about you. Matter of fact, if I didn't have use for you, I'd see that we became friends. You, and Dorothy Denton, and Hiram Rather, and all of them. But I'm not into that now."

"They'll be sorry to know what they missed."

He moved restlessly, without any real petulance, and said, "I wish you'd stop baiting me. I really find it annoying."

"I find you annoying, Colin," I said. "You have me in what I frankly admit is an untenable position. You obviously have use for me, and I know I won't like the use you put me to. You've involved me in all sorts of intrigues and murders. I've been compromised and blackmailed. I now find myself linked with another of your victims, Mr. Moriarity. And it all adds up to one thing:

I hate your fucking guts. Oh, I admire you, all right, Colin, I admire you for a sly, deceiving, conniving, evil, and basically vicious man. I really don't give a shit about your problems, and I don't care that you got fucked in the ass or whatever else happened to you in life. I find totally unacceptable your revenge motive, although God knows I'd like to try to get a little revenge as far as you and von Kleinschmidt are concerned. I hate your philosophy of life, and I don't accept your thesis that anyone can be bought. I think, Colin, that you're a goddamned crying shame and I wish I'd never met you and your pal in Baja California. That was a sorry fucking day."

I had said it all calmly. I had not been emotionally involved with what I was saying, which means that I had let my mind act for me and I had got it all out without feeling that rise in pressure that always came when I got angry. It was like saying something that had to be said but wasn't going to make any difference in the saying. I had spoken my mind, for all the good it did me.

Colin was pleased with me—so pleased, in fact, that he did everything but wriggle with satisfaction.

"That's what I would've expected to hear from you," he said, "nothing less. I'm going to like working with you."

"What work?"

"What we do. What *I* do."

"And that is . . ."

He smiled secretly, and said, "Not yet. You'll learn in time. I *can* tell you what I believe, and that's what's behind it all. I believe there're more pimps than teachers in the world, and I believe there're more whores than students. Let's begin with that."

"We're back to the everyone-has-his-price theory," I said.

"Oh, yes," Colin answered, "everyone has his price. For most people, it's money, and not very much of it, at that, which always surprises me. I think I could be bought out for a large sum, assuming I was in a position to be bought and wasn't doing the buying, which I am. Next we have power, and with that goes position. A funny thing I've found: power doesn't always go with money, or the other way around. Just to have influence over other people seems to mean a lot to some people. I wouldn't be at all interested in *that.*"

"What interests you?" I asked. "You haven't said."

"Money, of course, because I can buy anything I want or do anything I want. And power, well, I have that, don't I? It doesn't warrant discussion. But above all, I guess, it's position, to be where I can do what I want, to anyone I want, get what I want, be what I want, and never, never be touched. No one can come near me."

"There's one thing you don't know, Colin," I said. "You're vulnerable. I don't think you realize how vulnerable you are."

It was a thought he didn't like. It was so potent, in fact, that he suddenly looked frightened. All his barriers had been carefully erected, had, apparently, stood firm for years; then, suddenly, a simple mystery was presented to him and threw him into panic. He scurried to the bar and poured himself another drink.

"I'm not vulnerable to anything or anyone," he said as he poured.

"You think you know who I am. Maybe you've picked the wrong person." I gave him back his significant pause, and said, "We're enemies, Colin, I don't want you to forget that. Respectful enemies, if that makes you feel any better."

"I don't think of you as an enemy. I want you on my side."

He backed away from me, as if to study me carefully from a safe distance.

"You're not like the others," he said.

"What others?"

"Everyone who was at the party tonight: Mrs. Rabinov, Maestro Habich, that silly bitch Willy Maynard—I think he's a good columnist but I hate him, he's such a wimp—and all the others."

"What about them?"

Colin was still watching me carefully, but now he smiled. It was impossible for me to determine what that smile meant, but I knew it sprang out of pure delight and complete self-satisfaction. It was brilliant, it was certainly meaningful, and ultimately it was malevolent.

"They all work for me. They don't know it, but I have them under my guns."

"I don't believe it."

He shrugged. "Believe it or not, I don't care. I keep telling you, no matter how much they have, they all want more, and I know how to give it to them if they'll give me something in return. They're all only too eager to oblige. That's another reason you're different from the rest. You hate to be under obligation to anyone. I like you and your honesty, and I also have things for you to do."

"Let me go. You can do that."

"I can't. I need you; you're going to work for me."

"What is my work, Colin?"

"You'll know soon enough."

"It's something I do with Vincent Moriarity. I understand I'm writing his memoirs."

"You like that, don't you?"

"It's as good as anything, and better than most."

"I suppose you think Carl thought of it," he said waspishly. "Well, he didn't. *I* did."

"I didn't think one way or the other. As far as writing the book goes, I'd rather do it in different circumstances."

"No."

"Let me out, Colin."

"No. I can't. I need you too badly."

"I'm not like the others, you said so yourself. I'm not like the blond men and the dumb broads and all the people you call by nicknames and bought and paid for. It won't work with me. Let me out and let Mr. Moriarity out. We can go away and never think about you and von Kleinschmidt again. You blackmailed us, Colin, don't ever forget that. I know I don't have a price, and I don't think Moriarity has."

That proved to be too much for him. The pale face got whiter and the pink cheeks got brighter. The room was cool, but he began to sweat with the effort he made to stay in control. He managed it, but he was still little short of hysterical. He was no longer the pretty young man. I saw nothing now but the malice and fury. He was altogether ugly.

"You're not superior, David," he said. "You're just a little better than anyone else. Don't fool yourself. You have a price. It isn't money and it isn't power and it isn't position; you're right about that. Your price is cunt."

He let that sink in. It hit the rock bottom of me.

"I wouldn't have given you a second thought, if it hadn't been for Anna. If she hadn't hooked you that first night, you'd never've seen us again. But she got you cold."

There was no point in hitting him, and less point in killing him. I was already in enough trouble.

"When you went through customs in Los Angeles," Colin said, "you and Anna were in possession of two hundred thousand dollars in heroin and three hundred thousand in unset emeralds. Now, what do you say to that?"

I had nothing to say, and Colin must have known I was staggered by the knowledge he had just given me. I wanted to believe I saw a flickering of some compassion in him when he said, "I'm going now, David. Remember: I want your respect even if we can't be friends."

I had to say this for him: He was a wildly perverse little bastard!

I kept staring at the door after it closed behind Colin. I got to know that door very well, because I studied it carefully for a very long time, and concluded it held no answers for me.

The bell rang as I made up my mind to go to bed and forget the whole thing. It was a waiter delivering a carafe of coffee and all the trimmings that go with it. I was too tired to argue against the gesture; it seemed to be an exercise in futility to tell him I had ordered nothing, certainly not a pot of coffee so early in the morning when I had had no sleep and a new day stretched tiresomely ahead of me. I tipped him handsomely, thanked him, and watched the door close again.

It opened again within a minute or two, and Anna entered.

I noticed instantly that she was dressed in a very simple suit and wore no ornamentation except a pearl pendant that was pulled high and rested in the hollow of her throat. I had last seen her dressed in a flashing gown and loaded with jewelry. The change of costume was startling, to say the least about it.

"Good morning," I said.

She nodded, and waited for me to say something else.

"Come in," I thought to say. "Sit down." As she moved into the room, I said, "Your timing always surprises me. I guess I'd never get used to it in a million years."

"It's easy enough to work out," she said. She sat erect and composed at one end of a sofa. "Carl and I are staying here, too. We're ten floors below you. It didn't take much to learn when Colin was through with you."

"Is that how you think about it?"

"Through with you? Of course. That's the only way to think about it."

"Does Carl know you're here?"

She actually looked astonished, then recomposed herself, and said, "I don't know how to answer a question like that. I don't even know why you asked it. May I have some coffee? In case you were wondering, I ordered that, too."

"Help yourself. And pour a cup for me, please."

She brought me the coffee and presented it to me gravely. The dark eyes were desperately sober but showed no inner disturbance; the lovely mouth was composed but unsmiling; the set of her head was as precise as I had ever seen it, and more beautiful because it reflected Anna's wish to be direct and honest.

"Thank you," I said, and then, "You're some liar, you know that?"

"Yes," she said. "I'm some liar, all right."

"Why did there have to be so many lies?"

"Once you start, it becomes a way of life."

"You can't discriminate—when to lie and when not to?"

"It has nothing to do with discrimination. It becomes the truth because you believe what you're saying at the time, or else you believe you have to lie for whatever the reason."

"I don't understand that."

"I didn't think you would. You live by the truth, which must be just as hard, if not harder. You think there's something special about honesty."

"Isn't there?"

"No. It's frequently dull, and very often harmful."

"I don't give a shit about your other lies. I care that you lied to me."

She smiled at that, and said, "You wanted to be special to me. You were, David. You just weren't special enough." The smile faded, and she added, "You were more special than any other man in my life, now or before. If that means anything to you."

I didn't know if it meant anything, and I asked, "Did you know what you were carrying when we flew to Los Angeles?"

"I had some idea, but I wasn't sure. I didn't ask."

"I'm going to ask why you didn't ask. You weren't flying to L.A. alone."

"At the time, I didn't care who you were. I really honestly am terrified of flying alone, and you could have been anyone else."

"That you'd been to bed with the night before."

"That I'd been to bed with the night before."

It was all coming out very decently and rationally. No one could say we weren't being civilized, which was what bothered me most of all. I was behaving one way while fighting the desire to tear into her.

"What if we'd been caught?"

"I'd have taken the blame; I wouldn't have put it off on you."

"You say that now."

"I mean that now. David, listen. We can do this just as easily over breakfast. I'm hungry, and I know you must be."

"I don't know why," I said, "but I feel stubborn, even about breakfast."

"That's because you didn't get your way. I didn't lie to you about us; about other things, but not about us."

"True, too true. I find it hard to get that word out, but you're absolutely right."

"I never promised you marriage or a great time or even time together. I even gave you warnings. What I did with you, I did because I wanted to. It had its values for me, as I think there were values for you."

"You know that."

"I didn't want you to fall in love with me or be in love with me. I didn't provoke that."

"You did nothing to prevent it."

"Oh, for Christ's sake, David! I'd think you were less tiresome if you'd allow me to have some breakfast."

"I'll leave it to you," I said. "I'd like to wash up."

I left the room and went to the bedroom where Vincent Moriarity and I had had our talk. I stood looking at the chairs in which we had sat, and I thought about the distance I had come since that time in Baja California, and I thought about the places I had been. It's a sad fact of life that its balance is out of whack. It giveth and it taketh away, so to speak, and we'd better make our peace with that. It had given me Anna, and I had wanted to hold on to her, still wanted to. But I had been frustrated by a mating that was no mating. And I had been tantalized—still was, for that matter—by the knowledge that I was the best thing that had happened to her but I didn't have that extra measure of clout that made me more important to her than something else.

I hated myself for the situation I was in with Anna and my inability to pull out of it. Distance gave me some perspective and made the dilemma bearable. To be with her meant the struggle was intensified. It was a damned good thing we were both so civilized.

I shaved and showered and got into fresh slacks and a shirt. I had already decided to return to Los Angeles that day, on the first plane out that I could reasonably catch. That was a positive thing to do, and it was also protective. It would remove me from Anna, and I could go back into the sanity I found between our encounters. The thought reassured me.

Anna was pouring coffee when I returned to the living room. She had had the table set in a window that overlooked that astonishing city, and she had lowered the lights in the room so that we could watch the dimming of the lights in the world outside and the gradual spreading of dawn. I like to be abroad and walking at that time of the morning, to be a part of the phenomenon rather than a spectator to it.

I sat down to juice, a cheese omelet, rye toast, coffee. It was just such a breakfast that Anna had prepared for me during my first morning in Mill Valley. She remembered that I had enjoyed it, and I did so again. My hunger was greater than I had imagined, and I wasted no time in getting the food into me.

When I had finished, and Anna had finished whatever it was she had eaten, I sat back and turned my attention to her. She had taken off the coat of her suit, and I saw clearly now that she was wearing a blouse that seemed to catch against her skin as though it had been pasted to her. On anyone else it would have been a deliberate enticement, but, as always, it just happened to be a proper thing for Anna to wear. It was pretty, it complimented her body, it suited her. There was no possible argument against that, so I stopped thinking about it.

"I want to clarify a few things," Anna said, "clear up a few misunderstandings."

"I know the one I'd like you to start with," I said. "Are you Mrs. Carl von Kleinschmidt and were you always Mrs. von Kleinschmidt?"

"Yes, I am, and no, I wasn't. We were married a week ago, last Sunday to be exact. There isn't much else to say about it. It's an expedient marriage because it makes things look a little better. I don't like the word 'legitimate,' but that fits, too. He goes his way, and that's in a lot of directions, and I go mine. We're together when we need to be together, and I haven't any idea how that will work out."

"It's no marriage, then."

"In the eyes of God, David, yes. In mine, no." She laughed at that, and dispelled some of my intensity. She might not be in love with me, but she certainly knew me pretty well and maybe that was even better.

"Who are you?" I asked. "Who are you really? You've given me two versions and I'm ready for a third."

She laughed again, and said, as she poured me more coffee,

"Why do I have to be somebody? From somewhere? Why can't I *be?* A model, a failed actress, a smuggler, a petty criminal and maybe not so petty, a good lay, if so I am. Why do I have to have an origin?"

"It's like dealing with a ghost."

"But not like screwing one. I hope you know I'm there."

I smiled at that because it was a whimsical idea and typical of Anna as I first knew her. "I know you're there," I said, "but I don't know who's there."

"Would it help any if you knew I was a small-town girl from Shadows, Yukon Territory? A Canadian born and bred and almost educated. My parents were teachers and still are. They sent me out of the wilderness to England, where I was to learn manners and grow up to be cultured and intelligent. I was to meet all the right people and not end up the way they did, struggling with resistant natives and making out with next to no money. I got an education, managed to acquire a layer of culture, whatever that means, and met a lot of people, some of them the right ones my parents were thinking about. But *I* wasn't thinking about them because they didn't interest me, and they didn't have enough. Whatever it was they had, it wasn't enough for me. I went all over the world looking for more, sending nice newsy letters to my mother and father, telling them all the little things I wouldn't even have thought of doing. I sent them money to make things easier and promised I would come home soon, but I never made it. It's just as well. I think they were afraid of me by that time and were just as glad I didn't come home. It was better to imagine me as they wanted me to be." She stopped for a moment, looked at me for signs of a reaction, and asked, "How does that story hold up?"

"I'm just an inch away from believing it." And I was.

"Have it your way," she said. "Now, is there anything else you'd like to know? If there is, ask me. If there isn't, I'd like to get on with it."

I nodded my agreement, poured myself another cup of coffee, and she got on with it: "I didn't know Carl and Colin for three days or three years, so let's start with that. I told the truth when

I said I'd known them for three months. I met them in Jerusalem, of all places, and they weren't on any pilgrimage, either, I can tell you. It took only a night or two for me to get caught up in their way of life, which is really no way of life at all. It's an existence, and a marvelous one if you have nothing better to do. There's no order of importance for anything. You drink and you eat and you gossip and you meet famous people or not so famous ones and you screw here and there and you finally can convince yourself that there really isn't anything else to life. For most people, if they had their way, there isn't anything else. It's the sort of life you'd hate. You're a doer."

"So are you," I said, "I think."

"Yes, I am," she said, "but I'm also greedy. I want it all and as much of it as I can get."

"What is 'it'?"

"I really don't know." She said it without thinking, and then fell silent as she thought about my question. She looked away from me, then at me, and said, "It would take you to ask that question! "It" is all the material and beautiful things that spell security for me. Clothes, jewels, places to live, traveling first class, as much hot water as I want when I want it—things like that. Material things, David, which you—I really think you do—despise. You think it's shallow of me and I'm as inconsequential as things are."

"I keep proving that over and over again, don't I?" I asked, with what I thought was fine irony.

"You would think I was inconsequential if you weren't in love with me. I think I'm even proud that you are. I don't know; I don't think a lot about it."

"When I'm no longer in love with you," I said, "I'll find time to think about what I think about you."

"Fair enough," she said. She rose from the table and started to walk into the center of the room, moving nervously as I had seen her do before. "Now! I haven't got around to making things clear yet. So let's go back to Los Angeles airport." She was pacing now, not looking at me, and not avoiding me, either. She was inside herself, seeking it all out so she could make it clear to me. "I knew what I had, I didn't know how much of it. There was something about being with you that made it all very different. I remember holding your hand very hard a lot of the time, and the pressure back. Very sentimental, isn't it? But I remember it well. I was very disturbed when we got to L.A. and went through customs. I suppose I didn't seem as nervous as I was."

"Your poise was chilling," I said.

"It sometimes is. Anyway, something happened during those hours in the air." She stopped for an instant, then said in a quiet voice, "Being with you and sleeping with you made me see things differently, at least for that time. Perhaps it was nothing more *than* sentiment; it doesn't matter. What's wrong with sentiment?"

I was watching her closely now, searching her averted face for whatever I could see. I saw spots of color settle high on her cheekbones, almost directly beneath her eyes. They made her look younger, and, for possibly the first time I had noticed, at least a little open to the world.

She stopped her pacing to face me. "I've got to put some of the lies away, David, and I'm going to look at you when I do it: I did have the snake necklace. Oh, I also had the duplicate, which I bought with the idea of making a substitution. You see, I had learned a few things from Carl and Colin. I had the necklace, which is worth many hundreds of thousands—I don't know just how much. And I had all the other jewelry, all of it genuine." She flinched when she saw my reaction to that confession. "I don't know why I do it. It would have been just as easy to tell the truth, but I can't seem to do it. My mind seems to have a life all its own. It forces me to say what I don't want to say."

I put the rationalization away without comment. It was a miserable self-justification and unworthy of a lady of her intelligence.

"You don't believe that," she said accusingly. "I can't say I blame you, but it's the truth whether you like it or not. Now, where was I?"

"You were talking about the jewels and the necklace."

"So I was. Well, I don't know what I really had in mind, but I knew I wanted to break away and get clear of all of it. Anyone who works with Carl and Colin pays his way, you can believe that, and I had been put on a tight schedule." Again she made one of her significant pauses. "There was no appointment in L.A., David, and no fashion layout. I was supposed to go directly to San Francisco with the stuff I was carrying, turn the emeralds over to Mr. Klein and the other stuff to another contact I had never met before. I couldn't tell you that, now could I, so I wiggled out of it the best way I could and took off for San Francisco. On the way there, I thought about you a lot and couldn't understand why you had become so special to me. I've never felt any man was special. Do you believe that?"

"That I was special?"

"Of course! What else?" She was begging me to believe her, and I did.

I shrugged.

"Suit yourself," she said. "I'm not going to plead with you. She sat down again and stared at me defiantly. "Do you want to hear the rest of this?"

"No, I don't."

"I thought as much. And I don't want your good or bad opinion of me because of what I haven't said. Please let me say it, David." She went on without waiting for a response. "When I got to San Francisco, I did not—*not*—turn the emeralds over to Mr. Klein. I saw no reason why I should when I had finally decided once and for all to cut out. I really decided that, David, and I meant it. I don't know if you figured in my decision or not, and I guess it doesn't matter. I didn't have any moral feelings about what I was going to do. Is a thief a bigger thief for stealing from other thieves, or is he a smaller one, or no thief at all? That's another thought that came to me, but I didn't hang on to it for too long. I rented a safe-deposit box in a downtown bank and put the emeralds and my own jewels in that.

"I kept the other stuff, and I called another of Colin's ladies. Annette Graham. She was a show girl in Vegas when she met Carl and Colin, living with a small-timey gangster and just about making it, nothing more. I met her once when I was there with them, and I thought she was beautiful, as stupid as anyone I ever met, and, if I do say so, greedier than I am. She left Vegas and the gangster when she went with Carl and Colin. She's always been heavy into dope, which I have never been, and that's usually what they use her for. I knew she would be in San Francisco after making a jaunt to Hawaii. I thought I could count on her and it turned out I was right.

"I told her I couldn't make an appointment I had on the peninsula, and I made the point of telling her it was a heady one. It was, too. I asked her to substitute for me. What I didn't tell her was what I had gathered from careless conversations between Carl and Colin. It seems there're a large number of wealthy users in that long stretch between San Francisco and Big Sur, and the boys were planning to get into it, which meant taking it away from the local dealers. They knew it wasn't going to be easy, but they were counting on me to make the first entry with the help of my contact, whoever that was, and then slowly take it all over on a purely social basis. They were counting heavily on my charm school techniques, which have worked pretty well in the past. They knew the risks involved because that whole area was pretty well tied up, but they were prepared to sacrifice if need be, and that meant any people who happened to get in the way, such as me. Always keeping themselves in the clear, of course.

"Well, I wasn't prepared to be sacrificed." She was defiant again and verging on outright anger. "Besides, I had done all that thinking. So I finally persuaded Annette. She wasn't keen on doing it, because she had just started an affair with a Hawaiian beach bum and brought him back with her. I told her what I really believed, that it was a choice assignment and she'd only have to spend a night and a day in the halls of the mighty. When she said she didn't have anything to wear—her taste in clothes is slightly better than her taste in men—I threw in a fur coat and three dresses in the bargain. Anything to get her to take my place. The fur coat did it, because she'd never owned anything but a red fox jacket left over from her Las Vegas days."

The rush of words broke off, and she demanded my attention with the silence that followed. She was pleading in spite of herself, her eyes squinting with the effort of making me understand.

"I didn't set her up, David," she said. "I had no way of knowing she would die that way. If I had known, well . . ." She made a gesture of despair and helplessness.

"And Carl and Colin had no way of knowing it wasn't you. At first."

She nodded. "They thought everything was gone: me, the emeralds that hadn't turned up at Klein's, the dope, my contact, the Rolls, everything. And they decided you were tied in some way."

"Why me?"

"Who knows?"

"Do you know who did the killings?"

That time her gesture was one of exasperation. "How should I know? I suppose the rival gang they were competing with. Don't ask me to give you good reasons for any of this, David. They just came to the wild conclusion that you and I were in it together."

"Does that explain the dead animals?"

"And the beating they gave Dorothy Denton."

"You knew about her?"

"From almost the very first. It didn't matter to me if she made you happy."

"She did."

"I think I'd like her. She sounds sensible."

"Why the animals and the beating?"

"Colin. He's a mean little bastard. His perversity frightens me sometimes. He really didn't like me being involved with you in the very beginning, because he had nothing in mind for you then. All of that came later. When I disappeared, he thought you might've hurt him, and he wanted to hurt you back. Not any big stuff; just reminders that he was around and watching. He's like that. Completely twisted out of shape."

"Is Carl straighter?" I asked. "Are you?"

Her eyes narrowed angrily, and the flush heightened in her cheeks. "It isn't a game of superiority and domination with Carl or me, David. We just want things and we want to get them the easy way. Only it really isn't so easy."

"When did they catch up with you?"

"A matter of days. But they really didn't catch up with me. I overcame my nobility and went to them. They were a little put out at first, but I was still the best one they had, and the only real losses were the dope and the Rolls. True to his finer nature, Colin quickly decided that Annette and her companion were expendable, so he arranged to have the investigation quashed and then went on as if nothing tragic had happened. Not a pretty story, is it?"

"None of them have been so far," I said.

"There's an ending to part of this one." She shook her head in reluctant amazement. "You know, David, that little monster got control of the peninsula on his second try. Nothing ever seems to get in his way."

"Something will," I said.

Anna brushed that remark away impatiently, and said, "I thought of calling you several times after I got to San Francisco. I didn't because I suddenly knew where I really belonged. I don't mean I belonged with them. I mean I suddenly knew the *world* I belonged in, which wasn't yours. I tried again in Mill Valley. It didn't work, David."

"Is that what you were doing?" I asked. "Trying?"

"Yes."

"I appreciate that." And I did. It seemed to make it a little better that she had made an effort for me. It didn't solve anything; it just helped.

"Do you know what's going to happen to me?" I asked.

"No," she said, and then: "I want to say it again, David. Carl isn't in it with you, and he never was. We don't have a relationship and we won't have. If he wanted it, I wouldn't. He doesn't want it. What Carl wants is all he can get, and so do I. There's one thing you can say for Carl and me: we make a nice couple."

She smiled when she said that, then switched back to: "No, I don't know what's going to happen to you. I can guess, because they've worked too hard on you not to make it something dramatic and important. You're terribly important, and so is Moriarity. It's the damnedest thing, David—I don't feel sorry for you, but I do for Moriarity, who isn't as tough. You're tough, David, did you know that?"

I didn't know that, but I was finding out. I would find out

how tough I was when the gates were raised and the onslaught started.

"I don't want anything that's against you, David," she said. "I just want everything that's for me. That's fair enough, isn't it?"

"It's selfish enough."

She was a little irritated by that. "Of course it is. It's completely selfish, which I am. I never said I wasn't."

She got to her feet and walked to the center of the room. Her face looked serene and remote and self-contained and very beautiful. I didn't blame myself at all for feeling so strongly about her: love and dislike were in me like ebbings and flowings of great bodies of water. There were no lakes in my consciousness where she was concerned; nothing but vast oceans.

"It's going to be a beautiful morning," she said. "I'll be glad, for once, to be going out into it. But not yet. I'd like to go to bed with you, David. What do you say to that?"

"Not very much," I said.

She smiled and started into the bedroom, with me following her. I certainly was going to show her how tough I was.

My bags were packed and the bellhop summoned when the first call came. It was from von Kleinschmidt.

"I understand you're leaving today," he said. "I just called to wish you a nice trip."

"Nothing more than that?"

"Not right now. We'll be in touch with you within the week. You can expect to hear from us in plenty of time for you to pull yourself together."

I resented the implication that I would have to pull myself anywhere, much less together, but I kept my tone even, and said, "You could at least tell me what I can expect."

He chuckled a sly little chuckle and said, "The unknown, but it could be exciting, David. You'll hear from Mr. Moriarity shortly after you hear from me. You like him, don't you?"

"As nearly as I could tell from my one conversation."

"He seemed to like you. It's all going to work out fine."

He hung up after giving me that reassurance, and the next call came through immediately.

"Marie Stark here," a familiar voice said. "May I come up? I'm beginning to think I made a terrible mistake. I'm being mobbed."

"Come up or I'll come down, whichever is better."

"Up. Christ!" Then before the phone clicked off, I heard Dorothy's plaintive voice say, "Lady, what the fuck are you doing! You've got hold of my boob, for Christ's sake!"

She presented herself at the door minutes later, and she was an endearing picture of an idol of the silver screen who had just about had it. She was dressed in a vivid scarlet pants suit which was not guaranteed to preserve her anonymity; her floppy straw hat was so wide it would have overlapped the bottom of a barrel; and her sunglasses protruded two inches beyond the sides of her face. I laughed in spite of myself, and she laughed with me.

"Well, here I am," Dorothy said, "everybody's favorite camp follower. The girl who wears her heart on her sleeve and drips blood with every beat."

She made it into my arms and clung there for a minute or two. I pushed the hat off her head, and held her face up to kiss it. She wore no makeup, which made her look years younger than her thirtyish age, and she smelled of some fresh cologne that put me in mind of fresh fruits cut up and left in the direct light of a summer sun.

When she moved away, showing some slight embarrassment about the depth of her emotion, she said, "I'm going on the Wooldridge show tonight. He's giving me the entire hour and a half. Will you be sticking around?"

"If you want me to."

"I wish you'd put that another way."

"I'd love to," I said.

She noticed the bags then, and registered her dismay. "Jesus, but I take the cake! I barge in like a wife, and say things the way I say them, and—oh, shit!"

"No harm," I said. "I like the way you say things. I was ready to go, yes, but I can change that. I have to be back in L.A. in a day or two, but I'm not rushing to get there. I'd finished my business here, that's all."

She was still not happy with herself, but she rallied when the bellhop arrived and stood transfixed by the sight of Dorothy Denton, spectacular in the flesh. She was quickly the actress, poised and confident, and she went into her performance of lady-in-control.

"What flight are you on?" she asked me, and when I told her, she instructed the bellhop to see that my bags were sent to the airport and put on the proper plane for Los Angeles. As the bellhop gathered up the bags, Dorothy asked for a ten-dollar bill and tucked it into the jacket of the bellhop's uniform. "You're very sweet," she said, which broke me up, and sent the bemused man on his way.

"That's all I could think of at the moment," Dorothy said, and she sank back into a chair, her body straight, her head at almost a right angle to her body. She looked exhausted.

"It'll do fine," I said. "Now tell me the rest of our plans."

"A drink, please. Maybe just a couple of jiggers of gin on ice. Have you got?" When I told her I had got, she went on: "They sent the jet for me. God! The way some people live, it beats all! And I'll go back that way when I choose to. I told them no rehearsals and no priming with questions beforehand, none of that crap. All extemporaneous, and if Woolridge falls on his ass, that's just too damned bad. They accepted, and I'm out of all scenes for the next three days of shooting, and I thought of you, and, well, here I am. It all worked out."

"When do you go back?"

"Whatever suits you."

"I have no opinion."

"Then I'll tell you what. I'll do the show, I'll be through by ten, I'll order dinner for the plane, and we'll take off by twelve. Okay? That'll get us home in the middle of the night, which ought to screw everything up good and proper."

It sounded good enough to me; as a matter of fact, it sounded very good indeed. The whole childlike plan was so spontaneous and innocent in its conception that it allowed other considerations to fall away for the time being. I was beginning to be caught up in Dorothy's enthusiasm, which was mostly eagerness and partly calculation. There was an appealing immaturity about her, made all the more immature because of the role she played as film celebrity. She managed both parts of her life quite well, but I wasn't entirely sure which person I was associating with at any given moment.

"I'm going to wash up," she said, "just my face and things, and then maybe we can have a drink together before I go to the studio. Do you think I can get by with this outfit for the broadcast? I brought another suit, but this's the one that makes me feel bitchy. The other one's white and I always feel like the virgin whore when I wear it. What's your vote?"

I voted for the scarlet outfit, and she started off again, grabbing up her tote bag and purse, kissing me in passing. She paused at the door to the bedroom and faced me. She could not have been more sober.

"David," she said, "I haven't been very fair to you and I want to be. I know there's another woman; I've always known it. I don't know who she is and I don't much care, but I want you to know I'm competing with her. So far so good. She doesn't worry me. When she does, I'll let you know, and then we'll decide what to do about it. Until then, fun and games. But don't be surprised if I bring the subject up again sometime in the future."

Then she was gone, and the subject went with her.

I was in the audience during the broadcast, and my ego was filled and fulfilled. Dorothy was brilliant. She fielded all remarks about her private life, asserting at one point that she loved men but she loved women, too, not bothering to clarify the ways of her feeling about either sex. It was a sensational interview.

The flight home was unbelievable, as smooth as slipping on ice, and as sensual as eating a dinner of rarities and desserts. Dorothy had thought of everything, including the uses to which the reclining couches of a private jet could be used. Her enthusiasm always made sex an enjoyment; it was more so now that she had admitted knowing about Anna and had stated she was not yet prepared to make an issue out of the situation. I was reminded of what Anna had said to me: she had not lied to me, and she had promised me nothing. The same could be said of me in my relationship to Dorothy, although that knowledge didn't entirely free me of residual guilt.

We went directly to her beach house after arriving in Los Angeles, and we slept the sleep of the exhausted and just. I was the first to awaken in the midafternoon, and I phoned Hiram Rather immediately.

That voice closed in on me comfortingly, and it agreed that he and Cynthia would join us for dinner that evening.

I was home in L.A. again, and I felt a little safer, but I never allowed myself to forget that anything good in my present life was temporary. During dinner, I said as little as I could about my trip to New York, minimizing the hold von Kleinschmidt and Colin had on me, saying nothing about Vincent Moriarity. I knew I could trust Hiram with anything, but I also knew I had no right to expose a man of Moriarity's stature even to my best and closest, not to mention most close-mouthed, friends. I did, however, tell Hiram about Colin.

Dorothy and Cynthia were clearing the table and stacking dishes. Hiram and I were on the sun deck, chatting freely and rather aimlessly. It was comforting to be with that large presence, seeing the bulk of the man silhouetted against the moon-struck ocean, and knowing I had his understanding and acceptance. I had never known him to be critical of any friend.

"Colin Davenport alarms me," I said. "I'd never let him know that, but he does. I've known evil people in my time, Hiram, but he's a kind of distillation of all the evil there is."

"There's something about him that troubles you most of all," Hiram said. "You haven't told me what that is."

I thought about it for an instant, which was no longer than I needed to come up with the answer: "He values no one but himself; he has contempt for everyone but himself."

"That's not entirely true, is it? He seems to have singled you out as something special."

"That's right, he has. I think he's dealt with corruption for so long that he never expected to meet anyone with principles or ethics. I'm dumb about a lot of things, but I'm not corrupt. I think that's why he wants to know you. He knows you have integrity and I suppose he imagines some of it will rub off if he can strike up some kind of relationship with you—and me, of course."

Hiram smiled. "I think he wants a relationship with you more than of course. I think that's what it's all about. A relationship with you, for whatever the reason, and the rest of us come along just as a kind of window dressing."

"That's a heavy burden," I said, "and I don't relish shouldering Colin all by myself."

"You don't have to. He only has to think that's what you're doing."

"You're a wily devil, Hiram."

He laughed aloud, pleased with himself. "I never thought I was sainted. You laid that one on me. And anyway, David, you should keep one thing in mind. No matter how much he may want to have some of your integrity rub off on him, he doesn't want it so badly that he's willing to let you off the hook."

If I needed a sobering thought, there it was. I might mean a great deal to Colin, but his juggernaut drive to money and power meant more. He had already amassed a fortune and would add to it, maybe another skyscraper in Manhattan or perhaps some very nice and very large corporation that could cover him and give him the blanket of respectability he longed for.

"I want to meet Colin Davenport," Hiram said. "Let's give him that much at least."

"You're enjoying this, Hiram." I was beginning to feel better. I had the best of allies on my side.

"Enormously. It's Saint George slaying the dragon. It's decency slaying evil."

"You know," I found myself saying, "I must admit I have a

grudging admiration for the little prick. He's worked it out all by himself, starting with little more than an intense desire to set himself apart and above the world of man."

"Apart I'll go along with," Hiram said. "Above, no."

"You know what I mean. He made a business out of human greed. He found the common denominator, which was greed, for whatever people were greedy for, and he paid generously to insulate himself with power and money."

"A dubious distinction." The huge frame tightened and the massive face frowned with disapproval. "I don't like to hear you talking this way. It almost sounds as though you approved of him."

"I'll use another word," I said. "I'm not talking about admiration, then. I'm talking about appreciation."

"That's a little better," Hiram said, and his face relaxed into the benign expression I knew so well.

"You'll meet him as soon as he gets out here," I said.

"Meet who?" Dorothy asked, and she settled on the settee beside me, smelling of fresh fruit and soap and kitchen heat. It was altogether a domestic smell, and it made me comfortable.

"Colin Davenport," I answered. "Colin wants to meet my other friends, now that he's met you."

"I don't think that's funny," Dorothy said. "I don't think that's at all funny."

She was withdrawing from me, making an almost imperceptible move to lose contact with me so I would know how offended she was. I took her hand in mine and held her firmly.

"None of that," I said. "I wasn't talking about going over to the enemy. Tell her, Hiram." Then I turned to Cynthia as she joined us on the sun deck, "Or you, Cynthia, if you understand what we're talking about."

Cynthia stared at me with regal contempt. "Know what you're talking about! I could write your book, and I have very little to go on." To Dorothy, she said, "They're talking about practical considerations, darling. Davenport and von Kleinschmidt aren't going to go away by our pretending they're not there. It's better to draw them in and recognize them. They might expose some weak spots we don't know about."

"It's all right for you to talk," Dorothy said, and she was trying hard not to pout. "You haven't seen them, let alone have them threaten to blackmail the ass off you."

"A nice way of putting it," Cynthia said, and laughed. Then she said to Hiram and me, "You don't know this side of Dorothy the way I do. She'll not only cooperate; she'll put us all to shame."

Dorothy was mollified, or seemed to be, and sank softly against me again. I put my arm around her and sensed instantly that the tension had not gone, and that her rejection of me was still shakily at work inside her. Her vitality had turned inward; there was little of what she thought and felt to be seen on the outside. Her preoccupation with herself and what she was thinking was so deep, in fact, that she hardly acknowledged the moment when Hiram and Cynthia left for home.

We sat on in that quiet darkness, perhaps for half an hour, perhaps longer. I had been staring with such intensity at the quietly moving ocean that my eyes ached from the unblinking strain.

Finally I said, "Bed?"

"No."

"You're not hating me, are you, Dorothy?"

"I couldn't."

"I could. I often have, and this is one of the times. You can't imagine what kind of clod I feel."

"You're not a clod. Sometimes you're a silly bastard, but I can't hate you for that. There're two of us. I can be a silly bitch. How can I go around calling names?"

She sat up and lunged around to confront me. Her face was almost lost in the darkness of the night, but I could still feel the tension and, if I was interpreting it correctly, the underlying disappointment in me. I wasn't wrong about her disappointment.

"How'd you ever get us into this mess?" she asked.

"I'm too ashamed to say."

"When was the last time you were ashamed of yourself?"

"The time my mother caught me masturbating in the bathroom."

"How old were you?"

"Fifteen."

"What did she say?"

"I remember her exact words: 'When you get older, you won't feel the need to do that any longer.' "

"Was she right?"

"No."

She laughed at that, and I knew she was working back to her ebullient self. She said, "So how *did* you get us into this mess?"

"Can we go into that later?"

"Are you being a coward?"

"Yes, a big coward."

She leaned over me quickly, caught my mouth in hers, and massaged my lips with both energy and love. Then she pulled back again and stared at me, seeing my face because it caught the dim light from the living room, but hiding herself from me as she had before. I was amazed at the mass of vibrations that came from her and let me know almost all there was to know about how she was and who she was.

"You're the most honest man I know," she said. "You know, I never knew a completely honest man before, and it's what I like best about you. I'd trust you with anything. And even if you're also a good lay, I don't want to go to bed with you tonight. Is going to bed with me important?"

"Yes. Very. Always."

"Vital?"

"I don't know about vital."

"It doesn't matter, as long as you suffer enough tonight."

She kissed me again, swiftly, then disappeared into the house without a goodbye or a backward glance.

I went home that night feeling a great deal more secure than I had in long, troublesome weeks. I couldn't see my way out of the predicament, but I was starting to believe I would find the way. There was something about Dorothy's faith, more than my own stubbornness, that was driving me on.

When I reached my house, I checked my telephone service and got the full details of my trip to Japan. I was to rendezvous with an Air Force jet in San Francisco at noon on Thursday, was to anticipate a stay of five days minimum in Tokyo, and would be returned directly to Los Angeles, where Mr. Moriarity would vacation for a week before returning to Washington. It couldn't have been more simple.

The second message was even simpler: Colin Davenport would contact me within twenty-four hours of his phone call, which had been made at precisely six o'clock in the afternoon; Mr. von Kleinschmidt would not be with him. It couldn't have been more ominous.

I heard from Colin at the precise second of six o'clock the following day. He asked politely if I would be at home to receive him and when I said I would be, he told me he would be at my house within the half hour.

He arrived at six-thirty, looking radiant and pretty. He was alone, driving up in an expensive vintage Mercedes-Benz. It suited Colin, complementing his modish suit and carefully matched accessories. He looked so diminutive and refined as he stepped from the car that I found it hard to believe his interior was black and rotten.

He gave me a look-over and made a little satisfied smack with his lips at what he saw. "You look great," he said. "You don't know what a relief it is to see you without Carl and not have to pretend anything."

I didn't share his enthusiasm, decided not to say so, and got right to the point. "I leave for Japan on Thursday, as you know. What can I expect; what happens now?"

"I don't want you to think about it," Colin said. "You leave it all to me. I'll have someone here to help you pack, you'll fly to Frisco in my new jet, it'll all be taken care of. Will you trust me?"

The little man cocked his head to one side and looked at me appealingly. I don't know what role he was playing, but I knew he was trying to tell me it wasn't going to be as bad as I thought.

"Do I have a choice?" I asked. "What can I do but trust you?"

"It'll get easier as we go along," he said. "You know, since our talk, I've even thought of telling you more about what I'm up to. Maybe even taking you in with me."

"That's very reckless."

"Not really. I haven't done it, you notice." He giggled that silly giggle of his. "I'll know when it's right, and we'll see then."

"I can wait. And now what do we do?"

"I thought you'd tell me." He pouted, and it wasn't a pleasant sight to see that tiny monster playing coy and petulant. "I told you I was coming alone."

I made rapid calculations that came up with the right answer: "What I had in mind was maybe dinner someplace and then a visit with Hiram Rather. How does that sound to you?"

He was buoyant again. I had to admit the spontaneous decision to involve Hiram more deeply in my troubled affairs pleased me enormously. I honestly didn't know how to proceed any longer, and I knew I couldn't continue to go into and out of my rages. The human body was never designed to take such punishing fluctuations, and what were friends for anyway? In particular, friends such as Hiram Rather. I made the call to Hiram out of earshot of Colin.

I was careful in my choice of eating places, and selected a quasi-Italian restaurant that was newly opened, rather mildly recommended, and used to the sight of outlandish couples and groups. It seemed that Colin and I went beyond outlandish, possibly into weird or exotic.

I could see ourselves sitting in our booth in that restaurant, the rather grim-visaged man who had "no nonsense" written all over him, whose face would have broken into pieces if he had smiled; and the lovely white-skinned and black-haired manikin, who talked with graceful animation and would have made a better woman than man. If he had been a woman, his sex would have despised him and disowned him as completely as I did.

"We're doing this like friends," Colin said at one point in the dinner. "If I weren't careful, I might get carried away."

"Don't fall in love with me, Colin," I said, "or anything foolish like that."

He didn't like the remark, but wasn't enough disturbed by it to go into more pouting and petulance. He indicated by a tightening of lips that I was not to say such a thing again, and changed the subject to something else. I don't remember now what Colin found to talk about. I believe it had to do more with the people he knew around the world than with anything else. I do remember one thing—that his contempt of people came shining through. Nothing pleased him more than to recite the sexual varieties of his alleged friends, or their social indecencies or their moral weaknesses, or their small and large corruptions. It pleased him most of all that people had their prices and he was able to predict, like some ancient soothsayer, the price to be paid and the commodity to be received in exchange.

Our meal together did terrible things to my digestive system and had the opposite effect on Colin. He was ebullient with good cheer and flooding with excitement by the time we reached Hiram's. He might have been the acolyte going to see the bishop, and that is an accurate description of how he greeted Hiram.

Hiram had done everything to create the image and atmosphere of a bishop, and that was something I intended to ask him about later. He received us in the paneled, book-lined, and painting-hung study of his garage apartment. I had not been there since the birthday dinner with Dorothy and Cynthia, and I was knocked out by the progress that had been made on Hiram's new church and parish house. It was already taking on the shape of something grand, and our visit to the garage apartment was like a preview of the experience that would come later. A glance at Colin told me he was stifling with excitement.

Hiram looked as imposing as the newly forming structures outside, which was saying something. He was dressed, again for mysterious reasons that I would ask about later, in a tightly patterned silk shirt and a velvet smoking jacket, and he wore a loosely knotted cravat at his throat. I knew Hiram had never worn a cravat in his life, and I assumed it was hung around his neck now because it was part of the image he wished to project.

I know what I thought of Hiram in those clothes and at that time, which was that he looked pompous and faintly silly. I got the impression he struck Colin in a totally different way, since Colin's breathing got faster, his white face grew slightly pink with excitement, and his hand noticeably trembled as he thrust it out and it disappeared into Hiram's huge fist.

"It's my pleasure, Colin," Hiram said. "May I call you Colin?"

"I'd like you to," Colin said, suddenly shy. I had to give it to him: he was an astonishing little chameleon.

I was not so sure about Hiram at that moment. It was one thing to be polite to Colin, it was another thing to embrace him quite so completely and heartily. But I had learned to trust Hiram. He always had reasons for doing what he did.

Hiram suggested drinks, which both Colin and I accepted readily. It was, I knew, my cue to get the hell out of there for a few minutes, and I did so. I took as long as I could in Hiram's kitchen, stalling over finding the liquor, the glasses and ice; stumbling like an idiot through the simple-minded process of pouring liquor and mixes. I could have been gone seven minutes at most, and I returned to the study to find Colin and Hiram chatting with the ease of old friends newly met, with weeks of separation to cover.

"I don't make judgments, Colin," Hiram was saying when I rejoined them. "I deal with behavior, but only in terms of understanding it and suggesting ways to correct it if it needs correction. There're many people who behave badly who're quite happy with themselves. The same behavior in other people only leads to misery. Now, that's what I'm concerned with. Human misery."

He was sounding portentous and not at all like himself. I looked at Colin, and I saw the pink of his face go deeper and his smile take on an almost beatific beauty. He thought he was in the presence of the *presence* and it was feeding his ugly little soul. He was so quick to seize upon anything to excuse himself, and he was so obviously taking from Hiram what he needed for himself, that my hatred for him deepened at that moment.

"I'm not miserable," Colin said. "I'm actually very happy."

"You look it." Hiram's smile was loaded with the pleasure of recognition and as benign as the blessing of a priest. "I don't know many people at peace with themselves."

"I didn't say I was at peace with myself," Colin said a little querulously. "I just said I was happy. I can't say it's very peaceful running an organization as large and demanding as mine. I don't even know how many employees I have."

Hiram said, "I didn't get the impression from David it was that large."

"Hiram," I said, just to be saying something, "I never tried to give you an impression one way or the other. I don't know anything about Colin except the little I've seen and heard."

Hiram had listened very carefully to me. Then he turned the full intensity of his gaze on Colin, his massive head inclined to the little man like Jehovah giving his full attention to the world. I fully expected rays of light to shoot out from behind him and to hear his voice come thundering up like an eruption from the center of the earth. As well as I knew him, I had never seen him look so benevolent and godlike.

"You're quite astonishing," Hiram said to Colin. "When did you know you had such power and resources? I know David would prefer a different kind of relationship with you, which is understandable. But how he got to where he is with you, and what you expect of him, he's told me very little about. Do you have some kind of hold on David, Colin? He hasn't said."

Colin squirmed uncomfortably under the kind gaze, and his eyes worked nervously as he tried to arrive at an answer to a very simple and very direct question. I knew Hiram was artful, but I'd never imagined he could lie with such finesse.

"I wouldn't say I had a hold on David," Colin said. "He has an obligation to me." He brightened at his solution to the problem. "You could call it an obligation, yes. And when he discharges the obligation, I want us to be friends."

"That doesn't seem unreasonable." Hiram smiled pleasantly, as though he was satisfied and had no further thoughts on the subject. "Tell me about yourself, Colin. I'm sure David won't mind any repetitions."

Colin was eager to talk about himself and display his genius. "I don't really have an organization, and I do, if you know what I mean."

"No, I don't know what you mean," Hiram said.

"Well"—and I could feel Colin settle into it—"I inherited a paper-manufacturing company from my mother after her death, which was about ten years ago. And a small fish-canning company in Maine, and a few pieces of property here and there. It didn't amount to much, maybe around a million."

"You're very casual about a million dollars," Hiram said, and I detected a slight edge to his voice. If there was an edge, his appreciative smile belied it.

"I was used to that," Colin said. "I wanted a great deal more. There was only so much I could do with my inheritance, and I thought if I got the companies on a sound footing that would be enough for them. I did that, and I decided there had to be a more interesting way to make money. There was. I found it."

He paused an instant to make a decision, and finally said, "I don't think it's necessary to talk about what I do. As I told David, and I don't mind repeating it, I discovered people were bored and greedy. I also discovered I could supply them with what they needed, which was excitement and money or sex or whatever it was they wanted. It's not the same thing for everyone."

I interrupted to say, "Hiram knows I came through Los Angeles customs with dope and jewels. I told him that. Are you saying your business is smuggling?"

Colin was hurt. "That's very crude. You're putting it on a low level, and I'd never stoop to common smuggling, now would I? Do you think I would?"

I knew he would, but I didn't say so. I suppose what he was trying to get across was the thought that magnitude made the difference. If you smuggled a tin of marijuana you were a tinhorn; if you smuggled hundreds of thousands of dollars of dope across a border, you were in the upper fifth, or maybe tenth, or even the top echelon of splendid criminals.

"Do you smuggle?" Hiram asked. "Is that what you do?"

Colin looked on the verge of tears, and contented himself with a dramatic sigh at finding so little understanding in even the best of people. The pretty face worked nervously as he fought to frame a thought.

"I hate dope," he said sadly. "It's so nasty."

"In what way nasty?" I asked. "I can think of several ways it's nasty."

"So much bother," Colin said, "more than anything else. It requires so many precautions, and selecting the right people, and I just don't like it."

"Then why do you deal in it?" I asked.

Colin looked at me slyly, and turned away from me to Hiram, clearly indicating that I wasn't worth bothering with, certainly not if I was going to talk like that. "I didn't say I did," he said, and he asked Hiram, "I didn't say I had anything to do with dope, did I?"

He had made a point against me and I decided to stay out of it from then on.

"No, you didn't," Hiram said. "And I don't want to pry about what you do, although I think it's safe to say you do something that means traffic across the borders of foreign countries."

"You could say that," Colin said. He obviously liked the way Hiram had put it. "What I've learned is that people want *things*. Of course, everyone wants things. What I'm talking about are people with money. People with lots of money don't have much else to use money for except things, and they all love things they can't have, or think they can't have. You see, I don't think there's anything I can't have, and that makes the difference between me and other people. There're many differences, of course, but that's one of the big ones. Do you understand, Hiram?"

Hiram blinked at that first familiar use of his name and said, "Of course, Colin, I understand very well. What you're saying is that you supply people with what they feel they can't have in spite of their money and the power and influence it gives them."

"You're just saying what I said," Colin said peevishly, "only you're putting it a different way. It doesn't make it sound better."

"Oh, I was really talking to myself," Hiram said easily. "I wanted to make sure that I had the idea straight in my mind. You know, you are inclined to deal in subtleties, Colin, and I don't think you're entirely aware of it."

Colin swelled noticeably, and said, "I wasn't putting you down, you know; I was just letting you know that I'm not exactly dumb. I don't deal in words, the way David does, but I know what they mean and I know how to use them. How else would I be where I am?"

"Where are you, Colin?" Hiram asked quietly. "That's something I'd like to know."

The question was totally unexpected and certainly something of a puzzler. Colin gaped at it, and I again saw in his face that fight to get a thought out into some sensible form.

"I'm where I am," he finally said, almost gasping it out. "I'm, well, I'm successful and very, very rich. You have no idea how rich I am."

"Do you care to talk about *that?*" Hiram asked, indicating Colin had not cared to answer the other questions. "How rich are you?"

"Terribly." He was pouting again.

"You're not happy with me," Hiram said, "and I don't know why. I believe you wanted to meet me, and David made it possible for us to meet. I wanted to meet you. What do two people recently met talk about? Each other, of course—about who they are and what they think. If there isn't that exchange, there's nothing. You haven't asked anything about me, but I wouldn't refuse to answer your questions."

"I know all about you," Colin said, still sullen but beginning to ease up on his peevishness.

"Then you have the advantage."

"I know where you were educated and who your wife was and how she died, and who Cynthia Wallenstein is and where she comes from, and all sorts of things."

"If there's anything else you want to know, ask me."

"There isn't anything."

"Would you like another drink?" Hiram asked.

"No." And then, a little sunnier than he had been: "I was mad at your asking where was I. You made that sound as though I wasn't anyplace or I didn't know where I am. I know very well where I am."

"Why keep it to yourself?" Hiram smiled a shit-eating smile.

"I'm indifferent," Colin said. "I just don't care."

"I think you care very much," Hiram answered. "You care about money and things. I don't think you're indifferent to either of those."

"They're not as important as you'd think. What matters to me is what I can do with people. I like that. I can make them do what I want them to do. That's something most people don't know, Hiram. You and David know people will beg, borrow, lie, and steal to get what they want, or think they want. I know another thing. I know they'll grovel and they'll crawl."

"That's not a pretty picture."

"I didn't say anything about pretty, Hiram. I just said that's the picture, and it's up to you to decide what it looks like to you. To me, it's fun. It's the way I see people and it's the way I want them."

"I can't say I think that's admirable."

Colin was going to pout again. "I don't care if you think it's admirable or not. I don't even care if you like me. I think."

Hiram smiled at the "I think," and went on, "I suppose you're right, Colin, but I hate to think of a world filled with people like that."

"That's the way it is."

"Perhaps. How do you keep yourself from becoming a victim?"

"Meaning what?" Colin was defensive.

"How do you protect yourself? You have von Kleinschmidt, who does something for you, I can't imagine what. You must have others. How do you protect yourself from betrayal?"

It would be impossible to describe the radiance that beamed from Colin when Hiram asked the question. It was a massive smugness and just about as repugnant as any look I've seen on a human face.

"Layers on layers," Colin answered. "That's the way my business-affairs man puts it. He's very bright, which is why I have him, of course. He helped me with it. Layers on layers."

"I don't think I understand," Hiram said, but I felt sure he did, as I was beginning to.

"My business manager is very bright, which is why we get along. We're very much alike. He was a lawyer and then a politician, and you could say he wasn't quite as honest as he could have been." Colin snickered at that, and said, "In fact, he just missed going to jail, but I heard about it and I bought him off. Well, together we worked out layers on layers. Do you understand, Hiram?"

"I'd like to know more, if you care to tell me. This is fascinating."

Colin expanded at what he took to be a compliment and said, "For example, Carl doesn't handle money, and I don't. Carl has a lot of money, of course, but it's his. It's transferred to his bank account automatically, regular sums, and then any extra he needs.

"He accepts the responsibility in front. If anything goes wrong, and it never has, it's his fault, not mine. I don't know anything about it." Again the radiance. "And Carl charms and makes arrangements and goes to bed with people and arranges for accidents and so on. Do you understand?"

"Doesn't Carl know that's the way it is?"

"I don't think he thinks about it. He wants what he wants so much, I don't think he cares. If you're asking me have I told him, no, of course I haven't."

"What do you do with all your money? I take it you make quite a good deal of money."

"Legitimate investments, like the businesses and the building in New York, and stuff like that. And bank accounts and more investments in foreign countries. I could go anywhere, almost, in the world and live till the day I die with every luxury I ever wanted, and never have to leave anywhere I was for a minute."

"I'm impressed." Hiram was, and he was also appalled, as I could see. The idea of that repellent little creature manipulating the greedy and acquisitive to such an extent was frightening in itself. What was worse was the total lack of a sense of morality. He was preening himself at that moment, and I'll have to hand it to him: the pleasure he took from his rotten accomplishments made him look more angelic than I had seen him look before.

"I wouldn't want to stay put anywhere," Colin said. "I don't want to be one place; I want to be everywhere."

"Doing everything," Hiram added. "What do you think about the dead people—the man on Dorothy's beach, the dead man in David's house—the dead animals?"

The question didn't bother Colin. He didn't seem to see me at the moment or to be aware of me. I didn't matter for that instant and I doubt he would even have been able to interpret properly the intensity of the look on my face, which felt stiff and immobile.

"They weren't important," Colin said. "No one needed them. They became dangerous to us."

"They were murdered," Hiram insisted.

"Put away," Colin corrected him. "There was no point in their being around anymore."

"That seems cruel and unfeeling."

"You wouldn't think so if you knew them. They were takers and they'd been given a lot. We had no further use for them."

"That's playing God."

"Not at all. That was doing what had to be done."

"They were murdered," Hiram repeated.

"Do you miss them?" Colin asked.

"No, of course not. I didn't know them."

Colin was triumphant. "Well, the people who knew them don't miss them. What do you think of that!"

There was no answer to anything as primitive as that, and Hiram asked, "What about the animals?"

Colin's mood changed as he slipped from impatience to an uneasy defiance. He was aware of me again, feeling me sitting next to him, watching him. His eyes remained fixed on Hiram, but his body edged a fraction away from me as though he would feel safer outside my reach.

"That was different," he said. "I was very angry."

"Angry?" I asked. "You were angry at me, Colin?"

"It was Carl's idea," he said. "He was the one who thought

you'd gone off with the Empress. He said that was the last we'd see of what you were carrying. Anyway, that's what he thought, and Carl thought you should know who you were dealing with. He thought of the animals. I don't like to think about things like that."

"And then you found you were wrong," Hiram said.

"Yes."

"By that time, four animals had been killed, a woman had been beaten, a man was dead."

"Yes."

"And it didn't bother you?"

Colin shrugged, but his uneasiness was beginning to show clearly. "I told you, I can't think about those things. They bother me a lot. I'm too sensitive."

"Of course you are." Hiram said it quietly, nodding his head like the wisest of men who understood all things. But there was something lethal stirring in him. I could feel it without having felt it before. It was a new kind of power, and I found it awe-inspiring.

Hiram turned to me, and asked, "How do you feel about all this, David?"

"I've been trying to find out."

"No reactions so far?"

"Several. The first one is, I can't believe it's happening. The second, I'm frustrated because I feel so completely helpless. I *am* helpless." I looked at Colin. "Wouldn't you say I was helpless, Colin?"

The dainty little man wasn't liking this. He was, I knew, so accustomed to being impersonal that the intimacies of anger and frustration and indignation had no real part in his life and were never dealt with. He could cope with the brutality of murder and mayhem, but he had no knowledge of how to deal with the cruel subtleties of strong emotions.

"I don't know what you mean," he said, not looking at me directly.

"I mean, I can't do anything about you or what you've done. For example, I couldn't kill you, could I, assuming I'd want to kill you?"

The white face got whiter and I saw arcs of tightness fix themselves around the corners of his mouth.

"I don't know what you mean," he said again.

I was patient with him. "If I decided to kill you, here and now, I wouldn't get very far with it, would I? I'm not talking about the police or anything like that; I don't think they'd be much of a problem. I'm talking about your people, the ones I never see or hear you talk about, Colin."

Colin Davenport was on the verge of tears. He was looking at his hands, fumbling with the fine fingers, pushing at their nails as though he intended to erase them. He was unhappy. I thought for a brief and foolish moment that he was frightened, and I rejected the idea almost immediately. I had never seen Colin frightened.

"Why are you talking like that?" he said, and it came out as a whimper.

"Who knows you're here, Colin?" I asked. "Does anyone know? Someone must know."

"Why do you have to talk about killing me?" he asked. "I haven't really done anything to you. I want to help you. I like you, David."

"What would you be like if you loved me?" I asked. "I don't think I could stand that. Who knows you're here, Colin? Who knows you came to my house, where we went to dinner, where you are now?"

He looked at me then, and the arcs at his mouth had deepened into pits of defiance. I saw again how cruel beauty can be, because there are few cruelties as ugly as beauty vanished. Colin's face was just a white face, the hair too black, the eyes too wide and deep and empty, the mouth too full and red. There was nothing to read in it, certainly nothing soft and compassionate and fine. It *was,* without any reason for being, and I realized I neither liked it nor disliked it. I was merely tired of it.

Colin said finally, drawing it out of himself, "Why should I tell you? Why should you know the things I know?"

"No reason; only because I ask."

"That isn't reason enough."

Hiram spoke up then, and said, "Someone, or someones, know you're here; is that right, Colin?"

"Of course," he said. "Why wouldn't I let someone know?"

"Is it Carl?" I asked.

He snorted at that like a refined goat, and said, "I only trust Carl with what I want him to know. You certainly don't think I would trust Carl with me, do you?"

"You trust him to kill for you," Hiram said.

The snort came again. "Carl doesn't kill. What makes you think that? I don't trust him with that, either. Carl does what I tell him to."

"Who knows you're here, Colin?" I asked again. "Who is it who knows, and who would know if anything happened to you? If we were to kill you, who would know it was done here and nowhere else?"

He laughed at that. "You couldn't kill me, neither of you. You wouldn't know how to begin. Don't you know that?"

Of course, we both knew that. It takes a noncaring person to kill, or a highly charged one, and Hiram and I filled neither bill. We cared, and although we could be highly charged, it was never to a point where control was gone.

"I'm going now," Colin said. "I don't like this."

"You wanted to meet Hiram," I reminded him. "You've met Hiram."

"I don't like him."

The pout was there again, but the difference was in the kind and quality. I could see in Colin, as I had never seen before, how he could order a killing and have it mean nothing to him. I searched the grotesquely pale face for some sign of emotion, and there was none. It was, as it had been for the last five minutes, just a face, staring eyes and predatory mouth.

"No one's holding you, Colin," Hiram said. "You can go when you want to."

I was fascinated by Hiram, who had been acquiring a dimension to his personality unlike anything I had seen in him before. He was always impressive. At that moment he had become monumental and invulnerable; still kind, to be sure, but judgmental as a god would be judgmental.

"I don't want you to go, Colin," he continued. "I don't want you to stay. I am indifferent to what you do. I'm not indifferent to what you are. And what you are is vengeful and cruel. You're a creature without a sense of morality; in fact, I don't believe you'd be able to give me a definition of the word. Animals have more of a sense of belonging to their kind than you do. You've set yourself apart from everyone, and what's worse, you've set yourself above everyone.

"It won't always be that way, Colin. There'll be the one person who can't be bought or who can't be bought any longer. There'll be the slave who'll revolt. You won't know who, even as you don't know who it is now. But he exists. Or perhaps it's a woman; it could be a woman. But a person who reaches the end of whatever he has with you and decides to end it—or perhaps finish it is the better word.

"It could be Carl, Colin. It could be Anna or David. It will be someone. What will happen to you I can't say. But that something will happen to you, of that I'm sure. And your Cerberus won't help you, nor will your mercenaries. No one hates more than the person who has been bought; you have that to learn. I feel sorry for you, Colin, I really feel sorry for you.

"Other than feeling sorry for you, I feel nothing. I could sit here and watch David kill you. It wouldn't touch me. I don't hate you, Colin; I merely think you're hateful. There's a difference. And no one hates you more than you do."

The rich and resonant voice died out, leaving a painful vacuum in the room. The silence seemed to me to be more raucous than the worst noise.

Colin rose to his feet and left the room, the white face perched on its elegant body like a whitewashed pumpkin carried on the end of a decorated stick.

Hiram sighed, and I saw his eyes were filled with pain. He was unhappy with himself, but I knew him well enough to know he had acted with good reason.

"Why did you do that?" I asked quietly, not wishing to make more of my question than I had to. "You knew all along you were going to do that, didn't you?"

Hiram sighed again, and shook his head. "I had no intention

of doing it. I hope I haven't made him more of a villain than he is. I hope I haven't precipitated something. If I have, you'll have to find a way to forgive me."

I smiled at that. I couldn't think of a circumstance in which Hiram Rather would have to be forgiven.

I had heard Carl von Kleinschmidt give a toast to Archie, and I had asked him who Archie was. "Anything you want," he had said. "Anything you want out of life."

I was jammed into the corner of the back seat of a taxi, headed for home after that evening at Hiram's, when I thought about Archie. At the time, it had seemed like an innocent enough comment. What was wrong about wanting a lot out of life? Was there anything wrong in setting out to get what you want? The answer, of course, is that everything's wrong if someone is deliberately hurt in the process of your getting what you want.

Colin, we knew now, went after what he wanted with a staggering lack of regard for anything or anyone. I didn't want to give him credit for anything, even in a negative sense, but I was forced to admit he had covered his tracks well. He had already proved to be a master of organization, judging from the way he was able to keep himself completely clean and still in control of the people he manipulated. He was so wise in the ways of corruption that he seemed to know instinctively whom to corrupt, how to corrupt, and how much it would cost to corrupt.

I thought of the blond man murdered so neatly in my house, sitting there naked as though he were having a pleasant time at an orgy, and I wondered what that had cost, who had been paid, or perhaps how many had been paid, and how high on the scale of officialdom Colin had had to go to cover his spoor and position himself free of any involvement.

For a fleeting instant I thought that I must be very important to Colin to have him go so far in order to compromise me. Then on second thought, I knew I wasn't the important one. The indispensable man was Vincent Moriarity, who was immune from search and seizure and could cross any border knowing he did so with the highest authority in the world.

I didn't have to waste time in determining that my position was that of middleman. If I failed somewhere along the line, I could be replaced. It was doubtful if there would ever be another Moriarity.

An infinite weariness came over me when I finally reached my house in the hills, walked into my living room, and found my luggage in the center of the floor, neatly packed and ready to be picked up in the morning. A neatly printed note lay on top of the Val-A-Pak. I read: EVERYTHING YOU REQUIRE IS IN THE VAL-A-PAK AND GARMENT BAG. YOU WILL RECEIVE AN ADDITIONAL PIECE OF LUGGAGE WHEN YOU BOARD THE PLANE IN SAN FRANCISCO.

I had the awful thought I would never have to think again. A conviction like that deserves a stiff drink and I took it down in a gulp.

I called Dorothy and her sleepy voice didn't brighten as it usually did when she heard from me. She sounded groggy and thick-tongued, and a sense of alarm, even terror, jumped in me like a giant pulse.

"Dorothy, are you all right?" I asked.

"Yeah," she answered, "why shouldn't I be all right? Shouldn't I be all right, boychik? You're leaving for God knows where tomorrow, and I haven't seen you or heard from you all day, and everything's swell. Why shouldn't I be all right?"

"I'm sorry," I said.

"Sure you're sorry," she said. "I'm drunk and I've taken a couple of pills, and you're not to worry, you hear?"

I jumped at that, but kept the anxiety out of my voice. "What kind of pills?"

"Never you mind. Just pills, and if you think I'm planning my last dramatic exit, you got another think coming. When I do *that,* it's going to be good and it's not going to be in some lonely lousy beach house where I've been sitting all day because you didn't bother to call me."

"I'm coming right over."

"The hell you are. I haven't been this miserable in years, and I'm going to enjoy it. I've got something on you and I'm never going to let you forget it. Now, what do you think of that?"

"I don't like it," I said, and I didn't. But I began to feel better as I played this human game with Dorothy. She was tight enough to be more funny than accusing, and I knew exactly what she meant by getting a charge out of her misery. It was better to go along with it than have it do you in altogether.

"You're sure there's nothing I can do?" I asked.

"You can write or call me when you get where you're going. And you can bring me something back. You never bring anything back."

"I haven't been anyplace much," I said.

"That's no excuse." She wasn't letting me off the hook that easily.

"How did you know I was going someplace?"

"Cynthia."

"How did Cynthia find out?"

"How should I know? Hiram, I suppose. He *tells* her things, and you're such a dog about it."

"I'll tell you everything I can," I said, "from now on. If I feel I can."

"See! There you go again. Always conditions."

Her voice was thicker now, and sleepy-sounding. I had seen that pretty face often enough to know it began to close over like a child's at such times, eyes and mouth shutting like wings. She would drop off to sleep soon.

"I'm going to say good night, Dorothy," I said. "Please take care, and you will hear from me. I'll write, cable, call—I don't know. But it'll be something. Okay?"

She mumbled an echo of okay and the receiver clicked off.

I went to bed, and if I slept, it was in dozing periods of five or ten minutes. I listened to the noises of the neighborhood, trying to catch their rhythm so I would be knocked out by monotony. But there was no rhythm to those sounds. Dogs barked, cats fought, a baby cried, a noisy bathroom flushed, there was one sharp cry that sounded frightening as it tore into the stillness of that night. Then came the early-morning noises of the paper boys and the early risers and the late returners.

I was dressed and sitting in my living room by seven o'clock, feeling something like a child who is going off to school for the first time. I thought about my maturity, and wondered where it had gone. In many other ways I had regressed, shaken out of adulthood and my strong sense of self-determination by a pretty, white-faced maniac who was evil enough to be far smarter than I, particularly when it came to playing his game. It was a bad feeling.

A limousine picked me up, and I was stowed into its cavernous back along with my luggage. The man who drove the car was a blond, but a middle-aged one gone seamy and fatty. He was obviously one of those who had survived the early days of devilish pleasures, and perhaps that accounted for his ugly disposition. I was prompted to think that maybe Colin was right to get rid of the blonds as soon as they had served their purposes.

A small jet was waiting for me at International Airport, and I was put aboard ceremoniously and efficiently, as though I were a crate of priceless glass being secured for a long trip. I said nothing to the blond man who drove me to the jet and ushered me on board, and he said nothing to me; I doubt he would have recognized me had we met again. The same kind of acceptance and silence characterized the flight to San Francisco. I never saw the pilot or his crew, and it was another blond, this one dressed in the uniform of an airport employee, who hauled me off the plane and led me to the Air Force jet waiting at a far end of the field.

I was welcomed aboard by an enlisted man, who took my two pieces of luggage and then stood back to let me precede him into the plane. As I started to move past him, he said soberly and quietly, "Your luggage will be transferred from the plane to a waiting limousine when we reach Tokyo. You won't see it again until you're at your destination."

I looked at the man closely, trying to find signs of something in him or about him that would give me a clue to his identity. There was nothing I could see immediately. He was another young man in uniform, and I had seen many of them. He was not, however, a blond, but a swarthy Mediterranean type who looked and smelled of masses of perfumed hair. He was so unsmiling that I doubted even the vestige of a smile had ever broken the ludicrously curved lines of his mouth. He returned my look impassively and nodded with his head, indicating I was to go into the bowels of the plane and get out of the passageway.

I had never seen a plane quite like that. It was appointed like the expensive small second home of a multimillionaire. There were miniature staterooms on either side of the passageway, and the passageway ended abruptly in a large room that looked like a library and would have been a credit to anyone's home or club. It was planned and decorated with an eye to maximum comfort and beauty, and made me think of a hundred rougher ways to travel. I was suffering, all right, but I was certainly doing it in complete luxury.

Vincent Moriarity was sitting at the far end of that cabin library, talking to what I assumed were two of his aides. The two secret service men I had seen at the party in New York were not in sight, but there were two other men, who wore the jackets of stewards and were, quite possibly, secret service agents themselves. I really didn't care who they were, and I wasn't curious enough to find out, then or at some later date.

Moriarity got up the instant he saw me and came to greet me and pull me farther into the cabin. I was glad to see him, and it did me good to see genuine pleasure filling his face as his hand grabbed mine and pressed it.

"We'll sit over here," he said, indicating two leather chairs that were on swivels and could be moved to view any point inside or outside the plane. "We're taking off immediately, so I suggest you belt yourself in."

The plane was moving toward the takeoff area, and as Moriarity and I fastened our belts, the two stewards placed cigars, cigarettes, a plate of small sandwiches, a carafe of coffee, and another carafe of tea on a table near us, and asked if we cared for anything else to drink. We didn't and they disappeared into the forward section of the plane, followed instantly by the two aides.

As the plane took off, rushing into the air with a strangely joyous eagerness, Moriarity leaned toward me and hollered above the roar of the engines, "A superb pilot. We'll talk as soon as he completes his climb. You'll be surprised at how quiet this flight is. I'd advise keeping your voice low, not that you're a loud-mouth."

"No, I'm no loud-mouth, but it wouldn't offend me even if you thought so."

Moriarity smiled at that, indicated with a move of his head that he understood I had paid him a compliment, and turned to look out the window. I studied him, examining again the bush of red hair, the lean and devilish-appearing face, the lanky body, and the iron-knuckled hands that looked as though they could tear the meat off a man's bones. Yet there was a softness in him and by soft I certainly don't mean to imply weakness. Moriarity's softness would be any man's strength, because it was an expression of humanity and compassion and involvement. I supposed that was what made him a genius in his field of international, national, and personal affairs: He wasn't afraid to become involved.

We were at our cruising speed now, and he turned back to me, to say, "Would you like a drink now? I think I could use one. The sandwiches and coffee will keep."

We agreed to have drinks, and soon we were comfortably sipping at them, looking at each other, measuring the degree of feeling and trust that we now felt.

Suddenly, without preamble, Moriarity said, "There's a peculiar thing about me, and you might make a note of it for our book." He smiled when he called it our book, and I checked for bitterness in his voice and meaning, but there was none. Moriarity wasn't the kind of man to feel sorry for himself. "I never feel I do enough or that I ever realize my full capacity for whatever it is I do. I always feel I fall short. I haven't been analyzed, but I think it has something to do with striving for everyone's approval. What do you think of that?"

"It's not an unusual syndrome," I said, "but it surprises me in you."

"I married late," Moriarity said, "that is, later than most men doing it for the first time. I was thirty-five, eight or so years ago. I suppose it's a happy marriage. My wife, Theoni, is European and a liberated woman. She *does* things, you know, like painting—she's really rather good—and committees for fine arts and hospitals, things like that, anything that doesn't keep her tied to the house, which I would hate for her as much as she does. She doesn't take part in most of what I do. She's interested but inclined to be far more radical than I, and she gets emotional, so we decided to keep her out of things. At least she's not housebound, which she would hate. No children, but that's because her whole insides were torn out, practically, by a late miscarriage. But she survived, and we live together. What is a happy marriage anyway?"

I could feel how lopsided my grin was. "I wouldn't know. I've had three and I don't contemplate another. Unless."

"Unless?"

"I think anyone who makes hard-and-fast statements is an idiot, that's what. Who knows when the circumstance will come up that'll change the whole thing? I hope for the best and prepare for the worst."

"That dark-haired woman at the party? Anna?"

"You're very perceptive. I'm not surprised you noticed."

"She could make the difference."

"I think she could, but she won't. She's too caught up in herself."

"If you have to get caught up in anyone, I suppose she's the one to get caught up in, including herself. Narcissus didn't seem to suffer from it."

We laughed at that, and our laughter brought the steward. Our drinks were refreshed, and Moriarity led the conversation into a sobering turn.

He said, "Will you write my book? We share being blackmailed. Why not share something more profitable?"

"I'd do it in longhand, standing on my head."

He smiled. "I don't ask that. Just use whatever methods make you comfortable."

"I'm flattered."

"And I'm complimented. I don't believe David McEndree has

ever written the biography of anyone, has he?"

"No, and he can hardly wait to start."

Suddenly Moriarity's face turned sober, almost white. The contrasting red hair seemed to turn redder still and I actually believed it bristled with the energy of the man's mind. I learned later, as I got to know him better, that that curious phenomenon happened when his mind was clicked into higher energy fields and his computer brain went to work on a difficult problem.

"Excuse me," he said, and swiveled in his chair so that his face was hidden from me. He was staring out into the universe, lost to me and everything else in the plane.

I went to the bathroom, washed my face and hands, used the electric razor that had been left out on the counter. As I stepped back into the passageway, the enlisted man who had ushered me aboard came up to me with his robot efficiency and indifference and told me that the staterooms were available to me if I wished to rest at any time during the trip; I was to feel free to use any one of them. I thanked him and broke away from the encounter with the distinct impression that I didn't like the man. As a matter of fact, I was chillingly convinced that, although he was certainly a bona-fide enlisted man, his absolute loyalty was not to the U.S. Air Force. There was the smell of money about him, and I felt sure I knew where it had come from.

Moriarity was turned back in his chair, talking to one of his aides, when I rejoined him. He dismissed the aide, asked that lunch be served within the hour, if possible, and smiled at me. The florid face was reassuringly red again, the hair no longer bristled.

"We'll have lunch," he said, "then I'll have to spend time with my aides. I'm not the brightest man in the world when it comes to trade agreements, and I'll have to bone up on our past history with Japan. In such matters, my mind is a sieve, and it quickly leaks out."

"Please do what you have to do."

"And you the same. I brought along some family albums, which you may think is a peculiar thing to do, and I also brought letters I wrote to my mother and father during my school years. They may be of some help. That's all I brought, however, you'll probably be glad to know. Another drink?"

I agreed to another, and said, "Do you want a book or do you want several volumes, like the Churchill books?"

"Can we see how that works out? I hate to pin myself down to a formula. And in the long run, I'll want you to tell me. Now, while we're waiting for lunch, I want to be open with you, as you've been with me."

The face was instantly sad, the eyes moistening with remembrance but not with real sorrow, the good mouth turning downward.

"I haven't really given you a blow-by-blow account of the trap I'm in," I said. "But if you want it . . ."

"You told me enough," he said. "And I want to tell you enough, because if we're sharing the horror of the situation we're in, we should share the absolute horror of why we're in such a fix. I'll state it as quickly as possible, and you draw all the inferences and explore the subtleties like the good writer you are. All set?"

I said I was, and he said with considerable urgency, his voice low-pitched and husky with tension, "I hope I don't seem to be putting up a defense for myself, but the first thing I want you to know is that I've worked very hard to get where I am. My parents were poor farm people in North Dakota, and I worked the farm as well as at small jobs in town to get enough money for my education. I don't regret any of it, because the results have been so gratifying. My interests in school were unwavering. I loved history, devoured political science. It was a natural step for me to go to work for the Overton Corporation, where I could put my knowledge to good use, and even more natural for me to end up in Washington at an early age. I had studied my lessons well, and I deserve to be where I am, David. I worked for it, every single minute of it. I owe nothing to anyone. And now this."

It was a comment simply made, without bitterness. I understood its complete and exact meaning, because it really meant: "What in God's name did I ever do to deserve this? Where did I go wrong? What was my first mistake?" I had gone through that litany myself.

"I understand how you feel," I said, and could manage nothing more.

"Yes." He was reflecting, and I turned away to give him privacy for this thoughts. When he was ready to speak again, he gave me the full measure of his attention, those blindingly blue eyes probing into my own. He said, "Does the name R. D. Sparking mean anything to you?"

He might have asked me if I had ever heard of Hitler, Attila the Hun, Stalin. I had never met Sparking or any member of his family, had never had any desire to do so. All but the most ignorant Americans would have been able to identify that name, a very few with pleasure and applause, any reasonably intelligent people with fear and loathing.

I knew the basic facts about R. D. Sparking and his brood: Sparking himself born seventy-three years ago in a midSouthern state; sharecropper parents, illiterate, impoverished, bigoted in the way only ignorant people are indelibly and irrevocably bigoted. His education was minimal, his luck phenomenal. While he was busy filling his wife with one child after another, eventually to reach a total of eleven, he was also busy building an empire out of oil and real estate. As his wealth increased—he was a multimillionaire early on—so, too, did his bigotry. He hated niggers, kikes, redskins (which is what he called all Indians, whether East Indians or American), foreigners of any kind or description, greasers heading the list, and last but not least, anyone of the highly born or lowly placed who disagreed with him. In order to promulgate his opinions throughout the land, he owned papers, radio stations, television stations, and politicians. He also founded a good-size university, free to all who would allow themselves to be exposed to the special courses in the doctrine according to R. D. Sparking; it was even free to the minorities he hated, because he was convinced of his ability to point the way and prove to inferior peoples that they were indeed inferior. As a result, the school frequently exploded into large- and small-scaled riots, one of which had erupted three years ago, leading to the deaths of fifteen students and bystanders.

Yes, I knew R. D. Sparking for who he was. I nodded my head to Moriarity.

He said, his pain evident in his face, "My real name is Richard Dale Sparking, Junior."

"Holy shit!"

"Something like that." He smiled lamely. "That's about what I said when I first heard the news."

"First heard?"

"Two years ago, told to me by a sister who'd tracked me down."

He let that get through to me, then said, "I was the firstborn, and came at a time of lowest ebb for my real parents. For another thing, I wasn't expected or wanted. They sold me, actually sold me, within a week of my birth. I eventually was exchanged several times and ended up with the very decent people who gave me their name. The Moriaritys moved several times to cover the trail that might lead from my real parents to them, and eventually settled down on a small farm in North Dakota. They don't know to this day who I really am, and I trust you not to reveal a word of this."

"Not very damned likely," I said. "And that's the hold Colin has on you?"

"Not entirely. It's more complicated than that." The lame smile came again. "I think the knowledge that I'm Sparking, Junior, would be enough to cancel out everything I've worked for, and that my parents have worked for. I have to think of them. I don't include Theoni in this because she never did approve of my political career, and God knows, with her liberalism, what she'd do if she found out my true identity. Divorce me surely, kill me perhaps."

"How did you learn all this?" I asked.

"One of my real sisters was a lawyer and far less bigoted than the other members of the family. Actually, she was enlightened but terrified, in particular of one brother who apparently is like my real father all over again. He also bears the name R. D. Sparking, Junior, so there're two of us. My sister's name was Amalie, and she stumbled on the fact quite accidentally that Sparking's firstborn, who was supposed to have died in infancy, did no such thing. She set out on a search that took her years and led to me after I had already moved to Washington. I saw her once, she gave me proof of my identity, and then made a confession about something that had haunted her for much too long. She told me, David—and this is the frightening part—the truth about the last riot at the Southern Alliance College of Fine Arts."

Moriarity's ruddy skin looked inflamed, his eyes were streaked with exploding capillaries. His confession was costing him a great deal more than I could imagine, and I would not have been surprised if he broke down completely. But he was a strong man and determined to go on.

"My sister told me," he said, "that the brother who shares my name added expert riflemen to the state militia when they were called in to squelch the riot. They were all loyal members of his personal work force, as rabid as he was. Is, I should say. So the fifteen deaths weren't the result of hysteria or an unfortunate set of circumstances, as the jury found during the trial. They were calculated murder, and my sister could prove her accusation. After she told me that, she left for California. I never saw her again. Six months later, I learned she was dead, a suicide. Several days after that, I received a letter from her, and I never opened it. I know what it contains, and I'm afraid to face it. Do you know what's in that letter, David?"

"Yes," I said. "Proof of the murders, or information about where you'll find the proof."

"I think so." He let a long moment pass, then said, "I'm not much of a hero, am I, David? I should let the world know the truth, and I can't. Not yet, anyway. Maybe later."

"I don't think either of us deserves a medal for heroism. How do you suppose Colin got hold of this information?"

"I don't know. I can't even guess."

"He's an insidious little bastard. I'll give him that."

"So here we sit, flying to Japan, fearful of exposure, caught in a trap not of our own making. That's a switch, at least."

I asked, wanting to change the subject anyway, "Have you figured out what we're being used for, and how?"

"I haven't really thought about it."

"I have. You're nothing more than a shield hiding me. Where you go, I go, and with me, flying both ways, goes contraband cargo worth more money than I even want to think about, all of it pirated or stolen. I'm expendable; you're not. If I got caught, it's my ass alone. And you find yourself with a new biographer, or some other kind of aide. They want to keep you appearing clean and above reproach. I don't matter that much. Isn't it beautiful?"

"It's you and me," Moriarity said, "together. It's like an uneasy marriage, but better than living alone."

"I'll drink to that," I said, and I did. A long, hard swallow.

Tokyo is different now. I no longer feel the pleasure I used to feel in going there. The city has become a concrete swamp of pollution and disorder, the enchanting people are no longer unhurried and inscrutable. It's a scrambling place now, but, God knows, suitable to the mood I was in when we landed and were ushered into limousines that would take us to our respective destinations. The ushering was done with complete courtesy and care, but I felt pushed and shoved in psychological ways and was more than a little resentful of my reasons for being there, whatever those illicit reasons happened to be.

Vincent Moriarity was to be taken off in one limousine, I in another. He gave me a handsome portfolio, made some comment about seeing me when his schedule permitted and expressed the hope that I would be comfortable, then he was gone. I was not happy about his going, because he was my link to some kind of security and sanity in that strange country, but at least I knew he was as available to me as the nearest phone. I was, after all, his official biographer.

I was driven to the Imperial Hotel, which deserves special mention. I had always stayed in lesser hotels during my few visits to Tokyo, and I was not prepared for the magnificence of the building itself or the suite which had been assigned to me. The only word that properly describes it is sumptuous, and I again had the sensation of suffering in style. I could well imagine what it would be like to suffer in ghetto conditions, and I hoped I would never learn from personal experience.

In the center of the living room, which was one of the three rooms of the suite, were my Val-A-Pak and garment bag, and on a table near them, an item that didn't belong to me. It was a marvelously handcrafted leather case that looked like a woman's makeup kit. I found it was secured by a heavy brass lock; it would require a locksmith or some lethal and heavy weapon to open it.

The bell of the suite rang as I was examining the case, and I put it down before I went to open the door. I didn't know whom I would find on the other side of that door, and certainly I was not prepared for the two people I found there.

They were Carl von Kleinschmidt and Anna, both of them looking radiant, both of them looking like well over a million dollars apiece. It was indecent for two people to be so good looking, so vital, and so smashingly turned out.

"May we come in?" von Kleinschmidt asked, stepping back and motioning for Anna to precede him. Anna said nothing.

"Of course," I said. "I don't know why I'm surprised to see you, but I am. I thought I'd left you safely behind me."

"Did you have a nice trip?" von Kleinschmidt asked.

"Splendid, considering the circumstances."

Anna gave me a quick look at that moment, a studying and weighing look, but I could draw nothing from it that had special meaning for me. She walked over to one of the windows that looked down on the city below and sat on a sofa so that her back was to the outside light. Her face was caught in shadows, as she had wanted it to be, and I thought she was hiding from me. It was not like her to avoid inspection, and that seemed to be what she was doing.

Von Kleinschmidt was making a survey of the room, concentrating on doing something that was in the forefront of his mind. His face brightened with recognition when he saw the small leather case, which I had replaced in such a way that it was partially hidden by an ornate flower arrangement. He picked up the case with the assuredness of someone who knows what he's about and tucked it against his body with his arm curved to hold and protect it.

"I take it," I said, again feeling frustrated and inadequate, "that you were looking for that case. That's why you came here."

"Yes. That's why we came here."

"Will you tell me what's inside?"

"It won't do you any good to know what's inside."

"I'm curious."

"Don't be, David." Anna's rich voice was solemn. I could see little of her face because of the shadows, but I knew her well enough to perceive that she was gripped by either anxiety or some other kind of tension.

"I'm always curious," I said to her. "It's more than my stock in trade. It has a lot to do, at least in this case, with how I feel about playing courier when I don't know what the hell I'm carrying."

"You didn't carry it," von Kleinschmidt corrected me. "It accompanied you, just as something else will accompany you when you return to the U.S."

"I know how you feel about this," Anna said, and let it go at that.

"Do you?" I asked her. "I don't think you know what you feel about anything. I at least know I don't like the situation I'm in now, and there's no mistake about that."

"You don't sound as much bitter as angry," Anna said.

"At you or generally?"

"Either way."

I turned to von Kleinschmidt. "Well, there it is. I accompanied it, and you have it, and what're you waiting for?"

"Aren't you even going to try to be pleasant?" von Kleinschmidt asked, and I heard an intake of breath from Anna that was like the warning hiss of some reptile.

"You're a fucking idiot," I said. "Now, if you'll excuse me."

It was very playlike, I thought; it was all as though the three of us were playing parts in some civilized drama in which death and destruction were occurring around us while we remained untouched at the center of the vortex. My feeling of unreality was shattered by the ringing of the telephone. I turned from von Kleinschmidt, my eyes speeding briefly and resentfully over Anna, and I answered the call.

The sibilant voice of the operator told me Los Angeles was calling, and within a matter of seconds, I heard the heavy voice of Hiram.

"David," he said, "are you all right?"

"Yes."

"Are you alone?"

"No."

"Can you talk?"

"I don't think it matters."

"I'll make a guess. Carl and the Empress."

"Correct."

"It would figure out that way."

Then I heard it, the thickness of anger and sorrow and bitterness. I had rarely, if ever, known Hiram to give expression to such emotions, but he was doing it then. The mixture was as apparent as flags flying in a wind.

"How is everything?" I asked, attempting a cheerfulness I didn't feel.

"Would you rather I called you later?"

"No, not at all."

"I could."

"Not necessary."

"Then hold on to yourself. Don't react until it serves your purpose. Do you hear me?"

"Yes. And I understand. Go ahead. I'm glad everything's all right."

"Cynthia's dead."

"Well, that isn't too bad, is it?" I said, and I turned to von Kleinschmidt and managed a look that was remotely like a smile. "Can you tell me how?"

"She went over a cliff two blocks from her home. Crashed in flames. All I've been able to get so far is that a man in a sports car was seen near the scene of the accident at about the time it took place. Whoever saw him got the license number, but it was checked out. The car had been stolen from a garage, the owner is in Europe on a business trip. It was driven by a blond, David."

"Do you have any serious doubts?" I laughed, and I almost choked on that laugh. "I would say it's the end of the road, wouldn't you?"

"You know how I feel. I think I precipitated it by my attack."

"It would have been that, or something else, don't you think?"

"I suppose, but that doesn't help much."

"You can try a little harder. I know I'm going to. Beginning now."

"What does that mean, David?"

"It's in good hands."

"Meaning yours?"

"Don't you know it!"

"Be careful!"

"You know that, too. It was nice of you to call."

"Do you know how long you'll be gone?"

"Seven, give or take a few."

"Perhaps I'll know more by then, but I doubt it."

"See you then."

I hung up. When I turned back to von Kleinschmidt and Anna, I tried to be as I had been before, and I think I succeeded. My face was perhaps a little stiffer, that's all.

"Now, where were we?" I asked.

"We got to the part where I was a fucking idiot," von Kleinschmidt said easily.

"Things haven't changed since we last talked," I said. "When can I expect whatever it is I can expect next?"

"When you leave here," von Kleinschmidt said with that easy charm, "your luggage will be picked up and delivered to the plane. You don't have to worry about a thing."

"You make it all so easy," I said. "I don't even get the kick of being intimately involved in something illegal and exciting."

"You are, you know," he said, "whether you feel it or not. And if anything went wrong, you'd have some explaining to do."

"But you wouldn't."

"Very little, if anything. If I was to be asked, I'd be forced to say I hardly knew you."

"You were seen coming to this hotel suite."

"Casual acquaintances asked up for a drink. Or maybe not even that. We were never here, and we have witnesses to prove it. Why're we talking about this, David?"

"Playing the game, I guess." I was beginning to relax a little. The shock of Cynthia's death, and the knowledge of the impact it must have had on Hiram, were still with me and would remain for some time. I knew that. But I had other moments in life to live and other fish to fry. I smiled as I thought of that old adage, and I was able to say with something that could have passed for geniality, "I take it you'll be here for at least as long as I am, that right?"

"Yes. At least as long."

"I'll have free time. I suppose you will, too. Perhaps we can spend some of it together."

Von Kleinschmidt viewed that with some suspicion, but said, "If you feel up to it, fine."

"Anna?" I turned to the smoky figure sitting at the window, and as I did, she rose to her feet and started toward me. She moved across the room with that long, graceful line, her body enjoying the light suit it was wearing, her head held free and high, the beautiful face emerging from the darkness and suddenly appearing bright and colorful in its frame of dark hair. I knew I would never be entirely free of the temptation of that beauty.

"I'd love it," she said. Then to von Kleinschmidt: "Carl, don't you think we should go?"

He nodded at that and started for the door.

"How can I reach you?" I asked, addressing the question to von Kleinschmidt.

"We have an apartment near here. The phone is listed in my name. The hotel operator will get it for you. They're remarkably efficient, particularly at the Imperial. At these prices, they should be."

"I never heard you express concern about prices before," I said. "Isn't that something new?"

He laughed in the charming way that had first caught my eye

and ear in Baja, California. As it had been on that day, the blond hair was impeccably groomed, the tanned face was taut and handsomely defined, the teeth dazzled as his mouth broke into an open-mouthed grin. He might have been irresistible if there had been anything working inside him.

"I'm not worried about expense now any more than I ever was," he said. "I only meant the phone service here had *better* be good. If it isn't, let me know."

"I'll make do," I said, and turned from him back to Anna.

She was watching me, but broke from her scrutiny long enough to shoo von Kleinschmidt on his way in a gesture that said: Go on; I'll be right along. Then she faced me again, looked at me with intense concentration, and finally took my face in her hands and kissed me.

She pulled back from me, and said, "Whatever it is you have in your mind, please be careful."

I phoned Hiram as soon as von Kleinschmidt and Anna had gone, and was put through to him almost immediately. I dispensed with the usual greetings.

"Von Kleinschmidt and Anna were here," I said. "I know you understood why I was talking that crazy way."

"Of course."

"I don't know what they made of it, and I don't give a shit. But when they left, Anna hung back and said she didn't know what I had in mind, but to be careful. How about that?"

"She hasn't given up on you entirely. Do you have something in mind, David?"

"Yes, but first, tell me how you are. I'm really sick about this, Hiram, sick and mad."

"I've got over the worst of it. She'll be buried tomorrow, only not really buried because her will specifically stated no ceremony. She just wanted me and Dorothy and one or two others and the servants, of course. She was devoted to the people who took care of her."

"Of course; she was Cynthia. How's Dorothy?"

"She can't stop crying, and she's madder than hornets at you, David. You'll want to call her, but don't. Let her be mad and get it all out. She holds you responsible now because she wants you to be Superman and work it all out without problems. I told her you weren't Superman and couldn't work it out yet. She'll get the picture, and she'll call you."

"As long as the rest of you are all right."

"What do you intend to do, David?"

"What you did, Hiram. You pushed one monster to see how far he'd go. I'm going to push the other one."

"Are you sure that's wise? I'm not sure."

"I don't care about sure. I feel terrible about Cynthia, but I know you did the right thing. The trouble is, you did it for me and you were the one who got hurt, or Cynthia. I owe something to you, Hiram, like a lot. I'm going to see you get paid back. Okay?"

He said it was okay, and we hung up.

Hiram's devastating news sent me into such a state of anger and nerves that I drew on a sweater, decided against shaving and tidying up, and went out into Tokyo. Night had dropped over the city and I welcomed the cool air. It smelled as noxious as the air of Los Angeles, but that was all right with me. I wasn't out seeking perfection, only the kind of physical contacts and anonymity that would allow me to separate myself from the world and live for the moment within the exclusive atmosphere of my brain. I had to know what was going on up there.

I walked aimlessly, not caring what street I was on, and certainly I was oblivious to what was going on around me. If I noticed the differentness of the city, the smaller people and the marvelously odd faces, not to mention the incomprehensible language and hieroglyphed signs, I relegated it to the back of my mind, where it made no impression on me but could be called upon if I needed to remember someday. I found I was not actually thinking, as I had hoped I would. I was, on the contrary, carrying on some kind of lecture in my head, complete with slides. Single words, and phrases, and whole sentences, were moving around without logic or sequence, and since I was too tired to fight their lack of logic, I let them happen.

At one point in my walk, when I was pushing my way through a mob of short people who were thronging a main thoroughfare, I heard a horn and I turned to the sound, knowing it was intended for me. It was, and it came from an astonishing black car that looked as long as two limousines. Its interior was clearly illuminated from the crazy brilliance of the street and shop lights, and I looked into it to see Vincent Moriarity, who was sitting in the center of the back seat, flanked on each side by two ministerial young men who looked to be half Moriarity's size. Facing them in the jump seats were two Americans who were undoubtedly secret service agents.

Moriarity was smiling, his red face exploding with the pleasure of seeing me. He waved with almost childlike excitement, and I waved back. Then the limousine was gone, engulfed by that noisy city.

My first reaction to the encounter was a little sad, because I wondered what kind of life Moriarity led that would make him place value on having an association with me after such a brief acquaintance. Then I realized I had been equally glad to see Moriarity. Finding ourselves lodged in the jaws of the shark, it was comforting to know we wouldn't have to fight our way out of our predicament alone.

I felt better, and I discovered I was ravenously hungry. Tokyo suddenly became a place to me, blaring and glaring, and I walked without trouble or incident to a restaurant I had frequented on past trips. I took my time over that meal, savoring the raw and the cooked and the hot saki, taking pleasure from the beauty of the waitresses and the efficiency of the busboys, and I returned to the Imperial Hotel, prepared to sleep for a minimum of ten hours, but not holding myself to that limit.

I slept thirteen hours, and awakened only because of a call from Moriarity. He wanted to know if I was comfortable, if I needed anything, and if I knew anything. I told him yes, no, and maybe, which made him laugh. He wanted to know what I had been doing the previous night, and I said I'd been walking it off, meaning the largest load of fury and hostility that I had carried around at any time in my life. But seeing him had given me some direction, although I wasn't sure yet what that direction was, and I would certainly keep him informed if I committed a murder or even thought of committing one, which wasn't outside the realm of possibility. In the meantime, I assured him before we rang off, I was going to read his letters that day and would most likely start making some stab at organizing the approach I might take to his biography.

I read some of the letters while I had breakfast, looked at the highly interesting photographs while I had my second cup of coffee, and had to make a temporary postponement of any further work because of a telephone call from Dorothy.

"I'll bet your ears have been burning," she said in greeting.

"Yes, but I didn't know why."

"Guess."

"You've been saying wonderful things about me."

"Wrong."

"Then you haven't been saying wonderful things about me."

"Wrong. The answer lies somewhere in the cracks between wrong and right."

"That's called keeping me in suspense. How are you, Dorothy?"

"You never call me darling or sweetheart or honey."

"Do I have to say them if I feel them?"

"Yes. Saying them makes them really happen."

"Give me time and I'll learn. *Are* you all right? You know I heard from Hiram and he suggested it might be just as well if I didn't call you."

"That's right. There was no point in your being called asshole over all those miles."

I laughed, and said, "Not to mention the Imperial Hotel switchboard. Did you really think I was that bad?"

"Not really. When I got over the shock and got a grip on myself, I knew I couldn't blame you for what other people were doing. I must say, you seem to invite disaster."

"That same idea keeps coming to me. But I'm going to do something about it."

"Can I know what it is?"

"I don't know myself. But something. I'm not a stand-stiller, Dorothy."

"There goes that word again. Dorothy."

"Honey."

"It's not right yet. Don't work at it. It'll come in time. Have you thought of what you're going to bring back?"

"Yes, but I haven't decided. What do you want?"

"A Buddha, in ivory or wood or something, but not jade. I want something large enough to look at when I need to get myself quiet."

"You want a quiet Buddha, not a noisy one."

"One of each." She giggled. "I'm a creature of moods, and you're lucky you didn't see the last one I was in, the asshole-calling mood."

"I'm glad, too."

"What *are* you going to do, David?" The tone was serious now, no longer bantering. "If you really want to know how I feel, I'm worried sick. It's all been so lousy, and I don't want any more violence; I can't stand the thought of it. You wouldn't kill anyone, would you?"

"Yes, I would," I said. "But I don't think I'm going to have to."

"Thank God, because I love you. And don't say it back, please. I don't have to hear you say it, and I'd know if you did or didn't by the way you said it. I don't want to push that hard."

She hung up without waiting for an answer. I replaced the receiver in its cradle and sat staring at the phone for a long time. I had been very glib in making my statement about no killings. As a matter of fact, I wasn't at all sure what the future would bring for me. I knew beyond doubt that the kernel of my anger was both hot and poisonous, and it could spread inside me very quickly given the proper motivation.

I shaved and showered and dressed, postponing the work I would do on Moriarity's book. I went out for another walk, this time making my way through the daytime crowds of Japanese. My foreignness became a factor in the light of day and I let my mind run like an idling motor as I watched the faces that passed me, looking for the careful and often shy scrutiny that took me in and registered me as a stranger in that land. I wondered what they thought of the shaggy American who was stepping carefully between and around those small people, seeing only what he presented to them, unable to see the turmoil and torment washing around inside him.

I found the Buddha Dorothy wanted, an exquisite piece of yellowed ivory that stood about eight inches high and looked as if it would move if you touched it. He was a treasure, and as I carried him out of the store, I felt him pouring some kind of decision into me. I am not a believer in the occult and I've never been able to claim an extrareligious experience. I do know the Buddha was generating something in me, and I went along with it.

When I reached my suite, I unwrapped the little figure and put him on a table where I could see him from any corner of the living room. I studied him a long time, and then I called the hotel switchboard and asked to be connected with Carl von Kleinschmidt.

In two, perhaps three, minutes, I was talking to Anna.

"I asked for von Kleinschmidt," I said to her. "It's okay, though; I'm glad I got you."

"He's out doing whatever it is he has to do in order to get you ready for the flight back to Los Angeles."

"That sounds strange, as though I was something that had to be packed and wrapped for the long trip home."

"Isn't that more or less the truth?"

"That's very candid of you, Anna."

"I don't fool around, David, you know that."

"Is that how you think of me, packed and wrapped?"

"It doesn't matter what I think. You're being sensitive, and I don't think you should indulge yourself that way."

"Touché."

"Touché, my foot. There's nothing you don't know. There are

a few things you haven't faced yet. You're roped and tied, David, and what're you going to do about it?"

"You sound as though you don't like it."

"You bet I don't. What do you want to talk to Carl about?"

"According to the schedule I've been given, we're due to leave here in seven more days. That would make it next Saturday, or maybe Sunday if there's a delay. I think you and I should have an evening together. That's what I'm calling about."

She greeted that with a thoughtful silence, and when she had given herself enough time, she said, "You're not the social type, so I assume you're not just being pleasant and graceful. I hope, in other words, that you have an ulterior motive."

"I do."

"Splendid." She hung up.

I thought about her for a minute or two. She was beginning to wear off, and I was glad of that. It would be one of the great ironies of my life if we turned out to be just good friends.

The setting was made for dear friends or lovers, not for antagonists who could barely tolerate each other.

I had remembered a restaurant that overlooked a Tokyo park and temple, and it was there that I made reservations for my evening with Anna and von Kleinschmidt. It was one of those places designed to seduce and disarm: a partially enclosed room furnished in traditional and opulent Japanese style, service so impeccable and unobtrusive that it was almost magical, a view of gardens and bridges and gently flowing water that was like a sedative to the mind and emotions.

We were a little incongruous in that setting because of our size and general appearance, but otherwise we suited ourselves to it and not the other way around. Anna looked splendid, her black hair piled high on her head, her gown a modified version of a Japanese ceremonial kimono, her jewelry so minimal and fine that you saw it only at second glance. Carl von Kleinschmidt was All-American, Joe College, Mr. Junior Chamber of Commerce, resplendent in a khaki-colored suit with blue accessories, his blond hair shining, his skin scrubbed so that its fineness and brightness were almost too perfect to be real. It would have been a perfect social situation if we were all good friends.

"It's lovely here," Anna said. She turned away from us to look out into the park beyond, where the greenery was darkening with the falling night and the few small deer were becoming bolder in their forays after food. "You've seen it in better days," she said, not indicating she was addressing the remark to me. Her voice held a tinge of regret.

"And I've seen it in worse days," I said. "I came here for dinner the night I received word that a member of my family, very close to me, had been killed in an accident. The news had been brutal, and this place helped."

"Who was it?" von Kleinschmidt asked stupidly.

"It doesn't matter," I answered, "it was so long ago. Three years ago, to be exact."

"That isn't long ago," he persisted.

"In the natural course of life, or unnatural if you're inclined to think that way," I said, "that's ages ago. There've been other tragedies and other deaths."

Anna's eyes were on me then, moving away from the park and to my face in that slow, fluid way they had. I somehow knew she knew I was thinking of Cynthia Wallenstein, and I preferred to read some measure of concern in her eyes rather than complete indifference. She was not sentimental, of that I was certain, but she was able to dredge up real emotion from time to time and briefly join the human race. There was a kind of bitterness in that thought which I didn't like, and I put it from my mind.

"Will you let me order?" I asked. "I know the place and the menu, which has never changed. I'm apt to hit the exotic side of the menu, so you'd better stop me now if you have trouble with food."

They had none, and I ordered.

The eating ceremony began, and we went at it with enthusiasm, larding the parade of courses with small gulps of hot saki. There was conversation, but only of the sort that seems to accompany that kind of feasting. We talked of places we had been, people we had known, things we had done in the years of our lives. It was a deceptively comfortable time, but I had no trouble remembering I had a passionate hatred for Colin Davenport, a rousing contempt for the manufactured and unnatural specimen of manhood sitting there with me, and a slowly ebbing hang-up on the exquisitely beautiful woman who didn't have even the unique morals of a cat, because she actually had no sense of morality whatsoever.

We were onto tea and a remarkable dessert of multiple fruits when I said to von Kleinschmidt, "When I was in New York, I had quite a session with Colin. He was very interesting, more than I would have imagined. Among other things, he told me he owns and lives in the Action Building. I understand you've never been there."

His back straightened and squared itself, the tanned skin became a curious beige color, and the hand holding the teacup was lowered to the table as carefully as though it held nitroglycerin.

It took him more than a few seconds to bring a smile to his face, and it wasn't the easiest one he'd ever managed. He said, "What makes you think I've never been there?"

"Colin told me so. He told me so with considerable relish, I might add. Is there something wrong between the two of you, von Kleinschmidt?"

"Wrong how?"

"He's usually with you."

"He stayed behind."

"I know that. What I'm saying is, I've never known him not to be with you. Did your marriage to Anna have something to do with it?"

"With what?"

"Your relationship."

"I wouldn't call it a relationship," he said, considerably more at ease than he had been. "It's a partnership."

"He didn't give me that impression."

He said, "What're you getting at, David? I'm not very good at mysteries."

"I'm not getting at anything. All I'm really saying is, it was a strange evening in New York, and I learned a lot about you and Colin I didn't know before. I didn't know, for instance, that he's number one and you're number two, but two in Colin's scale is somewhere along fifty in any normal scale. You don't rate very high, von Kleinschmidt, do you?"

He said nothing, staring at me impassively, and quite possibly without anger. He had the look of someone alert and sensitive to the world around him. It was important to me that he listen, and I went on.

"Colin gave me the impression that he had little if any respect for anyone. I include myself in there somewhere. I wouldn't say it was contempt for me, as it seems to be in your case, but something more like a comfortable tolerance. I've been weak enough to fall into his trap, and he thinks I'm inextricably caught, and perhaps I am. The thing is, he *has* me—you know what I mean by '*has* me.' I belong to him, and he doesn't have to think about me anymore. I'm his, the way he sees it, and that might be right. But contempt, that's something else again. That's what he feels for you, von Kleinschmidt. That puts us all in there together, doesn't it?"

"Why're we talking about this?" von Kleinschmidt asked.

"*We're* not. I am. I am because there isn't much else I can do about it. It's like penal servitude, and all the inmates have to do is talk about how they got into it and how to get out. Isn't that so?"

"Not so at all," he answered. "I'm not *in* anything, and I don't feel like an inmate."

"But you *are* in something. I'm in it, you're in it, Anna's in it. We're all part of Colin's master plan and we all play our parts. You not least of all."

"I told you it was a partnership," he said.

"And I tell you that isn't the way Colin looks at it. He feels he owns you and pays you well to own you. He told me a lot that night, von Kleinschmidt, as much about himself as about you. How long have you known him?"

"What difference does it make?"

"It doesn't. I'm asking out of curiosity. I wondered if it was before he inherited the two companies or after?"

I didn't know I was taking a shot in the dark. But there it was, a shot that hit von Kleinschmidt in the vitals, jerking him to attention out of the casual state of indifference he had assumed. He hadn't liked what he heard.

"You didn't know that?" I pursued him. "He never told you about the inheritance, or that the two original companies still exist and that there are others formed since then. All of them legitimate businesses, von Kleinschmidt. That's quite some partnership you have with him."

"Why do you keep calling me von Kleinschmidt?" he asked. "I find it annoying."

"It's the only way I've ever thought of you."

"That's not much of a reason."

"I can't think of a better one. Von Kleinschmidt is how I met you, and that's the way it's always been. What difference does it make?"

"I don't know." He frowned as he tried to determine the difference it made. "Well, forget it."

"You know, von Kleinschmidt," I said, "I know you must have heard of the Action Building one way or the other. It's not exactly a pimple on the hide of Manhattan. But I'd bet my bottom dollar you didn't know Colin lives there in the penthouse and that he owns the whole shebang. Right or wrong?"

I felt Anna tense, but she managed to look merely indifferent. Her eyes had left my face long ago and were focused on the outdoors, as though they were seeking something there. She was not participating, and I doubted that she would.

"There's more to it," I said. "There's a whole floor below, and that's where he entertains and houses his guests and servants. I find it hard to think of Colin as having guests. I can't even think of his having friends, for that matter. What do you make of him?"

"He has his way of life," von Kleinschmidt said slowly, "I have mine. We don't bump into each other either coming or going."

I laughed at that because the image was such a strange one to apply to the fastidious and untouchable Colin Davenport. "I don't think anyone bumps into Colin. Judging from what he told me, he stands alone at the center of whatever you two are up to. And it might interest you to know that I know more than a little about what you do and how you do it. I'll fill you in. I know how I was used on the flight from Baja, California to L.A. I know it was only the purest chance, a freakish piece of luck, that got me any further involved with the two of you. It's the sort of thing that makes you wonder what sort of force plays such a large part in our lives. One minute it's clear sailing, and then bang! I've been in stormy seas before, but nothing like this. I can't say I like it, but I'm forced to admit I find it interesting. Interesting, hell! It's downright fascinating!"

I was smiling now, a kind of idiot smile, almost as though I was relishing the position I was in. I was, in fact, enjoying the turn in attitude taken by von Kleinschmidt. The man was separating from the boy. I had given him enough to think about, and he was going over it in his head, his eyes bleak and his mouth compressed with whatever was going on inside him.

Anna said, "Do you think it would be possible to get some coffee? Would it cause a catastrophe in a place like this? I don't want to upset the balance of things."

"Not only possible," I said, "but desirable."

"We could go," von Kleinschmidt said.

"I think not." Anna was looking at him fixedly. "I think it would be a nice idea to stay here until we've said what has to be said. It won't go away if we ignore it."

I ordered our coffee, and then said to Anna, "What won't go away?"

"I sometimes get more practical than I need to," she answered. "What I meant was, what you have in mind is going to be said whether Carl and I like it or not. One way or the other, you're going to say it, aren't you?"

"I'm persistent."

"That's more or less what I had in mind." She was talking to me exclusively then, not ignoring von Kleinschmidt exactly, but letting him know he wasn't a party to what was being said. "I don't agree with Carl. I think we're all joined at the hip. That comes out as quite a thought. All you have to do is think about it a little while."

She almost smiled, and added, "I have the feeling there's something farcical about this. Or maybe indecent is the word. The three of us sitting here, being terribly polite to each other, and knowing so much is at stake. Not really liking each other, either."

"I'll take your word for that," I said dryly, "although I don't have to agree. I'll take what you said at face value."

"Don't make it complicated, David," she said. "Don't go *into* it. I hate things when they're gone into."

Carl was looking better now, his face less a mask, his eyes a little less wary. He said, "No, I didn't know about the penthouse or the floor below or the building itself. I don't think it's important, do you?"

"Colin thinks it is. He even thinks it's important that you've never been there. It puts you in your place."

"We have separate lives," von Kleinschmidt said. "There's a great deal about me Colin doesn't know. He wouldn't think it was important to know all about me."

"I think you're wrong," I said. "I think he thinks it's important and I also think he knows all about you. Where you live, how you live, even who you're going to bed with. There's nothing he doesn't know. Do you think, von Kleinschmidt, that he would know as much about me as he does—and you yourself know what he knows—and not take the trouble to find out about you?"

He was going to think awhile about that one.

"Colin *is* the organization," I continued, "whatever that means. You only work for the organization. Anna knows that, don't you, Anna?"

"I don't mind listening to your conversation," she told me, "but I don't want to become part of it."

"Unfortunately, baby, you are part of it," I said. "Von Kleinschmidt is and you are and I am and even, in her way, Dorothy Denton is, because that's the way Colin wills it. Or better still, that's the way he works it out. We're all pigeonholed and we all have our price, and he places us where he wants us to be in the superstructure. But he's the only one at the top, and he's the only one in the clear. I don't know how he's in the clear, but if he says he is, I believe him. Now, what do you think about all that?"

"It's not very important," von Kleinschmidt said, "is it?" He wasn't asking a question, he was stating a fact as he saw it. "You're saying one thing; I see it all a different way."

"I'm only objecting to your word 'partner.' You're a paid employee, von Kleinschmidt, nothing more or less."

"What's wrong with that?"

"What's wrong is, you didn't know that's the way it is, and has always been. At least, you know you rate higher than I do. I'm the insect struggling on the pin. I don't even get paid for what I do." I switched the attack to a more intimate area. "I'll make a guess. I guess that Colin makes regular and large deposits to your bank account, or maybe it's bank accounts. All your travel expenses and living expenses are provided for. I'd be willing to wager you don't so much as pick up a check or buy an airline ticket—that is, when you fly on commercial lines. What I'm saying is, you've been lulled by the mechanics of payment, not to mention the generous amounts that filter into your bank account. Why wouldn't you be? But if you think that's all there is, you've got another think coming. You see a small percentage of the take. The rest is Colin's. All he has to do is see you're rich enough to satisfy you and keep you asleep. And there you are, marching out in front, for all the world to see. You're the prime target if it all goes wrong, and if he's asked, Colin will never know what you've been up to all this time. He'll hardly know you. Beautiful, isn't it?"

I paused long enough to order brandy and more coffee, and then I looked inquiringly at Anna and von Kleinschmidt. They were silent, Anna thoughtful, von Kleinschmidt morose. They weren't rushing away, and I took another step forward.

"That estate down in Baja California," I said, "the place where we all got acquainted. My instinct told me those Mexicans—Martinez y Ochoa, wasn't that the name?—might have given their name to the place as owners but they were in fact fronting for something else. There was a criminal odor about the place. The people were too varied and they came from too many places. When I look back on it, I remember it as a kind of clearing house, people passing through and some of them making it and others not. I suppose by making it, I mean becoming a part of whatever it is you and Colin do all over the world. Nothing to say?"

Von Kleinschmidt had a look that told me he had heard but had not listened to what I said. It was possible that I had left him minutes ago, and he was still chewing over some of my revelations about Colin.

Anna seemed to have checked out altogether. Her body had assumed a dignified and regal posture, the back straight, the head erect, the hands positioned easily so that their fingers rested together on the table in a pretty pile. She looked as unreal as porcelain, but I knew nothing was going past her or had been unheard.

"You've got to hand it to him," I said. "Colin's devilish and clever. I always thought H. V. Klein's existed by itself and for itself. Colin tells me that isn't so. He controls that, too. Now, you're not going to tell me you didn't know that, either, are you, von Kleinschmidt?"

The face became livelier, color coming back into it with a sudden flooding. He refused to look at me.

"You didn't know that, did you?"

"H. V. Klein's supports itself," von Kleinschmidt said stiffly.

"Not true. Colin didn't say as much, but he led me to believe that he controls the store, and that means your father as well as your mother; and your father knows it. That's why he hates Colin so much. You've taken too much for granted, von Kleinschmidt. Or maybe you just didn't want to see any of it. Maybe the truth wouldn't have made that much difference to you."

He remained silent, and I went on, "I met your father, von Kleinschmidt. After the animals were killed and Dorothy was beaten and the blond man was killed; after that. It made me curious enough to try and find out what, if anything, you and Colin had to do with it."

"Why do you keep going into all that?" Anna asked.

"I think it bears repeating. As you said, it doesn't go away by not being said."

"I see." Her hands locked and she again turned her eyes toward the darkness of the park.

"Your father," I said, "is not a nice man. As a matter of fact, I don't like him worth a shit. I can say one good thing about him, if it *is* a good thing. I think he worships you. He's very bitter because he sees so little of you, and he's more than bitter about your relationship with Colin."

"I don't like Mr. Klein," von Kleinschmidt said. "I go to the San Francisco shop rarely, and only on business."

"I'm curious about one thing," I said. "Why does he think it's necessary to pose as a Jew? Does he consider it good business?"

"He is a Jew."

That remark came into the room softly, but it had more impact on me than anything said that night. I knew it to be the truth because it stood out so boldly against the parade of lies that had gone before it.

"Is he your father?" I asked.

"No."

"He thinks he's your father."

"I know, but he isn't."

I decided to play a waiting game. I was thinking anyway, thinking that Jay Summerhill had investigated Klein and had said he was not Jewish. Now von Kleinschmidt was telling me he was Jewish and seeming to be angry about it. I didn't see that it made any difference one way or the other. If Klein was passing as a Jew for what would seem to be business reasons, then that got a little sticky, but it still wasn't important, and it certainly wasn't sinister.

"Klein was a minor Nazi official passing as Aryan," von Kleinschmidt said. "My mother was pregnant with me. She had to get out of Germany the best way possible. Klein blackmailed her. He would guarantee her safe passage to Italy and then into Africa if she did two things. My mother was a very beautiful woman; she still is. Klein said she had to turn over her money and jewels and sleep with him. She was carrying a great deal of jewelry, far less money. She didn't mind the jewelry or the money. She drew the line at sleeping with him. She had no choice. She slept with him and she never forgave him. I didn't, either, or anyone like him. He went with her. He thought the child was his, and she never told him. She told me."

His voice stopped suddenly, and I said, "I understand a great deal now."

"You don't understand anything!" he said, his mouth snapping open and shut angrily. "How could you understand anything?"

I said, "I don't mind easy explanations. You've just given me one that clears up a few things about Klein."

"I'm not talking about Klein! I'm talking about a woman he betrayed. I'm talking about my mother."

"That doesn't sound like much of a betrayal. Klein made a bargain and forced your mother to stick to it. What's so terrible about that?"

"Let's get on to something else," Anna said. It was the first time I saw her lose even a small measure of her poise.

"I don't mind talking about von Kleinschmidt's mother," I said. The atmosphere was getting thick, but I was enjoying it. "Do you mind my talking about your mother?" I asked him.

"She's a great lady," he said stiffly, and I suddenly saw all the German in him, or perhaps Prussian is the better word. "I take care of her. I see that she's comfortable and protected, and I see her when I can. She wants for nothing."

"That's a nice way of putting it," I said, "but I don't think Colin would agree with you. I think he thinks he provides for your mother. From him to you and Klein to your mother. That's the way he sees it. Don't forget, von Kleinschmidt, you're an employee, in addition to everything else you are."

Anna's hands moved on the table and their movement caused me to look at her. Her eyes were talking, and they were telling me to lay off. I could hear what she was saying, but I didn't listen to it.

"Who was your father, von Kleinschmidt?" I asked.

"He was a great naval officer."

"That should have been enough protection for your mother."

"He was killed in action."

"I still don't see . . ."

"They weren't married. His wife found out about my mother and the pregnancy after his death. My mother was reported to the Gestapo. She was branded as a whore."

"It seems to me," I said, and I said it carefully, "she *was* a whore."

He was across the table and grabbing for my head without having uttered a sound except for something guttural that rose from deep in his throat. I was ready for it, because I had been heading in that direction all along.

I was flat on the floor, my hands pushing at his chest, trying to heave that great weight off me. His hands were everywhere, but he was too angry and uncontrolled to do me any real harm. He kept pounding at me frantically, and I kept shoving at him, bursting with the effort of moving that bulk away. Another shove, and he was off, rolling away from me and crashing against the glass wall overlooking the park.

"My God!" I heard Anna say, and then I was on him. His hands were still flailing, and there was something funny about them, something that reminded me of an infant, angry in its crib, slapping at the world because it wasn't getting what it wanted. I laughed, and von Kleinschmidt's hands found my throat in that instant. His strength was greater than I had thought, and I was no longer in the mood for laughing. I grabbed his chin and pushed up on it, putting pressure on the back of his neck. He arched with it, his spine curving off the floor in such a wildly moving arch that his pelvis ground into my stomach.

He was in pain, and his hands dropped away to claw at the emptiness of the floor. When I released my hands from his head and neck, he went limp. He lay there, breathing hard, his eyes closed. If he hadn't been an enemy before, he was one from that moment on.

I got to my feet and looked first at Anna, then at the tiny waiter who was standing in the doorway of the cubicle, his eyes round and wide, his mouth grinning, my check held in his hand.

"He'll be all right," I told Anna.

She nodded, looking at me, not seeming to know or care that her husband was lying beaten and humiliated in the same room.

I inclined my head to her in farewell, and left with the waiter. I paid my bill and walked out into the night.

I set off for the hotel on foot. It didn't matter that I was unfamiliar with the outlying sections of Tokyo. I set my direction by the glowing of lights in the far distance, and I walked with such energy that I reached downtown Tokyo in less than an hour. I was on familiar ground there, and I slackened my pace, using some of my energy to think about what had been and what I would do next.

I thought of calling Moriarity and decided against it. It might give him satisfaction to know I had got the better of one of our opponents, but I couldn't predict how he would react to the news that I had made von Kleinschmidt a good deal more lethal than he was already. Moriarity had enough to worry about.

I decided it was time to stop thinking, and I hailed a cab and asked to be taken to the Ginza. It was livelier there, fast and bawdy, and I began to relax. It had some of the elements of Tokyo's notorious redlight district without having the same element of danger, and I felt safe there as well as diverted. I drank in a bar I wandered into; I watched a girlie show in which a line of extraordinarily beautiful and naked girls sang "Singin' in the Rain" in a hilarious accent that broke me up; and I stared at starers who were staring at me. All of it amounted to nothing, and it did me a great deal of good. The Japanese had always been high on my list of people of the world; their ability to charm and please made them go even higher before I set out uncertainly for the Imperial Hotel much later that evening.

I went straight to my suite, not bothering to pick up phone calls or other messages. I was at the tail end of the evening, and I felt let down. A shower helped a lot; I even bothered to comb my hair before getting into bed.

I had just pulled the sheet over me when the doorbell rang. A glance into the world told me it was still an hour or two before dawn, so it was inconceivable that anything but an emergency would cause anyone to arouse me at that hour. I was more curious than annoyed when I got out of bed, throwing on a robe, and answered the door.

It was Anna, looking surprisingly fresh. She was dressed as she had been, in the quasi-ceremonial robe, and her hair was still piled high, her perfume still retained its brisk freshness.

She came into the room, saying, "I've been waiting for you in the lobby. I saw you come in, and I couldn't make up my mind. You looked worn out, so I debated. What I decided was, I was less concerned about how tired you were than I was anxious to talk to you."

"I wasn't exactly tired," I said. "I was a little the worse for wear, but it had nothing to do with fatigue."

"You don't tire easily anyway," she said. "I'd like a drink if you have it. I was going to say it was a disgraceful hour to be drinking, but I'm not sure there's such a thing as a disgraceful hour to do anything."

"Right," I said, and I poured her a generous brandy. It took me little more than an instant to realize I could use one, too.

I turned off all the lights in the room except one in a far corner. Then I motioned her to a small sofa, and I sat facing her. I wondered what I was feeling, now that I had created both a scene and an atmosphere of old intimacy, but I couldn't find the pulse. We were the same people, yet something was missing. The good times had gone, what there was of them, and I was sorry about that.

She had been beautiful and exciting and sensual and gratifying and ego-building; she had made me appreciate my maleness in the best sense of that term. She was still beautiful and, in a different way, still exciting, and I supposed she was still sensual, but she was no longer gratifying, and my ego had been long since well fed. I didn't need that particular dinner any longer.

"You're different," she said.

"Yes, I'm different."

"I'm sorry to see that. I don't think I like your differentness."

"It has very little to do with you, a lot to do with me."

"Tell me about it." She took a long sip of her brandy.

"I really haven't thought about it much. It's like growing up. At one year in your life, you're five feet eight inches tall. A year later, you're five feet eleven, and your skin isn't broken out, your voice is deeper, you've stopped masturbating as much because you've discovered willing girls, you've outgrown your clothes and you're thinking of what you're going to do the rest of your life. You're not the same person you were, and you can't remember how you changed or what changed you."

"I was one of the willing girls," she said. "I have no regrets about that."

"Why should you have any regrets?"

"I do. I regret I'm not different or I can't become different. I don't know which it is. I tried being different, David."

"Yes, you did. We're thinking about the same thing."

"With all I had then." She stopped to think about it. "Even with all that. The house in Mill Valley, which could have been mine. All the clothes and all the mobility and all the money and jewels. Not to mention your money and your jewels." She smiled at that. "I had it all, and it wasn't enough."

"What is enough?"

"I don't know. I reach into a bottomless pit, David, and I pull everything out of it. But I always reach in for more, because I know there's more there, and I want it. It's greed. Pure and simple."

"Not pure," I said, "and God knows, not simple."

"Please don't moralize."

"I'm a writer, and writers tend to moralize. Or to be kinder about it, they attempt to put the correct construction on things."

"That's even worse." She finished her brandy and held out the glass to me.

"Where's von Kleinschmidt?" I asked. I poured in a larger splash of brandy and returned the glass to her.

"Dead to the world," she said, "and he might even wish he were dead. He took one of my sleeping pills. I use those a lot lately. You were very rough on him, David."

"He's been very rough on me."

"That wasn't criticism. I was merely stating a fact. I don't think he ever thought about where he stood with Colin. He was so sure it was a partnership and it was built on a mutual trust and affection. I think he's truly fond of Colin; perhaps in a way there's even some kind of love going there. It's a one-way street, of course. I've always known Colin was a voyeuristic crud. There's something about voyeurism that's always troubled me, particularly the kind that centers on cruelty. And with Colin it's so damned anal. He's unspeakable."

"You go along with him." I was stating a fact, nothing more.

"I was never a voyeur and never a participant. I could take offense at that, but I won't."

I got off that subject by saying, "Tell me why you're here."

"It is late, isn't it? I'll get to the point." She took a deeper pull at the brandy, a pull so greedy that I wondered if I was seeing something in Anna's future; it was a sad thought. "Carl said nothing to me when we left the restaurant. I don't think he resented anything you said except the remark about his mother. I've seen her, David, and she might have been beautiful but she isn't any longer. She's a dope addict, with all that means to the addict. I found her incoherent and crazy, but I didn't let on to Carl. She's one of his delusions, and I wasn't going to bomb it.

"If Carl feels anything ugly—and he does—it's all of it directed at Colin. He hasn't said so, but I know so. Carl is proud enough and stiff enough not to like being used. He believed you, David."

"I told him the truth," I said.

"I know, and he knew. We really don't have a marriage," she continued. "I told you that. But we live together and I've gotten to know him. Underneath that heavy tan and big smile lurks a dangerous man. I don't think he'll do anything against you, but he'll try to do something against Colin. It's not going to work, David."

for it, you may like to know. I can't tell you exactly what, but I'd guess at least half again as much."

"How does anyone pay for a thing like that?"

"I don't know, and Carl doesn't, either. Carl never handles the business transaction. He just handles the merchandise, and not much of that, I might add; only when it's necessary. I do know this Japanese businessman invests heavily in the United States. Maybe that's a clue to how it's done."

I shrugged it away, because it really didn't matter. "What will I be taking back with me?"

"I'm not sure. A temple hanging, I think, very old and priceless. It's for a private collection in Canada."

"A temple hanging isn't a diamond. It can't be duplicated."

"It won't be. It'll be stolen just in time to get it to your plane." She gave a short and unpleasant laugh. "You'd like to do something with what I've told you, wouldn't you, David? But you know you can't. That's what's so damnable about all of this for you. There's not one goddamn noble thing you can do about it."

She was beginning to slur, and her mouth looked less firm. A vulgarity was rising in her, and I found I was feeling sorry for her. I would never have imagined that possible before.

"There was a sergeant on the plane with me," I said.

"Yes; that was Sammy. That isn't his name; it's what I call him because he's a slick glick. Talk about greed! He sold out for peanuts. They're the worst, the cheap ones. They'll kill for a buck. He'd kill you for a buck."

"You seem to get a kick out of saying that."

"Don't make it worse for me than it is. I don't wish you harm, David. I envy you. All the crap is falling around you, and not a piece of it's going to touch you. No matter what happens, you'll always have a clear conscience about yourself. Don't get me wrong. I'm not going to have a wingding of guilt, not on your life. But I'm always going to wonder what it would've been like if I did it differently."

"I'm looking at a new you," I said, "and I don't like her very much."

"Tell me about her."

"She's feeling sorry for herself, for one thing. Let's leave it at that."

"That's not my feeling sorry for myself, David. That's nothing less than maudlin. I'm telling you things I have no right to tell you, and I don't even know why I'm doing it. Maybe because I think you'll want to do something *about* what I'm telling you."

"I intend to do something." As I said that, I knew that I'd do something, and I knew what it was I would do.

Her eyes were trying to find me now, but they had a problem focusing. She showed no other sign of drunkenness, except the looseness of her mouth. Otherwise she was dignified and almost regal, and certainly she was sad without being pitiful.

"I came here," she said, "not to talk my head off but to go to bed with you. You don't want that, do you? I can see you don't."

"You don't want it, either, Anna," I said, "not this minute you don't. I'll call for a taxi."

I did just that.

The following morning I received word from Moriarity that he had completed his mission sooner than expected and we would be leaving within twenty-four hours for Los Angeles. He would meet me at the airport and regretted our not being able to get together at some time during the trip. He would find free time, however, as soon as we returned, and he was looking forward to spending at least a day with me. He hoped I wouldn't object if he turned black Irish and got bombed out of his skull on rye whiskey. What else were friends for, if not to excuse the folly of other friends?

It was typical of Moriarity to be considerate and caring, even amusing, in the face of personal unhappiness. His phone call strengthened my resolve, and I felt as Olympian as Zeus when I placed my next call to Hiram.

He opened by eliminating the usual "hello"s and "how are

you"s and going to the heart of the matter: "I've been lonely and I've missed you. Dorothy has, too. We've spent a good deal of time together."

"How's your church and congregation?"

"Expanding a little faster than I care for. It's very flattering. One person tells another, and that's how it goes. It keeps me jumping."

In a sudden attack of conscience, Hiram declared we shouldn't be chatting long distance at those prices, and how soon could he see me after I got back home?

"Not immediately," I said, "and that's principally why I called you. I want you to do this for me, Hiram: I want you to leave your house now and don't return until I tell you to. I want Dorothy to do the same thing. It doesn't matter where you go, but I'd suggest someplace out of town. Maybe San Francisco or Palm Springs; someplace. I'll leave word with my message service as to when I'm officially home and free to see you. I don't want Dorothy calling, only you. When you call, please don't give even a hint as to where you are."

Hiram said, "You're telling me we're in danger."

"Not yet you're not. But you might be. I don't want to take chances."

"You're taking chances."

"I have no choice. You do."

"Can't I volunteer my services?"

"No!" I meant the rejection to sound as final as I intended it to be. "I'm not being a hero, Hiram. I'm fighting for my life, and I'm doing it my way. As a matter of fact"—and I laughed as I thought about it—"I really don't know what the hell I'm doing. I know what I'm *going* to do, but I have no master plan as such. I'm whistling in the dark, and all I know is I'm going to whistle up something but I don't know what."

"It sounds dangerous."

"Could it be another way?"

It couldn't, of course, and I hung up after getting Hiram's promise that he would evacuate Dorothy to a safe place. I felt better already.

I spent the rest of the day going over Moriarity's letters for a second time, and I worked into the night laying out a sensible approach to his biography. I was determined it would be the best such work to be published in the U.S. in the past two decades. I wanted to do that much for the man.

I received word that we would leave before dawn the next morning, and I was ready for departure: bags almost completely packed, my clothes laid out, nothing to do but shave, shower, and eat breakfast leisurely. I sat at the window as I ate, looking out on Tokyo and wondering, as I frequently had during my lifetime, how such beauty and power and magnificence could be so consistently corrupted by meanness, pettiness, deceit, and greed. It seemed to me it would be easier to live life straighter and enjoy more fully the richness of the world. But it was not to be, and perhaps it had never been. I had to make do with what was.

There was an old hardness at the center of me when the doorbell rang and I opened it to Slick Glick. He looked spruce and trim and hard-eyed, gave me a curt "Good morning," and went immediately to my bags, standing beside them as the Japanese bellboy loaded them into a trolley.

"Anything else, sir?" he asked me, before the Japanese took off.

"Just this portfolio," I said, indicating the case holding Moriarity's letters and photographs, "and I'll keep it with me."

He was stupid enough to let his eyes widen with interest and direct themselves at the portfolio.

"It wouldn't be anything you'd be interested in," I said.

His look was innocent and aggrieved, and he said, "I beg your pardon, sir?"

We started out the door, and I asked, "What's your name, Sergeant?"

"Horace Wellsworth, sir, on special assignment."

"On special assignment from where?" I asked.

"I'm attached to Special Services in Washington," he said.

"You're lucky to get this one," I said, "or don't you think so?"

"I think so, sir." He was a splendid robot, and what I would have expected to be incorporated by Colin Davenport into Moriarity's entourage.

I nodded to Sergeant Wellsworth, and said nothing further until we were at the airport and getting ready to board the jet. Then I said to him, "Sergeant Wellsworth, I'm very fussy about my luggage. I like it with me. When we debark at Los Angeles, I want all of it to go with me in the limousine. All. Got it?"

He looked puzzled, but accepted what I said wordlessly, inclining his head to me by way of saying my will would be done.

Moriarity was already in the cabin of the plane, hunched in one of the swivel seats, sucking at a long drink with curious slurping sounds that reminded me of a suckling infant. He seemed not to hear me when I sat next to him, and I said nothing. I did, however, study him covertly, and I was dismayed to see how gray his skin had become. It was clay-colored beneath the surface ruddiness, and the freckles stood out like dried blood splashed on adobe. I particularly noted the lines of his mouth, which were drawn downward and frozen in misery.

I signaled to one of the white-coated attendants for a drink, and sat nursing it along with Moriarity. I knew he knew I was there, and that was enough. We could start speaking in his good time.

Within fifteen minutes, the jet had rolled into position and was making its sweep down the runway. The flight had begun, but even then Moriarity continued his vigil at the window, staring out at a brilliant sky as though he would find answers in it. Finally he gave a quiet groan and turned to me, managing a bleak smile and shaking his head a little as though he were knocking something out of it.

"Welcome," he said.

"How did things go?" I asked.

"Better than expected. I had to correct months, if not years, of misunderstandings, and I think I managed it." He called for another drink, and went on: "The Japanese are not the easiest to deal with. They move slowly and their subtleties can be your undoing. I listen to what they say and then agonize over what they mean. I do pretty well, and if I live long enough, I may catch on to them. Then, Japan, watch out!"

His smile became brighter and more lively, and he asked, "And you?"

"I know more than I did, a great deal more, and I set something in motion. I can't honestly say I accomplished anything, but I'm on a course of action which may or may not prove out. How's that for conviction?"

"You have your own Japanese types to deal with. I'm sure you do it well."

"At least I know what you and I are up to, and why we're needed in the scheme of things." I told him about my dinner with von Kleinschmidt and Anna and my later meeting with Anna. "As I see it, it all adds up to a humiliated von Kleinschmidt and a confused Anna. I don't know what either of them will do, and I don't have to know. What I *must* do is be prepared for whatever comes from whatever direction."

Moriarity surprised me by saying, "I'm sorry about Anna. I'm sorry for you because you were in love with her. I'm sorry for her, and a hell of a lot more sorry for her than you, because she seems to know she's sold out. Usually—at least it's been my experience—the sell-outs make do with what they've bought and delude themselves into believing it's all they wanted all along. The occasional honest one takes a good look at his purchase and admits it's like holding a handful of shit after all." His laugh was sardonic. "Let's not kid ourselves; there're damned few of the honest ones. Anyway, it's sad about Anna."

"But not about me," I suggested.

He was amazed. "When you're so completely the winner! That's why I was so down at the mouth when you boarded the plane. I couldn't've talked if I'd wanted to. But seeing that you *were* the winner made the difference for me. I was on the edge of a decision, David, and the sight of you pushed me over. On the right side, I think." He signaled to an agent seated near us, asked him to get a portfolio from his bedroom, then turned back to me. "You're the only one to hear this now, David; the world comes later. You see, I'm going to open that envelope from my sister and I'm going to publicize its contents."

I said, thinking how tragic that exposure would be for Moriarity and the world at large, "What if its contents aren't what you think they are?"

"I'm right, I have no doubts."

"You know what this means to you. This is an unforgiving planet."

"But it forgets."

"I find it hard to believe even that."

"But you do. It means the end of one career and a new start on another. I can do it, David. As soon as I get over the first shock of disclosure, I'll be okay."

The agent returned then and handed a portfolio to Moriarity. That remarkable man and I exchanged a last look that locked us into an atmosphere of mutual liking and respect, then he left me, to take care of other business. We never spoke again during that return flight to the States.

The plane came in for its landing at L.A. airport and taxied to a far end of the field, where two limousines and three Air Force sedans waited for us. Moriarity said, "Please be careful, David. Be extra careful, because I'm beginning to be sentimental about you. It's my natural inclination to be fond of most people because I want to be trusting. That's a luxury I can't afford, and haven't since I learned my true identity, and when I've found someone I feel safe with . . ." He trailed off there, and ended lamely, "Just be careful. We'll be in touch. I'll leave it up to you to call me. No matter what happens, I still want you to work with me on my biography—autobiography?"

His handshake was firm and he held on to me longer than is customary. Nothing makes loneliness more bearable than the knowledge that you're not entirely alone.

We debarked from the plane routinely, but I ignored the young Air Force officer who tried to lead me to one of the limousines. I turned instead to Sergeant Wellsworth and said, "My luggage."

His reply was a cold, "Yes, sir."

I watched him as he went to the area beneath the plane where the luggage was being unloaded and assembled. It came off carefully, piece by piece. I saw my Val-A-Pak, then the garment bag, and finally I saw what I thought was the piece I'd been looking for: a cylindrical case made of very good leather, modestly appointed with a few strips of gleaming hardware, and fastened with a lock similar to the one on the case containing the diamond ring.

Sergeant Wellsworth grabbed my Val-A-Pak and garment bag and turned to me, indicating I should precede him to the car. I stepped past him, bent for the cylindrical case, and picked it up. I turned instantly to confront Wellsworth.

"You forgot this, Sergeant," I said.

"I didn't know it was yours, sir," he answered.

"It is."

I walked past him, and I believe I nodded to him in grudging admiration. He gave no sign that I had done anything out of the ordinary. I doubted for a second that I had picked up the right article.

I took the cylindrical bag with me when I climbed into the limousine and settled it on my lap. There was a few minutes' confusion, and then Sergeant Wellsworth came to me and said, "May I drive into town with you, Mr. McEndree?"

"I thought the Air Force sedans were for you and the crew."

"They are, sir. But none of them is going in my direction."

"I wouldn't worry about that, Sergeant." I smiled at his predicament. "If you wish, I'll order them to go in your direction."

"Would I be putting you out, sir?"

"Yes, Sergeant," I said. "You would be putting me out. Sorry."

I told the driver of the limousine to shove off, and we were on our way. I resisted the temptation to look back and catch the expression on Wellsworth's face. I was sure I wouldn't like it, and I was certain I would have little use for what was going on in his mind.

It wasn't good to be home, and I've never said *that* before. Although the place looked good enough, as comfortable and familiar as well-used clothing, it represented something very new to me. It had, I knew, ceased to be my home for the time being. I anticipated its becoming my fortress, and I was its sole defender. I was even unable to call in the police for reinforcements, because no crime had been committed and I had no evidence to suggest there might be one. It was a strange situation, and I found it exciting.

My pulse was up and adrenaline was pumping as I went through the cliché motions of opening the house for an airing, emptying my luggage, and secreting the cylindrical case in a reasonably safe place in my small attic. After I had done that, it was a natural thing for me to take a long-unused shotgun from a hidden place in my bedroom closet and to disassemble it for cleaning. I was sitting at a table in the kitchen, oiling and wiping its parts, when the telephone rang.

I left the table with caution, aware of what was inside as well as outside the house, and walked into the living room to answer the phone. I was staring out and down into the valley below me, darkening now with the coming of night, when I picked up the phone and asked who it was.

It was Hiram, saying, "I've been ringing you every half hour, David. I know what you told me, but I had to take that chance."

"I'm all right, Hiram. You're not to worry about me."

"I want to help."

"Of course you do. And I'd ask you to if I knew what I wanted you to help with. I don't, Hiram. So I wish you'd do what I asked and quickly."

"I'm not at home. I'm calling from a pay phone somewhere in the city."

"Great! What about Dorothy?"

"I told her you were delayed and wouldn't be back for a week. She told me I was to tell you you could fuck off, then she told me I was not to tell you that, instead I should say that she loved you." He laughed. "Then she said you could fuck off anyway, and she still loved you."

"That tells me how she feels, but not where she is. I don't mean specifically."

"It worked out fine. She was asked to do a one-shot on a variety show in England, and that will take exactly a week. I arranged for her to stay with friends, in London, and I told the friends that she was to be watched night and day. They'll take care of her."

"Where will you be? I want you safe."

"I'll be where I almost was. Call me if you need me, or better still, call me if you don't need me."

He rang off, and I hung up feeling easier than I had for the past twelve or more hours. Hiram would be at Cynthia's house in Bel Air. It gave me a great sense of security to know he was only twenty hard-driving minutes away from me.

I finished cleaning the shotgun, loaded it, put a box of shells beside the gun on a table in the living room, and then made a tour of the house. I checked windows and doors, drew drapes where there were drapes, closed shutters where there were shutters, and turned off all lights in rooms where there were neither drapes nor shutters. Then I flooded the exterior of the house with lights, turning on those in the garage and on the porch and walks in the front; putting on high-voltage globes in the patio and gardens and the hillside to the rear. To be inside the house was like being blind with a bright world all around you, but I knew I was the one who would have the advantage if I should come under attack.

I turned on the stereo to a station that played undistinguished music very softly, switched on the oven and shoved a TV dinner into it, and went upstairs to shower and shave. I told myself I should be tired, but I had no sense of fatigue. I was waiting, and the longer I waited, the greater the tension grew. But the tension was that of preparedness and had nothing of anxiety in it. Whatever was going to happen, I wanted it to happen quickly.

An hour wore away. I had had a drink, I had eaten. I was sitting in the patio, listening to the stillness around me. A week before, I had listened for other sounds. Those were of the morning, and the ones I was now hearing were either going-to-bed sounds or let's-get-something-going sounds. There was an occasional sound of a laugh or a laughing voice, but for the most part I could hear only complaint and dismay. The world around me was troubled that night.

“Do you mind if I sit down, David? I don’t think Colin will be coming along the next minute. I’m sure he’ll take a little time out to think about shooting Carl and what he’ll do next. And I’d like another drink. The booze doesn’t seem to be touching me, but I keep on wanting more of it.”

“Don’t go out of control. It could hit you fast.”

“It won’t; not this morning it won’t.”

She added whiskey to her generously filled glass and sat on the arm of a chair. It was the chair in which Dorothy and I had found the very nude and very dead young blond man. There is more than one way of being dead, and Anna, it seemed to me, was demonstrating one of the variations.

“Don’t feel sorry for me, David,” she said tiredly. “I don’t feel sorry for myself, but I do feel sorry for you. You don’t deserve to have all this happen to you.”

“What did happen?”

“Wellsworth was supposed to deliver the scroll to Carl, Carl was to pass it along to another contact. You took off with it, and Carl had to tell Colin. We went to the apartment they use out here, I guess it’s the Westwood Summit, I’ve never been there before, all white and mirrored. Colin was getting it off watching two young men screwing a dreadful creature named Carmen. He didn’t seem to mind my being there and he didn’t tell them to stop. That was at first.

“Carl didn’t say a word on the flight home. I think he thought it all through and decided he had no choice but to go along with it. The stakes were always high, but they went out of sight when you and Moriarity came into the picture and made Colin more ambitious. Maybe Carl was thinking he’d go along and ask for a bigger cut. I know he didn’t like discovering he was a second-rater, and even *I* believed he was right in there with Colin. I had no reason to think otherwise.”

She put her glass down abruptly, rose to her feet, and walked out of the room, going into the kitchen behind her. She was gone a minute, certainly no more than that, and returned showing faint signs of agitation but otherwise with her composure reasonably intact.

"Something gets to me," she said. "I don't know what it is, but it overwhelms me like nothing I ever felt before." She took a careful swallow of her drink, smiled, and said, "I think I could get to hate this stuff; it really tastes vile right now."

"Don't drink it."

"You really want to see me do right, David, don't you?" She looked at me fondly, and spoke what had shown on her face. "I really like you, because you're decent and caring. Well, let's get on with it.

"Carl told Colin it was important he talk to him, and Colin got rid of his circus. He didn't like it, let me tell you, and so we all got off on the wrong foot.

"As far as I know, the three of us were alone. There might have been somebody else in the apartment; I just don't know. Carl had let himself in with a key. I guess we can assume there was someone around somewhere, can't we? No difference. What matters is, Carl told Colin what had happened, and Colin learned I had told you about Wellsworth and the scroll. I volunteered that because it had to come out one way or the other, and I was perverse enough to do it. It just came out of me, and Colin showed us there was something worse than the fury of a woman scorned."

She indicated her face and the mess her hair and clothing were in, and said, "Something worse is what happens when Colin is getting his lumps. He attacked me the way a woman might've, all hands and nails and screaming. There was too much going on for me to protect myself very well, and I guess that's what broke Carl, who doesn't exactly hate me. He pulled Colin off and threw him to one side and went at him in a few well-chosen words. He let it all come out, and it really didn't take all that long."

She stopped long enough to give herself time to think, and continued, "Carl told Colin what he expected in the future in a kind of 'or else' way, and we left. We took the elevator down to the basement garage, and we got in, Carl on the driver's side. He had just started the car, and Colin appeared, looking very calm and I must say quite beautiful, the way he can. He came over to the car, reached in, and fired once into Carl's chest. Then he walked away as if he'd just been saying good night.

"I got around to the other side, and helped Carl heave himself over. He told me he was all right, not to worry, and directed me how to come here. So there! Isn't that a nifty story?"

She was crying now, and I hope I never see anything like that again. It's one thing to see a weeper cry, because you expect it of him. It's another to see the strength go out of a strong person in a flash flood, leaving nothing but the vulnerability that was always there to begin with. It becomes a crying for all the lost things of the world and all the anguished moments that were never admitted to before.

I left her crying and went upstairs to climb into my attic. After retrieving the scroll, I returned to the living room, to find Anna repairing the ruin of her face and hair. She was herself again as I had always known her, and was ready for anything I proposed.

"Just tell me," she said, "and I'll do it. You don't know how cooperative I can be."

"No, I don't know that," I said, grinning at her, "so show me. I'm going to turn out the back lights and you and I and the scroll are going to climb up the hill as fast and as quietly as we can. There's the back end of an old estate up there, and a shed that used to be used as storage for gardening tools and suchlike. Kids use it now to hide out and maybe screw a little. They're a little more advanced than they were in my day. I want you to hide there. I'd like to send you away, but you'll be safe, I think, and you'll be near if I need you to run for help. Or something. Okay?"

Nothing about her would surprise me. She was out and up the hill in faster time than I could make it. I was panting when I reached the top, and she was waiting for me calmly. I pointed the way, and she found the little path that led to the shed. I handed the cylindrical bag to her and we stood there silently for a moment, just looking, having no need to say anything.

Finally she said, "What do I do with the scroll?"

"If I can handle it," I said, "you won't have to think about it. If I can't, you can turn it over to Hiram Rather. He's in the book."

"That sounds fine. Be careful, David."

I started back and she said to me, "If it all works out, I don't think I'll want to see you again, David."

"That makes sense to me."

I went back to the house.

My pulses were on the move again, and excitement was collecting in me like rain water in a steel barrel.

Again I sat in the living room, all lights out except for the ones outside, my body listening for the night noises which were beginning to be diluted by the sounds of the city coming to life again. It would be dawn in another hour, and nothing had happened. I doubted Colin would make a move in full daylight.

I thought of von Kleinschmidt, slumped in his rented car, grossly dead in an impromptu casket that would have symbolized luxury for him. I thought about his poisonous father who was no father, and wondered about a relationship, based on a fantasy, that was no relationship at all. There was nothing much else to think about. I couldn't even dig up more than a shred of wonderment that Colin and von Kleinschmidt had been so close and yet von Kleinschmidt had never been curious enough to find out what his buddy was really all about. It all came down to one thing: the lust for money, power, and position was the world's biggest blindfold.

I broke the shotgun open, and closed it again. The sound was hard and metallic in the stillness of that house, and I thought I heard its echo across the canyon. But it wasn't an echo. It was another sound, another hard and metallic sound, coasting up the walls of the canyon and coming to me from a distance that I could not judge. I listened for it again, and it didn't come. I listened harder, and I heard a flat sound of something dull striking another dull object.

I shoved the living room drapes to one side, and then I pulled them open. It was becoming lighter now, and the power of the few street lights and the illuminating lights of my front yard had begun to fade. That half light which was neither one thing nor another was tricky, but I was not deceived by what I saw.

A man was coming up the street toward my driveway, and as he approached, I heard the dull sounds again: his leather heels pounding against the asphalt roadway. I couldn't see him clearly enough to be certain as to his identity, but I knew he was familiar to me. There was something about his rigid posture and the stiff way in which his head sat upon his shoulders.

I looked beyond him, and I first caught the glint of the chromium headlights of an automobile; it was almost hidden by trees and underbrush, but I knew it was an automobile and I guessed it to be a very large sedan. A harder look, and I saw three men, one very small, the other two large and threatening even at that distance. The little man was dancing nervously, and there was no mistaking who it was. Colin Davenport.

The first man started up my driveway, hands in the pockets of his coat, walking steadily toward me, negotiating the steep road with a plodding pace that left no doubt as to his determination to reach his goal. I could make him out now: Sergeant Wellsworth, dressed in civilian clothes.

It was time to show myself, and I stepped out onto the porch, walked to the edge of it, and stood there with the shotgun resting along my arm, pointed to the ground. I had a wild impression of that scene, seeing myself as the pioneer defending his home against the outlaws. There really wasn't anything wild about it, after all. The years had gone by since the days of pioneers, but the days were still lawless and growing more so. I had a real kinship with those pioneers I was remembering.

Wellsworth came to the foot of the stairs, and said, "I came for the leather tube you took at the airport, Mr. McEndree. It isn't yours, and if you give it to me, I'll leave and you won't see me or any of them again." He made a vague gesture to indicate the men behind him.

"What if I told you it wasn't here?" I asked.

"I wouldn't believe you."

"It isn't here, Sergeant, and you can go back and tell Mr. Davenport that. If it were here, I wouldn't let you have it."

"I'm not going to tell Mr. Davenport that, Mr. McEndree," he said. "That isn't what he wants to hear."

"Then you'll have to think of something that's going to satisfy him. I can't help you there. The scroll is not in this house."

He had been watching me closely, and I knew he believed me. He didn't like me, and he sure as hell didn't like the position I was putting him in. But he was astute enough to size me up correctly. If I said the scroll wasn't in the house, then it wasn't there.

"I don't know how I'm going to handle this," he said.

"You'll think of something."

"I doubt that I will. Is it foolish of me to ask you where the scroll is? Mr. Davenport wants it very badly."

"It's very foolish of you. And I don't know how you could persuade me to tell you where it is."

"I can't argue with that."

His eyes pulled away as though they'd been glued to my face, and he started back down the driveway. He was moving more slowly now, reluctant to deliver my message. But there was courage in him, and he was calling on it then, forcing himself to return and confront Colin.

They met, and there was an exchange. Colin's dancing grew more furious, his hands and arms moved with the boneless goofiness of a puppet. He was talking furiously, and Wellsworth threw up his hands suddenly and started in the direction of the hidden car. I heard a popping sound, and Wellsworth dropped to the ground, falling out of my range of vision. So much, I thought, for Sergeant Wellsworth.

As far as I knew, that made two killings for the evening, and I wondered how many more there would be.

It was light enough then to see the world more clearly, and I could almost distinguish Colin's agitation. I thought of that antique way of describing a highly disturbed person as "beside himself," and that was how I saw Colin. I knew him well enough to know how he could be. The person I was seeing at that moment was a totally different man, as though Colin had stepped outside one personality to reveal another. His frenzied ballet was remarkable to behold.

I was so fascinated by the charade being played out below me that I almost missed the man who had circled through the underbrush and had now disappeared into the overgrown hillside behind my house. I could do nothing about him without abandoning my position on the porch. I knew I would hear him if he tried to enter the rear of the house through the locked windows or door. To make sure he didn't surprise me by sneaking up and taking a shot at me from the side of the house, I stepped back into the safety of the doorway.

A second man started up the street to my driveway, and I saw he was holding a gun, ready in his hand. I recognized him instantly: the "survivor," the aging and hardened blond man who had driven me to the airport on the day I flew to Japan.

I maintained my position. I had no choice. Short of killing me, anything they would attempt would be designed to draw me away from the house. There was no safe or sure thing I could do. I had to stay put.

Anna's voice rang out over the canyon, not so much a scream as a warning yell.

"David!"

I smelled the smoke and heard the cracking of dry wood. The hidden man had fired something at the rear of my house. My brain raced up to the study, where files and folders and tables were loaded with thousands of manuscript pages. Everything I had written or planned to write or had started to write was up there.

Anna's voice came again.

"David! He's coming for you!"

I could see Colin dancing his frenzied dance, driven crazy by the sound of Anna's voice and my own implacable stand. I had a fleeting thought of Hitler dancing triumphantly in the French forest.

The aging blond was at the foot of my driveway now, starting up. He raised his gun, there was one of those strange popping sounds, and a bullet hit the wall beside me. Another pop, and a second bullet hit on the opposite side of me.

I could see it all: The aging blond, who was, I realized gratefully, a rotten marksman. Colin pirouetting in the distance, flanked on either side by two more of his men. I even caught a sidelong, flashing glimpse of the hidden man, who was maneuvering carefully as he tried to get a clear shot at me.

It was unbelievable, and I was nerveless.

There were too many of them, and only one of me. Nothing seemed more logical at the moment than to take out the leader of them all, leaving them without motive or direction.

I raised the shotgun, and it must have been clear to anyone who saw me that Colin Davenport was my target. A profound silence settled over the canyon. Colin continued dancing and exhorting his motionless henchmen. My finger tightened on the trigger of the gun. I never pulled the shot off.

A barking noise sounded and was instantly lost in the stretches of the canyon. Colin Davenport dropped to the street in a gangling heap of arms and legs.

I was conscious of movement around and before me. I knew, without seeing him, that the hidden man who was stalking me had withdrawn in a great hurry. I saw the aging blond rush to the car, passing Colin's body, shouting to his companions to "get the hell out of here!"

I heard the car start up, saw it pull away. But more than anything else I saw a large figure walk slowly into view. I could see the pistol in his hand, but I could not connect that weapon with the man who carried it.

Hiram Rather!

I found it hard to believe that the Hiram Rather who approached me so slowly, so heavy with fatigue and despair, was the old friend whose buoyant spirits and optimism could make the most serious problem seem trivial and transitory. He had lost something of himself, and the loss gave him the appearance of someone aged and vulnerable. I felt infinitely sorry for him, without knowing why; it was an unpleasant reaction, which deepened when he came to the foot of the stairs and looked up at me with the dazed expression of a poleaxed bull.

"Are you all right, David?"

His face was white, his eyes anguished. I glanced at the pistol that hung from his right hand. It was unreal. It was an impossible fact that Hiram Rather stood there holding a murder weapon. The minister to dependent and loving people was a killer. I took it all in, but I could assimilate little of it.

"Yes," I said. "I'm okay."

"You should call the police."

"I will."

"Then do it."

"There's a fire going on in back. I have to take care of that first."

"Go ahead. I'll call."

It didn't seem odd to me that we were behaving so reasonably in a totally unreasonable situation.

As Hiram started up the stairs, I turned from him and entered the living room. I put the rifle on a table, then continued through the house and out onto the patio. There was a nice little blaze going, eating its way slowly up the hill and creeping through the underbrush at the base of the house. Flames were chewing at one of the window frames, but the house was not in any immediate danger of being destroyed.

I turned on the hillside sprinklers, grabbed a heavy garden hose, and started playing water on the most avaricious of the devouring flames. Water ran down the front of me; my shoes were soaking it up. I needed a new pair anyway, and now I had an excuse to get them.

I looked up, to see Anna making her way down the hill, the cylindrical case held close to her body. She reached the patio and moved past me toward the house. She turned at the door to face me, and I saw she looked ghastly in the revealing daylight.

She was a morbidly pale, lank-haired female, her clothes filthy and torn, her poise crumpled and ready to be thrown away. Rarely had I felt the compassion that overwhelmed me at the sight of her.

"You called the police," she stated.

"No. Hiram Rather did. He's inside."

"I don't think I want to see him."

"I don't know how you can avoid it, but whatever you say. Would you like a drink?"

"There won't be time. They'll be here in a minute. I'll wait out in front."

"It's up to you."

She disappeared into the house, and I finished the watering. The fires were out and I said one of the few prayers of my life, thanking whomever you thank these days for not sending a wind my way.

When I went inside, I found Hiram standing in the front doorway, staring at the outside world. He turned slowly at the sound of me, and I saw there was a curious twist to his face, almost a grotesque grimace that was like a last agony.

"That was Anna?" he asked.

"Yes."

"I don't think she saw me. At least, she walked past me without seeming to see me."

"Where is she?"

"Outside. She's leaning against the Cadillac, looking inside. I think she's crying."

"She's looking at Carl. He's dead. Colin shot him."

Hiram nodded and said, "I killed Colin."

"We're very polite, Hiram," I said. "Do you think we can stop being so fucking polite?"

"I guess it's time." He moved his head nervously at the sound of a far-distant siren. "I guess everyone's being polite. Your neighbors aren't out there, and there're two dead men lying in the street."

"That's not politeness or lack of curiosity. It's fear."

"You're right, of course. I think you're more often right about people than I am, David. You should have been the minister. You're more reliable."

I didn't know what he meant by that, and I didn't know how to answer him. I said, "I asked you not to come here, Hiram. I was doing just fine, and it was my show all the way. There was no good reason for you to get involved."

"I was involved, David."

"I know you did it for Cynthia, but I could have handled it my way."

"I didn't do it entirely for Cynthia. I also did it for you. In a way, I did it for myself."

Hiram's face twisted again. It was working to keep his eyes in control, but I saw the wetness that began to seep along their lower lids. It disturbed me to see a man of his strength express deep emotion in such a way, which says something about one of the idiocies of our American society and its emphasis on manhood.

"Try me, Hiram. Maybe I'll understand."

"I don't want you to hate me, David. We've been good friends, haven't we?"

"Off and on, considering the traveling I've done, I'd say we were pretty close. Not in daily communication or anything like that, but close." I was being cautious, keeping it light because I didn't know how to handle the situation.

The siren sounded closer, and I guessed the police were near to their turnoff on Hollywood Boulevard. I was cold, possibly because I was anticipating the arrival of the police and the messy aftermath, certainly because I knew I was faced with something I would not be able to understand after all.

Hiram said, "Cynthia was one of them."

So that was it. No. I didn't understand it.

I thought of something to say: "So that's how they knew every move I made."

"Yes," Hiram said. "But that's the least of it, David."

"Why would Cynthia be involved with them, for Christ's sake!" It was a big imponderable and impossible for me to grasp. "The

Wallensteins had money. She inherited all of it."

"There was no money, there was no inheritance. The only thing Cynthia owned was a reputation for having money. She couldn't live with that."

"I hope that's the last of the surprises, Hiram."

"No." The siren was louder and his voice went faster. "Colin Davenport set Cynthia up as a recruiter. Everything she had—the house in Bel Air, the servants, cars, everything—they all came from him. I was only one of her targets, and she sought me out because of my connections with the high and mighty, and the promise of more to come."

"I don't believe you knew that from the beginning, Hiram."

"I didn't."

"When?"

"The night you first met Dorothy and Cynthia. She told me then, and told me she was getting out of it. She had fallen in love with me, I with her. I told her to stay put."

I said, "Now we're getting to the good part."

He was finding it hard to look at me, but he found the courage to keep his eyes fixed on my face. "Things were moving too slowly for me, David. I had a certain amount of power and influence, but not enough to satisfy me, and I was going heavily into debt. I didn't want to wait. I thought, As smart as Colin Davenport is, I'm smarter—and I knew there had to be a way to get to him, maybe even take it all away, perhaps even join forces with him. I had no real plan, but I wanted in."

I was half listening to him, half going into my own mind to search for reasons and answers. It had been a long struggle; I had fought long and hard to get myself in the clear and back to the reality I used to be comfortable with. Now it was painfully obvious that there was no reality for me to go back to. I suddenly found myself in the infancy of my understanding of the life that circled wildly and unpredictably around me. I wondered if I was wise enough to make my adjustment to it.

I said, "If there's more, Hiram, you'd better get it out. This could be the last time we'll have much to say to each other."

"I understand," he said, "and I know it can't be any other

way. There isn't much more. Amalie Sparking Houghton became a member of my congregation months ago. She told me—confessed may be a better word—about her brother Moriarity and the riot at Southern Alliance. I tried to help her, David, but I couldn't hold on to her."

"So you get the credit for pairing me off with Moriarity?"

"Yes. It was my idea, David. And I want you to know Cynthia was against it."

"But she went along with it."

"At first. Then she changed her mind." His speech was slower now, thicker, as if every word had become an effort. "I had never seen Colin Davenport before that night you brought him to my place. You might as well believe that, David. He had no idea I was the one responsible for setting you up with Moriarity. He gave Cynthia full credit for that, which is the way I wanted it to be. I wanted to keep myself out of reach for the time being."

"You have talent, Hiram. I believed every word of that performance you put on for me and Colin Davenport."

He nodded, and said, "I'm a role player, David. But I wasn't playing when I got angry with Davenport. That was the real thing. I suddenly began to see myself in that little man, and I didn't like what I saw. But I didn't see myself clearly enough."

"I'm sorry you didn't, Hiram, for both you and me. And for Cynthia."

"Late that same night, Cynthia called to tell me she was pulling out even if it meant losing me. She had already told the same thing to Colin. She didn't seem to know or care that you just don't pull out on someone like Colin Davenport, but there was nothing I could do about it. Her death hit me hard."

"You're a late thinker, Hiram," I said, "a too-late thinker. And you're some bad friend, all right. I'm glad I have only one like you."

The siren was howling in the canyon, and I went outside quickly. Anna was still leaning heavily against the car, her arms folded on its roof, her head bent to her arms. She stood there without moving, and I judged that she had finished with her tears.

I went to stand beside her and put my hand on her shoulder. "You didn't tell me about Cynthia."

"I had given you enough heavy stuff to carry. I didn't want to add to it."

She pulled away from the car and faced me. She was unrecognizable; I would not have known she was the Empress. All the years of her conniving to get the things she wanted had piled into her eyes and over the lines of her face. I no longer felt anything about Hiram Rather. I felt a great sadness about Anna, and realized at that instant that I had never learned her last name. She came into my life anonymously and was going out the same way. But I refused to believe it had all been just another hustle.

The police car rolled to a halt at the bottom of my driveway and two young officers leaped out like a pair of gymnasts. Instantly I saw bits of movement in and around the houses nearest me. The cops had arrived, and now my neighbors, who must have heard the racket, could safely put in an appearance and feed their curiosity. I wanted to think about that later, when other problems had been resolved.

I went back into the house, to find Hiram standing at a window watching the scene below. He was composed and silent, and made no move to look at me.

"What time is it in England?" I asked. I looked at my watch. "It's seven-thirty here."

"About the middle of the afternoon. Dorothy might be at the Forsythes' now. Do you want me to place the call for you?"

"If you will."

While Hiram was busy at the telephone, I went to the door and watched as the young officers inspected Carl's body and then asked Anna a battery of questions. She had mustered sufficient poise and self-possession to deal with them directly and with authority. I had decided she would never be able to surprise me again, and there she was putting the lie to my conviction.

Hiram said, "The circuits seem to be fairly clear. The operator said she thought the call would go through in just a few minutes."

I turned to him, and said, "Thanks. I need to talk to Dorothy because she's the only one there is. She's the best, Hiram, but it took something as drastic as this to get that idea into my thick head."

"What have we learned from this, David?" Hiram was appealing to me, and I didn't have the proper answer for him.

"Only one thing so far," I said, "speaking for myself. Cynthia's dead, Carl and Colin are dead. But Archie isn't dead, Hiram. Archie was the word Carl and Colin used for anything you want. And Archie is very much alive in you, Hiram. You still want it all, don't you?"

He flinched at that, and asked, "Is there any point in asking you to forgive me?"

"You're asking me to be noble, Hiram," I said, "and I'm not ready for that."

The two policemen started up the stairs and entered the house. They looked very young and sober. I thought about all the years that stretched ahead of them and hoped they would recognize and appreciate the bright moments when they came.

They looked inquiringly at us, and Hiram said, "You'll want to talk to me."

"We'll want to talk to both of you," one of them said, but they moved to Hiram just as the phone rang, its shrill sound startling all of us.

I answered the phone, and that voice that had no equal asked, "Who is this?"

"It's David. Hi, honey."

"Say that again," she commanded. "Say it exactly the way you said it the first time."

"It's David. Hi, honey."

"You did it." Her voice was thick with emotion, and, I thought, with a collection of tears that had not yet spilled over. "My, you finally did it."

"Did what?"

"Said 'honey' as if you meant it, you fool. I told you I'd know the difference. So tell me what's up."

"The jig is up. The scene has played itself out."

"When will I see you?" Her voice was bright again, choked

now with an impulse to laugh or sing or shout out loud. "Can you come here? I have five days to go."

"I'll try."

"Do better than that."

"I'll try to do that, too."

"When will you know?"

"Maybe later today."

"Before you hang up, tell me."

I knew what that meant, and I said, "I love you—at least I think I do."

She laughed, and I heard the phone click shut.

The policemen were still questioning Hiram, and I refused to look at the sight of that ruined man. As I headed for the kitchen, I thought it would be possible to forgive him, and Anna, and all the rest—in time. It would be a little harder to forgive myself.